PSI/Net

PSI/Net

Billy Dee Williams
AND
Rob MacGregor

TOR®

A TOM

NEW Y

PSI/NET

Copyright © 1999 by Billy Dee Williams and Rob MacGregor

This book is printed on acid-free paper.

A Tor Book
Published by Tom Doherty Associates, LLC
175 Fifth Avenue
New York, NY 10010

Tor Books on the World Wide Web:
http://www.tor.com

Tor® is a registered trademark of Tom Doherty Associates, LLC

Designed by Lisa Pifher

Library of Congress Cataloging-in-Publication Data
MacGregor, Rob.
    PSI/Net / Billy Dee Williams & Rob MacGregor.—1st ed.
       p.   cm.
    ''A Tor book''—T.p. verso.
    ISBN 0-312-86766-2
    I. MacGregor, Rob. II. Title.
    PS3563.A31113P78   1999   99-24477
    813'.54—dc21

First Edition: July 1999

Printed in the United States of America

0 9 8 7 6 5 4 3 2 1

*To Mom—Loretta Anne Williams
and my children—Corey, Dee, and Hanako Anne*

*To my late father, Donald MacGregor,
who always listened and encouraged and who
shared my interest in the realms of
the unknown*

*Special thanks to remote viewers
Joseph McMoneagle, David Moorehouse,
and Angela Thompson Smith for their
encouraging comments on the manuscript*

THURSDAY

One

The raft surged through the rapids, water splashing over the bow. Four sets of oars flailed the air and slashed the foaming white river. Helmets glinted in the midday sunshine and orange life vests bobbed across the rough waters. The rafters bantered back and forth.

"Now don't fall out again, Sam. I'm getting tired of dragging your ass back in here," chided a broad-shouldered man with hair tied in a ponytail to the chunky, bearded man on his right.

"Knock it off, Art. It's getting old. At least I keep my screwups to the river and not the office."

"Oh, touchy, touchy."

At the stern, river guide Trent Calloway tightened his grip on the rudder. His anger surged with each caustic exchange; he wanted to tell them both to shut up. Take it easy, he told himself. He'd talk to them as soon as they reached the rest stop. He shifted the rudder, moving the raft closer to the right side of the river. All the rafters, except Calloway, worked for a California software company and the trip was a company perk that they'd chosen.

Calloway peered out at the sandstone walls that rose on either side of the river. The rushing waters had etched out shallow caverns so that the walls seemed to lean over the river. He spotted a well-known petroglyph of Kokopelli, the ever-present hunchbacked flute player whose image had been carved on walls throughout the Southwest by the ancients—the Anasazis.

Not far now to the last rest stop, he thought. Then, they would make the final run to Mexican Hat, the end of the two-day trip from Sand Island.

Calloway had been hired as a guide last summer after taking a trip down the San Juan River with a local outfitter. The company had been short of help for the high season and Calloway simply said he wanted the job. He'd told Ed Miller, the outfitter, that he was retired from the air force and that was good enough. If Miller wondered why the Afro-American, who was still in the prime of his life, lived alone in a twenty-foot Airstream that he hauled behind an aging pickup, he didn't ask and that was fine with Calloway.

The San Juan ran high and fast, good for thrills and less chance of hitting rocks, but there was always the danger of losing a rafter or two over the side. The men wore helmets and life vests, but a tumbling rafter could still be seriously injured. The eight men with him, all in their twenties and thirties, enjoyed the challenge. But Calloway was glad this one was almost over. Twice now, Sam had fallen over the side. Fortunately, he'd clung to the lines and had been pulled back into the raft. The last incident had happened an hour ago and he was still taking heat from Art. Calloway was ready to tie him down and maybe stick a rag in Art's mouth.

"Okay, work hard now, concentrate," Calloway barked. "This is a tricky rapids coming up. We're going to drop down fast so hang on tight."

"Hear that, Sam. That means keep your fat butt down," Art yelled.

"You too, pal!" Calloway shouted, then impulsively leaned forward and smacked the palm of his hand against Art's shoulder. At the same moment, the raft dropped down. The dip was faster and steeper than even Calloway expected. Icy water sprayed over everyone. The raft bounced hard, everyone lifted up, and when the raft came down, Art was gone.

"Oh, shit!"

He jammed hard against the rudder to keep the raft from going into a spin and when he looked over his shoulder, he glimpsed a blob of orange surrounded by foam ten feet away. He hurled a safety line back, but Art missed the rope. The raft hurtled through the white water and Calloway lost sight of him.

"Great. Just great," Calloway muttered to himself.

"Art went over!" Sam yelled. "Where'd he go? I don't see him."

Calloway veered around a rock and into a pool of quiet water near the wall. He spotted Art floundering in the rapids fifty yards downstream. The others shouted and pointed. "Okay, paddle hard. Let's go get him."

He nudged the rudder, turning the raft out into the middle of the river. Art still bobbed in the strongest part of the current and drifted farther and farther away. Then he disappeared around a bend. They paddled furiously. When they rounded the sandstone wall, the chop diminished, the water turned so calm that it felt as if the place were under a spell.

A flat, sandy area opened on the right, sheltered by low cliffs—the rest area. Calloway knew it as one of the better sites for viewing Anasazi petroglyphs on the cliff walls. Art stood in knee-deep water. He waved and hooted when he saw them and the sound echoed eerily around them.

"What a rush! That was great!" Art chortled.

But Calloway didn't pay any attention to him. Ten yards beyond Art stood three Indians—a man, woman and boy—near a fire. One of them, the man, held a fish on a stick, and all three ignored the rafters, acted as if they weren't even there. The man and boy wore loincloths, the woman was bare-breasted and garbed in a skirt that looked like deerskin. Long, scraggly hair added to their primitive appearance; they looked as if they'd just stepped out of the past. Suddenly, the man locked gazes with him and Calloway felt a sharp jabbing pressure against his solar plexus.

Feeling like an interloper, he looked away, and turned to Art, who trudged up to the raft. "Are you okay?"

"I'm fine. Did you push me?"

Calloway ignored the question. "C'mon. Get in. Let's go."

"Hey, why don't we stop here?" Sam said. "This place looks great."

"No, let's not bother them."

"Bother who?" someone asked.

Calloway looked up. No Indians. No fire. As if they'd never been there.

Two

Gordon Maxwell stood in front of the full-length mirror, a towel slung low around his waist. After staying fit all of his life, he now had trouble keeping the extra pounds off, even when he stayed with the goddamned low-fat diet. He could only imagine what he'd look like if he still ate all those big, juicy steaks, the baked potatoes slathered in butter and sour cream, even the salads covered with high-caloric dressings. In the old days, he could get away with it. Not anymore.

Maybe it was part of the male menopause thing. If the hormonal change in men actually existed, as some people claimed, Maxwell figured he was experiencing the symptoms. He never slept eight hours anymore and he got up to go to the bathroom once or twice. Then there was the usual aging process, the graying around his temples, the balding spot at the crown of his head, and the loss of his ability to focus on anything in front of him without reading glasses.

He fought hard against the slow physical deterioration. He worked out regularly, even though he kept straining muscles and ligaments that seemed to take forever to heal. He looked at his long face, straight, thin nose, and his gray, hooded eyes. He smiled. At least he remained handsome in the same mysterious sort of way that had always intrigued women. But how much longer would that last?

He didn't like thinking much about the future, at least not when it dealt with his own mortality. The irony, of course, was that he called himself a futurist, someone deeply concerned about coming events. When he spoke tomorrow at the Western Governors Conference, he'd be introduced as a retired air force colonel and a futurist who had served government agencies during his military career. Upon retirement, he had started a private consulting business and had begun teaching part-time at the University of Colorado.

He straightened his back, inhaling deeply, smiled as he imagined the crowd applauding as he approached the podium. This was clearly his chance to make an impact, one that would ripple across the nation, and he wasn't about to pass it up. He stared into the mirror, tightened his hold on the towel, and practiced his opening lines.

"Not long ago, one of my students asked me a curious question," he began. "She said, 'What good is the future, anyway? Every day we wake up to the present. The future always remains out of our reach—in the future.' "

That was when he expected to hear a few laughs. A silly story, but it would loosen them up. Then he would continue. "She made a good point. What good is the future? More specifically, what she meant to say, is: 'What good is studying the future?'

"I answered by telling her that we are presently living in yesterday's future and yesterday we wondered how we could be better prepared for today. Of course, that's what futurists attempt to find out."

He would start soft and touch on the academic world's perspective, and show how the futurists of the mid-sixties had accurately predicted a "greening" of America. "Over the past thirty years, we've seen a growing interest in the environment, holistic medicine, natural foods, and vegetarian diets. We recycle our garbage, work to save our rivers and wetlands and celebrate Earth Day. We spend billions of vitamins and herbs each year. We eat far less meat, and watch our diets as never before. Meditation, relaxation, and yoga are practiced by millions. Blah, blah, blah . . ."

Then he'd tell them how inaccurate the futurists had been regarding technology. "For the most part, the futurists of the sixties did not foresee the widespread use of computers in the home or the development of the Internet as a viable mass communications system. They saw people living on large space stations and colonies on Mars, but they didn't foresee that millions of us would spend hours each day in something called cyberspace. That was a big miss, a very big one. So how can we expect anything better from today's futurists?''

He would move on to the hard-edged, life-and-death scenarios of the military and their use of psychics. He would give them several examples of how remote viewers—many of them military officers— had tuned into future events as well as present events occurring elsewhere. Then he would finish with a startling prediction that would leave them buzzing. By evening, he would be featured on the national news, then the interviews would follow. He would gain national stature, the visibility and power that he longed for. Of course, he couldn't talk about everything. His most important projects could never come to the public's attention. But the publicity would bring in new clients interested in remote viewing.

He glanced once more at his reflection, then moved over to the closet, where he pulled on a robe. Maxwell expected a waiter to arrive with his dinner at any moment. He walked across the luxurious room and looked out the eighth-floor window of the Brown Palace Hotel onto downtown Denver. He'd never stayed here before, yet there was something about this hotel, something from the past, something significant, that he was forgetting. He'd been trying to remember it ever since he'd checked in two hours ago, but for some reason he couldn't pull it out of his memory banks.

A tap on the door distracted him. He walked over, opened it for a man in a white coat with a dinner cart and covered platters. The waiter kept his head obsequiously bowed, as if he were studying the carpeting. He muttered something about dinner.

Maxwell frowned, stepped aside. ''Okay, bring it in.''

The waiter moved into the room, then slowly unloaded the cart onto the table. Maxwell slipped a couple of dollars from his billfold. ''Okay, I'll take it from here,'' he said impatiently. ''Here ya go.''

The man turned and stared at him, but didn't take the tip. A handsome, but tough-looking man of forty or so, the waiter looked more like somebody's security chief than a food server. "Hiya, Max. How are ya?"

Maxwell, stunned, took a step back and stared at the stranger. "Who are you?"

Then he recognized the icy pale blue eyes. He couldn't believe it. His heart pounded, his face flushed. He felt confused, disoriented. "General . . . ! I mean, George. Is that you?"

George Wiley laughed. "You can still call me 'general.' Most people I see these days do. But to them, I *am* their general." He turned his head to the side. "So what do you think of my new look? It's a work in progress."

Several seconds passed and Maxwell started to recover, but now his surprise shifted to fear. Any moment, federal agents might burst into the room. His hands trembled. His stomach twisted in knots. They would drag both of them away and Maxwell's hopes and plans would be instantly extinguished, forever gone.

"Jesus Christ. What the hell are you doing here? I'm trying to protect you and you intentionally walk right into a hornet's nest."

Wiley, whose picture graced the top of the FBI's most wanted list, just smiled. His nose appeared thinner, his dark hair several shades lighter and longer, and his mouth seemed fuller. But if Maxwell recognized him, so might his pursuers.

Hell, everyone knew about him. His notorious career had all the making of a Sunday night television movie. The young officer who had risen rapidly under the wing of General Norman Schwarzkopf during the Gulf War. A general at thirty-five. But two years later, he'd faced charges of sexual battery by four women officers. He'd evaded conviction, but had been forced to resign his commission in disgrace. He'd disappeared from sight for a year before emerging as the elusive leader of a white separatist militia based in several western states. Within months, he faced two murder charges in the death of men associated with Freedom Nation, the political umbrella group associated with the militias.

During the Gulf War, Wiley had secretly engaged Maxwell's remote viewers—psychic spies—to gather information that he used to
make his recommendations to General Schwarzkopf. By the time Wiley
had gone underground, Maxwell had retired and had started his private
remote viewing operation. When one of the ex-general's lieutenants in
Freedom Nation had approached him, Maxwell at first had begged off.
But the money had been too good to turn down and the challenge of
using remote viewers to protect someone like Wiley had intrigued him.
Besides, he had missed the feel of power, the sense that he could manipulate historic events.

But now, just as Maxwell was about to make his big break, Wiley
showed up. He wanted nothing to do with him. He had to get rid of
him.

"Don't you understand the danger, George? The president is going
to be here tomorrow. The place is probably swarming with Secret Service agents by now."

Wiley looked amused. "Don't panic, Max. I won't be here long."
He picked up one of the covers on the cart, revealing a pasta dish and
steamed broccoli. "Very healthy. I told the waiter that I was a friend
and that I'd deliver the meal myself as a joke. When I gave him a
twenty, he didn't complain about me borrowing his coat and cart."

"What if he recognized you?"

"He didn't."

"What do you want?"

"I've got an assignment for you. What else? I need your boys to
play some games with the new G-man in charge of finding me."

"Did you have to do it this way?" Maxwell stuttered. "I thought
we had an agreement. No face-to-face contact."

"We also had another agreement," Wiley snapped. "While you
worked for me, you would remain low-key. Talking to these governors
doesn't quite fit my idea of low-key."

Rage flickered within him. Deep, long-held resentments surfaced.
One of the women who had accused Wiley of sexual misconduct had
been Maxwell's courier, a lieutenant whom Maxwell himself had taken
to dinner a couple of times. He'd been hoping the relationship would

develop further when he'd found out from Wiley himself how he'd forced her to perform for him on her knees after she'd delivered Maxwell's secret sheath of papers.

"I've got my own agenda, George. I'm not one of your fat-ass, racist soldiers. I think for myself and I act for myself. I've helped you out long enough. If you don't like it, that's tough. Now you better get the hell out of here while you've got a chance."

Wiley laughed. "Ah, a little hot under the collar, are we, Max?" He shrugged off the tight-fitting white coat. He filled his chest with air, showing off his admirable physique. Wherever he was hiding, it must include a weight room. It looked as if he spent a couple of hours a day working out.

"I'm going to walk right out of here as if I own this place. And guess what? If I'm caught now or tomorrow, or the next week or next month, I'll blame it on your petty aspirations. You will go down with me. That's a promise, Max. So you better pray for me. Pray hard."

Three

Calloway hunched over the picnic table outside his silver Airstream, a beer in front of him, a couple of empties to one side, and a portable radio on the other. The software guys had packed up and left the Sand Island campground for an all-night drive to California. A troop of Boy Scouts and their leaders who'd arrived earlier in the day had settled into their tents. Calloway quietly thanked the Scouts for rafting on their own without a guide. That meant he could sleep in the morning. He sipped his beer and listened to the yammer on AM radio.

"You keep blabbing about this great, nonviolent movement, about all the people in the West someday coming to their feet and turning away the federal government by referendum . . ."

"Hallelujah!" the talk show host interrupted.

"That's all fine and good. But it ain't gonna happen that way. You seem to think that all the Jewish bankers, the corporate internationalists, and world government promoters are going to just sit back and let us create Freedom Nation and go our merry way. Uh, uh. No, sir. I'll tell you that now. They won't allow it."

A distant flicker of lightning followed by a rumble of thunder interrupted the broadcast. Calloway cast his eyes upward. The sky appeared clear overhead, but he knew that thunderstorms could come up suddenly.

"So what do you think is going to happen, Joe?" the broadcaster asked. "You've got all the answers. Let's hear it."

"Now I know you're not going to like hearing this, Brian, you being the moderate voice and all and trying not to make this a race issue, but let me tell you what I've picked up on the Internet. The government has a special program in Los Angeles, New York, and Chicago in which they are training black gang members in techniques for invading houses and disarming residents."

"Ha, ha. That's a good one, Joe. Do you think they really need to be trained?"

Joe wasn't laughing. "I tell you that the last straw will be when they come to get our guns. That's when I end my nonviolence and so do my neighbors. We're not going down without a fight and we're getting ready now."

Calloway turned off the radio and reached for another beer in his cooler. Ever since the talk show hosts had gotten wind that the president would be going to Denver this week to speak at the Western Governors Conference, the rabble-rousers had been taking their potshots. Brian Hawkins's show, in particular, attracted militia types who wanted to form their own country in a few western states.

"So, Calloway, you like listening to that racist shit?"

He turned and saw Art standing in the shadows a few feet away. Tall and lanky, his hair in a ponytail, he wore an unbuttoned flannel checked shirt over a T-shirt.

"I thought you guys left."

"A couple of us decided to leave in the morning. I was thinking of visiting your boss before we left and having a little chat with him."

Christ, the bastard was going to tattle on him like a damned schoolkid. Calloway wasn't about to apologize. Or beg him not to tell Miller what happened. That was exactly what Art wanted to hear.

"You know, if those militia guys ever got their way, the whole country would probably fall apart," Calloway said. "It would be like the end of the Soviet Union—American-style—the West, the South, Northeast, the Midwest, all separate little nations complaining and pushing and shoving each other. What a fucking mess."

Art stared at him. "Yeah. I suppose."

He turned and walked away into the night.

Calloway thought back to the incident and admitted to himself that pushing Art had felt good—at least for half a second. His thoughts drifted to the Indians on the riverbank. They had looked like flesh-and-blood beings from the past who had somehow penetrated time. Normally, such a mystical experience would intrigue him. But the startling appearance and disappearance had left him feeling uneasy and he couldn't figure out why.

Ask the river about it. He smiled at the thought. A couple of weeks ago, as he'd sat here with a beer, an old Navajo had wandered up to him. He'd looked out at the river, then turned to Calloway. "You know, a river will never lie to you," he'd said in broken English, then walked on.

Calloway ambled over to the riverbank, beer in hand, and gazed down into the swirling torrent. "Okay, river, I need some answers," he said tentatively. He felt foolish talking aloud to the water and looked around to make sure he was alone.

Then he squatted on the riverbank and continued, "I need to know the truth about something. Why did I see those Indians? What was that about?"

He stared intently at one spot in the river and watched the flow. Minutes passed. He felt the power of the water pumping like blood through the land. He listened to the gurgling that lapped at his ears, listened for several minutes. He felt chilled in his T-shirt; his legs ached from squatting. A river may never lie, but it might not talk to you, either, he decided.

He reached for his beer, stood up, and crushed the nearly empty can in his fist. He started to hurl it into the water when a blinding flash of lightning strobed the night, instantly followed by a pummel of thunder that slapped hard against his chest. His left foot slipped on the loose gravel. He lost his balance, slid down the embankment. He bounced his head, scraped his palms, and plunged into the icy water up to his knees.

He groaned, dragged himself out of the water, and lay back against the embankment. He gazed up and something shimmered in front of him. He blinked his eyes. Not an angel, not a glimpse of heaven. No uplifting message from the gods. Just a number. It stood out against the dark sky and seemed to hover in front of him.

962-033.

It wasn't a phone number, or part of his social security number, or any number he recognized. Yet, there was something familiar about it, something vaguely upsetting.

He rolled over and crawled up the embankment. He smelled sizzled wood and saw a thick, lower limb of an immense cottonwood split open. Smoke wafted from the tree; an electrical charge hung in the air. He brushed the dirt off his clothes, noting that he'd been standing less than ten feet from the tree. Too close.

Once was enough. He'd been hit by lightning years ago while on leave in South Florida, and he'd survived. But his life had taken a dramatic shift after that. He'd recovered, but even though he could function as a normal person, he'd never been quite the same. At first, he thought his air force career was over. But when he discovered that he knew what people were thinking and he could see what was going on elsewhere, his career had taken a new turn.

He walked back to the trailer, tugged off his boots and jeans, then peeled away his T-shirt. He leaned over his sink and splashed water in his face. His nut brown skin looked grizzled in the mirror.

"You're lucky you're still alive, Calloway," he told himself. "That was close."

He gently probed the tender spot where his head had struck the ground and winced at the pain. He lay back on his cot and took several long, deep breaths and with each exhalation he imagined the throbbing sensation receding. He relaxed, allowing his eyes to close slowly. Just as he started to drift off, he saw the numbers again: **962-033.** They loomed on the underside of his eyelids—white digits on a black background—as if they'd been tattooed there.

Stop ignoring it, he told himself. Maybe the river had spoken to him after all, reminding him of his past. He'd wanted to dismiss the numbers as unimportant and now he knew why. Six-digit numbers played a major role in the world he'd once lived, in the world he'd abandoned and had tried so hard to forget. From time to time he thought about using the skills he'd gained during his last several years in the air force, but that inevitably brought back bad memories of how it had ended. Memories of Colonel Gordon Maxwell and the death of Bobby Aimes.

He sat up in bed, kept his eyes closed, and focused on his breathing. He figured the numbers related to one of the targets that he'd been given. But what target, and why had they appeared to him today? He gradually sank into his zone, the state of mind where the body was relaxed, the mind quiet but alert, his launchpad for finding targets. When he had worked in Project Eagle's Nest, he'd always been guided by a monitor. They'd typically followed a rigorous protocol—an established set of procedures—so that as he sank deeper and deeper, he gradually perceived more and more difficult information about his target. But he didn't want to go through stages now. He just needed raw data on the numbers.

He repeated the six digits to himself over and over again, waiting for an image to appear. Nothing happened. Maybe after his four-year hiatus, he'd lost his ability to remote view. He realized he was thinking again. He released his concerns and focused on his breath. After several minutes, he noticed pillars and wondered how long he'd been staring at them before the image had registered. The instant his thoughts kicked in, the pillars vanished.

Calloway is working again.

He blinked open his eyes and looked around, half expecting to see someone standing in the trailer. "What the hell was that?" he asked aloud. The words had sounded as if they'd been spoken by an invisible person standing next to him.

First, the Indians, then the numbers, and now a voice. The appearance of the Indians from the past had foreshadowed the numbers, and the numbers indicated something else, something more than he'd glimpsed. But where did that voice come from? He'd even sensed emotion—surprise and concern. But it must've been a part of him, his subconscious thoughts surfacing, expressing his own feelings about what he was doing. It certainly wasn't the river and he doubted that it was the Indians.

He stared at the ceiling of his trailer, too restless to sleep. He still felt a dull pain when he touched the spot on the back of his head, but the throbbing had vanished. At least the remote viewing had resulted in something positive. That was more than he could say for his years of psychic spying for the military and CIA. He'd changed from his easygoing old self, a man who loved his wife and had looked forward to starting a family, to one more and more obsessed with his work and suspicious of everything outside it.

He and Camila had carried on a long-distance relationship, even though both lived in the same house. When they did see each other, they'd argued. Sometimes, he'd inadvertently brought home his work and had actually taken on some of the traits of the people he'd remote viewed—terrorists, drug dealers, megalomaniacs. Not only did he and his colleagues psychically spy on their targets, but at times they sank into the persons, assuming their thoughts and emotions, literally donning their self-images.

He recalled the day that he'd nearly assaulted Camila just an hour after targeting Saddam Hussein. He was supposed to remain in the facility for three hours after going into a subject, but he'd snuck out a back door and rushed home, certain that he would catch Camila in bed with another man. He'd found her folding clothes in the laundry room, but that didn't deter him. He'd accused her of having affairs, of plotting to end their marriage. She'd denied the accusation and he'd barely stopped himself from grabbing her throat and throttling her.

He'd blamed Saddam for the incident and promised it wouldn't happen again. But a week later, he'd renewed the accusations when Camila had come home late from work. Even though, he hadn't remote viewed that day, he'd raved and nearly grabbed a butcher knife from the kitchen drawer. That did it. He knew the next time he might lose control, and so he'd left.

Since then, he'd feared getting involved with another woman, and after retiring, he'd taken up the nomadic lifestyle, constantly moving to avoid commitments.

Four

Calloway gradually became aware of a vehicle moving slowing into the campground. He rolled out of the cot and headed for the door. Halfway there, he stepped on an empty beer can.

"Ouch. Shit."

He danced a couple of steps holding his barefoot. He pushed open the door, expecting to see Ed Miller's white pickup. Instead, he gazed out at a blue Explorer. The engine shut down. The door opened and a woman stepped out. He couldn't see her face well, but he glimpsed her short hair and wide girth and that was all he needed.

"Oh, no," he muttered under his breath. "Doc? Is that you?"

"Trent Calloway!" The big woman's voice boomed across the campground. She moved into the light and a smile stretched across her features. "I just knew I'd find you here."

He held up a hand. "Hey, don't wake up the Boy Scouts."

She laughed, moved forward, and hugged him, her pillows of flesh pressing against him. "Great to see you, Calloway."

He stepped back, forced a smile. After four years, she just drops by. "Yeah. So how are you?"

"I'm okay." She studied him a moment in the faint light from the trailer window. "You don't look so good. Are you all right?"

"You woke me up. We go to bed early here."

"Sorry. But you're awake now! I got your card, you know."

"What card?"

"The one last Christmas. I sent a card to your P.O. box in Albuquerque and you sent one back, said you'd be here this summer, and that I should stop by. So here I am."

Yeah, he remembered, but he never figured she'd actually look him up.

"We've got to talk, Trent. It can't wait any longer."

"What can't wait?"

She looked past him to the trailer. "Can we go inside?"

He shrugged. "I wasn't expecting company, but c'mon in."

She followed him into the Airstream and took a seat at one end of the narrow table. "Do you want something to drink, a beer or water, Doc?"

"Water's fine."

He moved over to his tiny kitchen area and filled a glass of water from a bottle in his compact refrigerator and popped open another Bud. "Doc, is it something . . . something from before?"

"Of course it is."

Her words, or rather the way she said them, reminded him that he had often found Doc an overbearing, know-it-all from their days at Eagle's Nest. She seemed about to say something further, but held back. Not like her, he thought. Reticence had never been one of Doc's traits.

He thought again of the voice he'd heard when he'd tried to remote view and its cold assessment of his action. He realized it wasn't exactly an invisible presence, nor was it his subconscious. Someone had been looking in on him from elsewhere, remote viewing just like he used to do. But why on this night? That person, in one manner or another, had addressed a third party, and Calloway had picked up the message. *Calloway is working again.* A chill raced through him. He thought he'd left the world of psychic spies behind forever, but maybe he was kidding himself.

Doc sipped her water and began by telling him about her quiet life in the precipitous town of Ouray, Colorado, high in the Rockies, where she and a niece ran a bookstore.

He recalled that her real name, Miriam Boyle, rarely had been used during her tenure with Eagle's Nest. She held a Ph.D. in psychology, and after she'd been introduced as Dr. Boyle on her first day she'd been dubbed Doc. The name, it turned out, had fit her well because, in her own way, she had been a healing force within the secret project—a know-it-all who mothered "the psi-gang," as she called the other remote viewers.

"I've been cutting down on my hours lately, though," she explained. "Actually, I try to stay in the house as much as possible. I can do the accounting and ordering new stock right from home."

He guessed that something was missing from the story, and waited patiently for her to get to the point of her visit. But she seemed content to dance around the matter.

"So, what do you do when you're not leading these rafting trips?"

"I only do the trips in the summer. Then I drive from campground to campground, town to town. Down to Baja. Then in the spring, back up here."

"You're a free bird, Trent. But I don't think I could live like that. Not for long."

She finished her water and gathered her thoughts. "Have you talked to any of the others?"

He shook his head. "You're the first since I left."

She nodded. "That's what I thought. You need to know what's happened with everyone. It's important."

Good old Doc, he thought. Already telling him what was best for him. He didn't need it. "I'm not interested. I've put that time behind me."

"Like hell you have."

"What's your point, Doc?"

She leaned forward. Her hand shook as she raised it. "We were psychic spies, remote viewers, who could see what was happening on the other side of the world, but you know what? We couldn't see what was right under our noses."

"I believe it. But so what? That's over."

"Do you remember when we found out that the Fort Meade group was getting the same targets we were?"

"Yeah, we thought it was a lot of useless duplication, as I recall, and it was. But that's the military."

"It was more than that."

"Okay. So what's the story? I know you didn't drive all the way here from Ouray for a late-night chat about old times."

"About three months ago, our old buddy, Eduardo Perez, showed up at my door."

"Ah, Eduardo, the lotto king. What's he doing with his millions, building bunkers?"

Perez had been the only remote viewer who had won a lottery. He had attempted to see the winning numbers week after week, but always missed, rarely hitting more than one or two. Then one night, as the story went, instead of numbers, he glimpsed a name: Yaro Lu. He didn't know who it was or what it meant. But he changed the letters to numbers, according to their placement in the alphabet, and played them. Yaro Lu hit a jackpot worth eight million dollars.

"Not a bad guess. I'll get to that. After the project ended, he tried to find out more about Eagle's Nest. So he invoked the Freedom of Information Act and got his hands on a document that referred to the Fort Meade remote viewers as a control group."

"Perez was a conspiracy nut. He was always talking about enemy remote viewers attacking us. I remember he was convinced that the Chinese were using remote viewers to psychically force cooks to poison the take-out Chinese food that we ordered on those days we targeted Chinese installations."

Doc seemed in no mood to make light of Perez's past. "Do you want to hear what he found out?"

"Okay, I'm game. So if they were a control group, what were we?"

"The experiment."

Calloway frowned. "What experiment?"

"Do you remember that civilian technician, Jenkins, who always took our blood pressure at the beginning of each session?''

"Yeah, the skinny kid with the glasses that always slipped down his nose. We used to make fun of him because he wore surgical gloves, like he was worried that we might be contagious.''

"That's it!'' She grabbed his hand and squeezed. "Those gloves were key!''

He took back his hand. "The key to what?''

"One day I noticed that he painted something on the inside of the blood pressure belt. He usually did it in his tech room before he came into the viewing room. But on that particular day he forgot and did it in front of me. When I asked him what it was, he seemed sort of evasive, at first. Then he called it a transmitting gel that helped give a better reading.''

Calloway clearly recalled that the inside of his forearm was often damp when the belt was removed.

"I'd forgotten all about it until after Eduardo showed up and told me about that document,'' Doc continued. "I think we were being subjected to a drug that was absorbed through our skin from the inside of the blood pressure belt. I tried tracking down Jenkins to verify it, but there is no record of a James Jenkins ever working at the base in Colorado Springs.''

"And the other group didn't get the drug.''

"That's my guess. They were the control group.''

Calloway stared out the window into the darkness. "So what does it mean? Did it make us any better psychic spies?''

"Maybe. But that's a moot point. The important matter is the side effects.''

"What side effects?''

"They seem to vary. Mine relate to crowds. That's why I moved to Ouray.'' She hesitated, bit her lower lip as if she wasn't sure she wanted to continue. "I hate small towns. I'm a city girl. I grew up in Chicago. But now if I go into a city or around a lot of people, I just lose it. It starts with a dull headache that gets worse, then I start shaking and gasping for breath. Sometimes, it even happens when I'm in a room with more than a couple of people.''

"How do you handle the bookstore?"

"I only work mornings when it's slow. I stock the shelves and put in orders. If some customers show up, I close my eyes for a few seconds and imagine that I'm all alone at the top of a mountain. That usually works for a while. Then I have to call Marla, my niece, to take over the shop."

She shook her head, tears came to her eyes. "I've been incapacitated, Trent. I hate it. I came here at night so I could avoid running into a bunch of campers. It's that bad. When Marla left town for a week, we closed the store and I had groceries delivered to the house."

"And you think that's from the drug?"

"It actually started while we were still working together. You remember how I made up excuses to avoid meetings. I'd monitor you in the viewing room and do paperwork. I managed to hide it pretty well, but even then it was on my mind all the time."

"I didn't know. I'm sorry."

"I'm not the only one." She sipped her water. "With Johnstone, it's driving. He goes into a trance and forgets what he's doing. He also thinks that the government is beaming him with some sort of invisible rays. Timmons developed an obsessive fear of germs. He washes his hands all the time, changes his clothes five, six times a day, and won't touch anyone."

"I wouldn't want to get stuck in an elevator with those two," Calloway said.

"Henderson is into animals in a big way."

"He was always talking about his dogs."

"I know, but now he's got fifteen or twenty of them, at least a couple of dozen cats, and a horse with its own bedroom in his house," Doc explained. "He likes animals better than people and spends most of his time dealing with his menagerie."

"What's the horse doing in the bedroom?"

She smiled. "Glad you asked. He says that he and the horse are in telepathic communication, and the horse requested an in-house stable."

"I wouldn't be surprised if he thought the horse came from Arcturus," Calloway said. "Henderson always wanted to do UFO targets."

She nodded. "I remember that. You asked about Perez. He's a rich survivalist type. He lives in an underground mansion he built near Crested Butte Mountain with a five-year supply of food. He told me he's concerned that an asteroid is going to hit the Earth and that it'll cause the poles to shift."

"He can support his paranoia in style now. What about Steve Ritter?"

"Remember how he always talked about trains?"

"Right, especially steam engines that ran on narrow gauge rails." Calloway also remembered him as being competitive and antagonistic.

"He lives in a room in a nineteenth-century hotel in Durango, Colorado, and once or twice a week rides the old train to Silverton and back. He rarely leaves the hotel except for his train ride."

Calloway thought about his own nomadic life, drifting from one campsite to the next with no long-range plans and his obsessing about the past, about Camila and Bobby Aimes. He leaned back in his chair. "I guess I do feel handicapped from what we went through. But I don't know if it relates to any drug. Maybe it was the remote viewing itself."

Things had gotten strange during the last winter in Colorado Springs. Doc had left and told him he should do the same. But he'd stayed on another three months. With the support for the project collapsing, Maxwell had been desperate for results. He'd pushed Calloway beyond the limits of anything they'd done, and Calloway had never gotten over it.

"I thought about that, too. So I checked on the control group," Doc said. "There are a couple of eccentrics among them, but none of them are exhibiting the mentally dysfunctional behavior of our gang. Several of them have turned their experience into profitable businesses. They teach and do contract work."

"Gordon Maxwell, too?"

She nodded. "He calls himself a futurist now. He gets contracts with corporations and uses remote viewing to pick up on trends. At least, that's the cover story. Eduardo thinks he's involved in corporate spying and who knows what else."

"You mean he's doing it himself now?"

"Not exactly. He's got the old gang involved, all but you, me, and Eduardo."

"So they can still do it?"

Doc shrugged. "They're obsessive, paranoid, and antisocial, but that apparently doesn't stop them from hitting targets."

"I'm surprised that Maxwell hasn't come after you."

She folded her hands on the table. "He called about a month after Eduardo stopped by. He wanted to know if I'd like to start doing some targets again. I wouldn't even have to leave home."

"That sonofabitch better not approach me. I hope you're not going back to work for him."

"The money is good, Trent, and he would like you to get involved, too."

Calloway pushed away from the table, stood up. He suddenly realized that Doc had come here to lure him back. "Are you crazy? What about that drug?"

"It could be interesting."

"Interesting? No! You don't understand everything that went on between me and Maxwell." He pointed to the door. "Go back to your little mountain town, Doc. I don't want anything to do with it. Or you, for that matter."

"Trent, sit down," she bellowed. "You've got it all wrong, you stupid sonofabitch. I despised Maxwell when you were still defending him."

He took a breath, slowly exhaled, calming himself down. He sat back down. "So what is it?"

"Look, he didn't give up easy. So I played along with him. He even gave me Ritter's phone number and told me to talk to him if I wanted another perspective. That was how I found out about the others. Ritter, in his usual arrogant way, told me about their quirks as if to say that if *they* were doing it, so could I."

Calloway leaned back in his chair. "Okay. So what's your plan?"

She smiled. "I think we should infiltrate the bastards. See what they're up to, then go public, expose Maxwell for what he is. There's a lot of money involved. That makes me think there's something crooked going on.''

Calloway already knew what his answer would be. "Sorry, Doc. I'm not going back and I'm not really interested in finding out what Maxwell is doing with his boys.''

"Trent, we might be getting dragged back into it, whether we like it or not. I've been hearing shit in my head. Voices. I catch words, phrases. At first, I thought I was going nuts. None of it made sense. Then I realized it was them. I'm picking up on the other remote viewers while they're working. It's like I'm overhearing pieces of their conversations.''

"How do you know that's what it is?''

"I don't, not for certain. That's why I wanted to talk to you. Have you had anything like this happen to you?''

Calloway is working again.

"No. Nothing like that.''

She watched him closely. "What aren't you telling me? C'mon, out with it.''

"For chrissake, Doc.'' He knew he couldn't fool her, not for long. He told her about his day—the Indians, the lightning, the numbers. "I tried the numbers. All I got was a brief glimpse of pillars. But then as I came out of it, I heard a voice, as if someone was talking about me.''

He told her what he'd heard.

She frowned, shook her head. "It was them, Trent. You've got to go for that target again,'' she said, emphatically. "Let's do it now. I'll monitor you.''

"No way. I'm not getting involved. Besides, I'm tired. It's late.''

"Hey, I drove all the way here from Ouray today. Five hours. I'm tired too, but we need to do this now.''

Calloway ran a hand through his short, natty hair. "No we don't. Look, Doc. I've got tomorrow off. I'll take you out on the river.''

"Like hell you will. Listen to me, you sonofabitch. This morning I was working in my garden. I looked up and there you were standing by a stone wall with hundreds of petroglyphs on it.''

He nodded, surprised by both her vehemence and her accuracy. "You're right. I was there. That was where I saw the Indians."

"But you spoke to me. I heard your voice in my head."

"What did I say?"

"You said that we had work to do, that we had to stop the bastards before it was too late."

"I said that?"

"I interpreted that to mean we should infiltrate Maxwell's gang."

"Let's talk about it tomorrow. You can sleep on my cot. I'll take the hammock."

"Damn it, Trent." She raised her voice again. "You need to hit that target. Those numbers didn't appear for no reason and some part of you did reach out to me."

He scowled. He'd almost gotten hit by lightning, he'd fallen into the river, and now he was getting berated by a fat lady who wanted him to remote view in the middle of the night and maybe even go work for his old boss—a man he never wanted to see again.

"I'll tell you what, Doc. I'll shoot for that target. We'll see what I get. But I'm not going to go to work for Maxwell, even if it is to expose him." He waved a hand in front of him. "That's the end of it."

Doc looked disappointed. Tough, he thought.

He sat on the cot, a couple of pillows propped up behind him. He began breathing deeply and slowly. Doc handed him a notepad from her purse. "Write down the numbers you got," she said quietly. "I'll feed them back to you once you're down."

The numbers came easily to mind. He jotted them on the pad and handed it back to her. He drifted down into his zone and this time he pictured a dark hole to one side. He tossed all of his concerns into it, including his worries that he wouldn't succeed and his regrets about the past. To top it off, he tossed a metaphorical six-pack of beer into the hole and sealed it shut. Then he redirected his attention to Doc as she slowly read the numbers aloud.

He cleared his mind and focused. After a couple of minutes, Doc repeated the numbers and told him to take his time. He'd always been known as the quickest one to pick up images, but now he wasn't getting anything. He tried again. This time he pictured the numbers hovering in front of him, as he'd seen them by the river.

The image of the pillars reappeared. They took on dimension and he realized that they were in front of another structure. "I see a building with pillars. But something's wrong here."

"Is the building occupied?"

He didn't feel good about the place. He moved away until he gained a better perspective. The pillars tilted precariously, little remained of the building.

"It's in ruin. Devastated."

"Okay. Move further away, get an overview."

"I don't see anything recognizable. It's rubble, pieces of buildings in every direction."

"How old are the buildings?"

"I can't tell," he said slowly. "There's no reference here."

"I want you to go deeper now, Trent. Down to stage two. You can do it."

He took several slow, deep breaths, feeling himself sinking further and further down, but maintaining his view of the site. When Doc spoke again, he felt as if he were actually among the ruined buildings. At the same time, he remained aware of himself sitting in the trailer.

"Okay, Trent, now tell me exactly where you are. Let's start with the big picture. What continent are you on?"

"North America." He answered without hesitating, even though he wasn't sure how he knew.

"Where in North America?"

This time he took longer. "I think it's Washington, D.C."

"Are you sure?"

"I see something in front of me now . . . more broken pillars and a figure, a statue. I think it's Abraham Lincoln from the shoulders up."

"You mean a part of the Lincoln Memorial?"

"Yes."

"Is it the same building you saw before?"

"No. That was the White House. What's left of it." At one level, he responded quietly to her questions as if he were simply a knowledgeable observer. But on another level, he felt numbed with shock by the realization.

"Is this a future event?" Doc asked.

"I don't understand. I'm here now. I see smoke or clouds. I can't tell. The sky is odd. Very low. It's green, yellow, red. It's windy. A swirling wind."

"Trent, do you want to come back now?"

"No, not yet."

"Okay, let's go down to the third level. Take your time. Sink into it, to that place where you will have greater knowledge than what you can see or even what you can sense."

He imagined lead weights attached to his legs as he sank deeper and deeper. He remained bilocated, but also aware of another layer, an abstract place of knowledge, an invisible library. He couldn't tell how much time had passed when he finally heard Doc's voice.

"Move your finger up and down if you're ready," she told him. "Good. Now, tell me what time frame you're viewing."

"Near future. Very close."

"How close? Be specific."

"Days. Not many. Four or five more days."

"What happened to the capital?" she asked.

"A nuclear bomb exploded."

"How did it get through our defenses?"

"Oh, it was already here. Carried into the city in a backpack. Powerful, but small."

"Can you move back to the time when the bomb arrived in the city?"

"I can't move back there, but I can see things related to the explosion." He spoke in a matter-of-fact tone. "A kid is carrying the bomb to Washington. He's eighteen or nineteen. He only has a vague idea of what he's doing. It's a complicated matter."

"Are there others involved?"

"The kid is a courier for somebody else."

"Who?"

He felt as if someone were watching him, the same way he'd felt earlier, before Doc arrived. He pushed away the thought, concentrated. But it was no use. "I can't tell. But it might be a group of people involved."

Stick to your rafts, Calloway. It's safer. Much safer.

"I know you're tired, Trent," Doc said. "But this is important. Can you get a name of the kid?"

"Name. I don't know. Wait. Okay. Matthew."

"Can you get a last name?"

Watch it, Calloway! The voice sounded darker this time, threatening.

He reached toward the fuzzy image of the kid named Matthew, searching for a last name, but the annoying voice rattled inside his head. He came up blank. He shook his head. "I'm losing it."

"All right, Trent, I want you to come back now. Take your time."

Calloway withdrew from the target and settled completely into himself again. The other presence vanished. Doc's skin and hair seemed to glow in the lamplight. Everything in the trailer seemed to vibrate. He'd experienced such phenomena other times after returning from third-level sessions.

He moved from side to side. He winced as he felt tingling in his legs and feet. His lower back ached. "How long was I down?"

"Two hours and forty-six minutes."

"That long? It felt like minutes."

"Yes, and you came up with a week's worth of material. I just don't know . . ."

". . . if it's true," he finished.

"I didn't say that, Trent. I don't know what we should do about it. But we've got to do something. We can't sit back and wait four more days to see if it comes true. We may be the only outsiders who know what's going on. Or at least have an inkling about it."

He closed his eyes. Everything would've been a lot simpler if he would've sent Doc on her way and gone to sleep. But he didn't and she was right.

"Doc, let's go right to the top."

"What do you mean?"

"The president is speaking tomorrow night in Denver. Let's get some sleep and drive there tomorrow."

Now Doc seemed uneasy. "The president? Maybe we could just call the Secret Service or the FBI."

He shook his head. "We need to be there. We've got to do more sessions to pinpoint the location of the bomb and I want to do it right in front of them." He might be rusty, but he still trusted his abilities.

Doc sat back, frowning. "Jeez, Trent, suddenly you're very gung ho on this thing. Does this have something to do with your ex, Camila?"

"She can open doors." If she'll even talk to me, he thought.

"But do you think she'll be there?"

"She seems to go everywhere he goes." She'd been on David Dustin's staff since he was a senator.

"When did you last see her?"

"Six years ago," he said without hesitating.

Doc nodded. But now her confidence seemed to waver. "It's a good idea, but maybe you should go by yourself."

"Wait a minute. I need you to monitor me. I've never worked well by myself."

She rubbed her arms, made a face. "There's going to be a lot of people there, Trent."

"I need you there, Doc," he said, emphatically. "I'm not going to do it without you."

She stood up. "I'm going out to my Explorer. I've got a sleeping bag and cushions."

"I'll take that as a yes," he called after her.

FRIDAY

Five

She wandered around the ballroom of the Brown Palace Hotel in downtown Denver, a glass of Perrier in hand, greeting old friends and casual acquaintances and moving on, searching for Harvey Howell. She needed to talk to Howell, the president's national security advisor, about a matter that had arisen during the afternoon.

"Oh, you must be Camila Hidalgo. I've seen you lately on CNN."

She turned and smiled at Barry Greer, a CNN reporter. "Hi, Barry. What's up?"

He beamed back at her, showing perfect teeth. A handsome, square-jawed man with clear blue eyes, Greer combined aggressive reporting with a friendly, I'm-your-pal approach. "That's what I was going to ask you, Camila."

Two weeks ago, she'd been appointed as acting spokesman for the president, an imposing position with endless responsibilities. She'd once yearned for the job, but when it had been offered to her, she'd reluctantly assumed it and only with the understanding that it would be temporary. She didn't feel comfortable standing in front of the cameras day after day and looked forward to returning to her behind-the-scenes work as a special assistant to the president.

"The president is going to speak on the new outlook on the federal-state relations."

"Oh, that's so dull, dull, dull. Do you think he'll take any questions afterwards?"

"I doubt it. What do you want to ask him?"

"What he thinks of that talk by Gordon Maxwell this afternoon. Specifically, Maxwell's prediction that several western states will break from the union in the next five to ten years."

She'd heard the talk. She'd gone to the luncheon not so much out of duty, but out of curiosity to see the man who had been her ex-husband's boss during most of his career in air force intelligence. "That was a rather dramatic statement. I wish he had made it at a meeting of futurists rather than before the Western Governors Conference."

"He'll get better coverage here."

"If you're any indication, that's certainly true. But don't count on the president to say anything about it tonight. He won't take questions and he's leaving for his vacation immediately after the speech."

Greer smiled. "Then again, David Dustin sometimes does the unexpected."

"Don't count on that, either."

"Well, I suppose we can always shout at him outside, if all else fails," Greer added after a moment in his usual breezy manner. "By the way, you got any plans tonight after the dinner?"

"My plans, Barry, are to go to bed and get a good night's sleep."

He took a step closer. "Did I hear you say something about going to bed?"

"Yes, by myself."

"Sorry to hear that part. You know I still wear my heart on my sleeve for you."

You mean you've got something up your sleeve, she thought. She liked Greer and had gone out with him several times. But she'd cut off the relationship when she'd realized that Greer wanted to tangle himself in her life, something she didn't need or want. Not now at least, and not ever with him. Greer was just too good looking, too perfect. Mr. Everything. Everything but modest and subtle. His ego would probably swallow the relationship whole. She preferred men with some rough edges. At least, that was her history.

She spotted Howell moving across the ballroom. "I gotta go." She touched his sleeve. "Put it back where it belongs, Barry."

"Two hearts together are better than one," he called after her.

She walked over to Howell, who held a half-empty glass of red wine in his hand. He looked distracted, as if he needed to be somewhere else. In his early fifties with short-cropped hair and round wire-framed glasses, Howell had climbed through the ranks of the National Security Administration, then spent four years as director of the intelligence agency before being picked to join Dustin's staff.

"Harvey, we need to talk about this bombshell that the futurist dropped this afternoon. I'm sure I'll be asked about it at the briefing in the morning."

He waved his limp hand and twitched one shoulder as if a fly had landed on it. "Oh, don't worry about him. What does he know? Maxwell can say anything he wants from his ivory tower. Who cares?"

Even though Howell had been married for the better part of two decades, he occasionally displayed certain affectations that Camila associated with gay men. But if he were gay, he carefully hid that side of his life.

"Is that what you want me to say tomorrow?" she persisted. "Should I say that's from you or the president?"

Howell hesitated, reconsidering.

Bluntness often worked well for her. She hadn't become the youngest member of the president's inner circle by being pushed around, or ignored. Whenever she doubted herself, Camila simply looked back on her past accomplishments for reassurance. She'd been the only girl among six children in a Mexican-American family and learned to assert herself to get enough to eat. During her first six years of education, she'd gone to five schools as the family worked its way from Texas to Colorado, and although she excelled, there was no money for college, especially for a girl. But that hadn't deterred her. By graduation, she had won academic awards and scholarships that had paid for most of her education. She had learned early to confront adversity head-on.

She became a congressional page the summer of her junior year of college and returned after graduation to work as a press aide for then—Colorado senator David Dustin. She later served as a press liaison during his campaign for the presidency. After the election, she joined his staff as a speechwriter.

She frowned as she realized that Howell seemed to be studying her outfit, a sleek, off-the-shoulder black cocktail dress that reached the middle of her calves. She glanced down to see what was so interesting.

"Is something wrong?" she asked.

He shook his head, then raised his gaze. "No, nothing. You're on the fourth floor, right?"

She nodded, wondering what that had to do with Maxwell's view of the future.

"Good. I'm in 411. I need to go up to my room and change for dinner." His gaze fell to her body again.

Maybe he wasn't gay. "Harvey, are you all right?"

He blinked, and nodded. "Of course. I'll give David a ring and see how he wants to respond to Maxwell's comments. I'm going to suggest an attack on remote viewing. It'll be from me. I've had some experience with remote viewers and know how fallible they can be. Why don't you stop by in about twenty minutes. We'll go over my comments and go down to dinner."

"Okay." She frowned. On one hand, he seemed to be acting normal, taking charge of the situation. On the other, he seemed troubled and acted oddly.

She set her Perrier on a table and decided to head back to her own room to check her messages and make a couple of calls before meeting Howell. She walked down the hallway of the elegant nineteenth-century hotel with its gold onyx wall trim and marble floors, then crossed the lobby that featured stunning Italian Renaissance architecture. As she rode the elevator to her room, she wondered if she was overreacting to the Maxwell matter. Maybe the less attention paid to him, the better. Then again, she needed to be ready with a response if the issue started attracting attention.

The phone was ringing as she entered her room. She decided to pick up, rather than take a message.

"Hi, Camila. It's Gina Weston. *Insider* magazine."

She wished she'd let Weston leave a message. "Hello, Gina. What can I do for you?"

Weston was a rumormonger and often started her conversations with the phrase, "Is there any truth to the matter . . . ?" She liked short quips rather than lengthy, deep explanations. If she brought up Maxwell's comments, Camila knew how to respond. *You don't plan for the future of the nation by calling a psychic hotline.*

"I'm glad I caught you in your room. I hear that Darcy Mitchell wants out."

"Wants out of what?" Camila feigned ignorance.

Weston paused as if reveling in her knowledge. "Her marriage. She's had it with Mitchell. Too much smoozing with a certain singer and up-and-coming actress."

"Says who?"

"It just came over the AP wire," Weston said, smugly.

"Can you read it to me?"

"Of course. Can you respond to it for me when I'm done?"

"Read it and I'll tell you."

"Okay. Here it is. It's not long." Papers rustled. " 'Could the vice president and his wife, Darcy, be heading to divorce court while he's still in office?

" 'Darcy Mitchell, the wife of vice president Rollie Mitchell, said Friday morning that she is considering divorcing her husband unless he settles down. Mrs. Mitchell refused to expand on the comment, but said, "Rollie will know what I'm talking about."

" 'Vice President Mitchell has been seen in the company of Grammy Award winning singer Sarati Finders on several occasions. When asked last week about their relationship, Finders said they were simply friends. Mitchell was unavailable for comment on his wife's remark ' "

"That's it?" Camila asked.

"Isn't that enough? No one ever gets divorced while in the White House." Weston sounded annoyed with Camila for not getting excited or astonished.

"The vice president doesn't live in the White House," Camila replied, dryly.

"You know what I mean, Camila."

"All married couples have their spats, Gina," she replied evenly. "There's nothing unusual about that. Darcy often says exactly what's on her mind at the moment. Sometimes that's commendable. Other times it's regrettable. I suspect this is one of the latter instances."

"Off the record, Camila, don't you think he's got something going with Finders. I mean, why else would Darcy be making a big stink about it?"

"I know very little about Rollie Mitchell's private life. I certainly wouldn't comment on it or speculate about it, Gina. As for Darcy, I'm not sure she's making a big stink about anything."

"Well, I got the feeling this is going to be a juicy one. That we'll be hearing a lot more about it."

"I hope not."

After she hung up, Camila sat down on the bed. Mitchell had spoken to the governors yesterday on his approach to repairing urban decay. Then he'd promptly left. But where was he now? She picked up the phone, called the vice president's office, and asked to be put through to his chief of staff. She left a message and told him to call her right away.

Camila regarded Mitchell as a better-than-average vice president who had come under more scrutiny than any other vice president in history. As the first Afro-American to attain the office, he was enormously popular among minorities. Yet he had successfully avoided being labeled the president of black America. Nor had he tried to upstage the president. He'd worked hard helping Dustin forge his positions on welfare, health care, race, and crime. He remained a strong advocate of the poor, yet he frequently compared long-term dependence on welfare to slavery.

She glanced at her watch. Time to get Howell and go to dinner. She hoped he had talked with Dustin about Maxwell, as he'd promised. She knew she wasn't going to be able to speak to the president herself until tomorrow. She knocked on his door and wondered if Howell knew that her ex-husband had been a remote viewer. Maybe she should mention it to him.

Answer the door, Harvey. She knocked again. Had Howell forgotten about her?

The door opened. Camila stared, but didn't move, didn't say anything. What she saw left her speechless.

"I'm almost ready, I think," Howell said in a soft voice.

"Ready for what, Harvey?" He wore a pale green gown with falsies, a wig, and high heels. He just needed makeup.

"Aren't we going to dinner?"

"Is this a joke, Harvey? What's going on here?" She stepped into the room and quickly closed the door. She leaned against it, eyes wide, and took in a deep breath.

He moved a couple of steps back, gave her a puzzled look. "I'm not sure."

If he didn't know, then she certainly didn't either. She cautiously stepped closer to him as if he would collapse in a heap if she moved too abruptly. She took his arm and carefully guided him over to the mirror. "Is that how you really want to go to dinner?"

He stared for several seconds. "Oh, my God. What am I doing?"

Stay calm. Humor him. "You're wearing a dress, Harvey. It's a nice dress," she babbled. "But I don't think it's your style."

"It's one of my wife's. She's a size fourteen."

She folded her hands in front of her to keep them from shaking. "Not a bad fit, but wouldn't you rather wear your tux to dinner?"

"I don't know how this happened, Camila. I came in here to change and . . . I don't know."

"Why did you bring a dress to the convention?"

"I don't know."

"Have you worn it before?" she persisted.

"That's none of your business," he blurted, straightening his back. "No, of course not. Now do you mind leaving the room so I can change?"

She folded her arms. "Not yet. I want to know why you did this. Is it something I did, or said?"

"It's got nothing to do with you. Okay, I do cross-dress sometimes, but it's a personal thing. I don't do it publicly. I don't know what possessed me. I simply forgot myself. I'm sorry. Now are you satisfied? Have I sufficiently groveled in front of you?"

"You don't have to apologize, Harvey. I'm worried about you. Do you realize what would've happened it you'd gone down to dinner in a dress?"

"I wasn't about to do that."

She wasn't so sure that was the case. Even if they'd said it was a joke, it would've been a tasteless one that would damage Howell's credibility and raise new questions about David Dustin's administration.

Howell sat on the edge of the bed. "I'm not feeling well. I think I'm going to get room service tonight."

"Room service is a good idea, but . . ." She frowned at the dress.

"Yes, don't worry. I'll change as soon as you leave. Like I said, I really don't know what got into me."

"I better go." She stopped at the door.

"Camila," he called after her. "You won't tell anyone?"

"No, of course not."

"Promise?"

"Yeah, promise."

She headed along the corridor toward the elevator, her head throbbing. That was one promise, for the good of the nation, that she might have to break.

Six

Matt Hennig stood motionless in the dark, cold tunnel guarding the entrance to the ice cavern. A few feet away, Gary Burke, the other sentinel, leaned against the wall, sullen and angry that he'd been assigned guard duty. Hennig didn't like it much either, but he didn't gripe like Burke.

Instead, he occupied himself by thinking about how warm and soft Jill felt when he held her close as they lay naked under the quilt in the back of his camper. They'd done it nine times in two months. He kept count in a journal where he described his encounters with Jill along with his thoughts about the militia and Freedom Nation. Love and duty. Sex and pride. Fun and more fun.

Suddenly, he snapped alert and tightened his grip on his Swiss-made SIG automatic rifle. He stared intently into the dark tunnel that curved away in front of him.

Burke pushed away from the wall. "What's wrong now, Hennig?"

"I thought I heard something," he whispered.

Laughter echoed from the cavern behind him where the men were gathered.

"I hear guys having fun. This is rinky-dink guard duty. No one's going to bother us down here in this goddamn icebox."

"We've got to be prepared for anything," he said, earnestly.

"This is the militia, not the Boy Scouts, Hennig."

Burke, a beefy guy with a shaved head and a swastika tattooed on his shoulder, had recently become a sheriff's deputy. So now he thought he could boss him around. When he'd asked Burke about the tattoo, he'd said the swastika stood for discipline and racial purity and those weren't bad ideals to live by.

Matt thought he understood the need for Idaho to become independent and a part of Freedom Nation so that the feds wouldn't invade their privacy, take away their weapons, and rob more and more of their earnings through taxes, but he was confused by the racial issue. Some people, like Commander Sudner, said the new state would be all white. Separate and white. But others, like Commander Boswell of the North Division, said it would be easier to make a separate nation if they didn't call it a white nation and avoided the race question altogether.

"There, I heard it again. I heard ice cracking," Matt said.

"So what? It probably cracks all the time by itself with changes in temperature. Day and night, you know."

"The temperature doesn't change," he answered. The caves were always thirty degrees, day and night, year around. Matt knew all about it. He worked twenty-four hours a week leading tours in the public section of the caverns.

"Take it easy, will ya, Hennig? You're still a goddamn kid. You got the jitters, that's all."

Matt knew he still looked like a kid, what with his reddish blond hair and freckles. But he stood six foot one and weighed a hundred and eighty pounds. Big as most men, bigger than many. Muscular, too. And he knew a hell of a lot more about these caves than Burke.

He held up his hand. "Listen! There!"

"Yeah, I heard it." Burke didn't sound so confident now.

A faint ghost light gleamed off the icy walls. Matt worked his finger over the trigger on his SIG. "See that?" he hissed. "It's from a flashlight." Footsteps crunched loudly against the icy floor.

"Someone's coming," Burke said. "Stay here. I'll alert the commander."

"Thanks a lot," Matt muttered as Burke lumbered away. He tightened his grip on the rifle. More than one. Maybe three or four. Right around the corner.

He wanted to bolt after Burke, but held his ground as he'd been trained. "Halt! Who's there? Speak up right now!"

"It's General Wiley."

"Prove it!"

He moved forward, sticking close to the wall. It could be a trap. The war game had supposedly ended two hours ago with the capture of Commander Boswell, but maybe some of his men were coming to free him. Only now, he was armed with a rifle and live ammunition, not a paint-ball gun.

"Cat's paw," the man called out.

They knew the South Division code. He didn't like the situation. It still could be a trap. "Okay. Come forward, slowly."

Two men, large and muscular like bodyguards, appeared in his flashlight beam. They aimed automatic pistols and a light at him.

"Take it easy, son," the man behind the guards said. "You're doing your job, but now lower that light and your weapon."

Matt had heard Wiley speak several times and recognized his voice. His hand shook as he followed the orders. Another man, unseen by Matt, moved in from the side and grabbed his rifle. Shit, he'd allowed himself to be disarmed.

"It's okay, son," Wiley assured him. "You did fine."

He looked different than the pictures, but the commander had hinted that Wiley had changed his appearance. Matt knew it was him. He stood at attention and saluted the most important man in the West. Wiley told him to relax and shook his hand. Matt's heart pounded. Just standing near the former U.S. Army general, the hero of the Freedom Nation, the man who would be the first president of the new nation, made him feel incredibly privileged.

Just then Commander Sudner rushed into view, rifle in hand, followed by several others. When he saw Wiley, Sudner looked startled and relieved at the same time. Overweight and out of shape, he huffed as if he'd just run a mile. "How did you find us, sir?"

"I had an observer at your war game. We followed you here after you took Commander Boswell captive." Blond and muscular, Wiley focused his sharp features on Sudner. "If you want a safe hideout, you don't bring the entire squadron in a wagon train, even at night with your lights out.''

"Yes, sir."

"Where's your prisoner? I want to see him."

"We'll go get him, sir." Matt heard an unfamiliar tightness in Sudner's voice. "We'll bring him right out."

"Nonsense," Wiley bristled. He strode past Sudner and into the cavern. Two of his bodyguards followed close behind, the other—the one who had taken his weapon—remained in the tunnel. The man motioned for him to go with the others, but kept the SIG. Matt hesitated, but then hurried after.

Everything looked confused in the cavern and it took Matt a few seconds to figure out what was going on. The men had been drinking beer and had made a belated effort to hide the evidence when they heard that Wiley had arrived. But several cans remained visible. One had tipped over and slowly drained into the hard-packed dirt floor.

Wiley took it all in with a sweeping glance, then his gaze froze on the figure leaning against the wall. Matt turned and saw Boswell sitting up. The hood had been pulled from his head and someone had covered his face with greasepaint. A sign hung around his neck. It read, "ROL-LIE MITCHELL'S BEST BOY!"

"Get that sign off him," Wiley ordered. "Clean up the man's face. Commander Sudner, I want you to apologize to Commander Boswell for exceeding your designated powers, and then I want you to drive him home."

"Yes, sir."

Wiley's penetrating blue eyes peered at the men as if he were sighting them through a rifle. "As for the issue of race, everyone listen very closely to me. We are not white supremacists. We're not trying to oppress any other races. We just want to live in an all-white territory where there would be no need, desire, or for that matter, ability, to oppress people of any other race.

"The fact is, we now have white supremacy under David Dustin's liberal regime in Washington, D.C. They import cheap labor from the

Third World, because the white American man and white woman won't work that cheap. It's a conspiracy between the left-wing state bureaucracy and right-wing international corporations."

Matt tried to follow Wiley's logic so that he could repeat it. But if Dustin was a white supremacist, why did he pick a black man for vice president? Matt wondered.

Wiley apparently knew that question would be asked, if anyone had dared. "Dustin selected Rollie Mitchell for his vice president so he could appease black people. What black people and everyone should be wondering is why Dustin and his coconspirators are so anxious to encourage blacks to speak broken, miserable, semiliterate black English. Any true friend of black people would insist they obtain a classical education in the Holy Bible, Latin, Greek, a modern foreign language, chemistry, physics, Western literature, higher mathematics, and classical music. Instead blacks are being sold out on the lowest common denominator of mis-education. That way they'll be easier to control and enslave."

Matt wondered what the hell Wiley was talking about. He didn't get that kind of education. Did that make him easier to control, too? Maybe things would change in Freedom Nation. But if that was the case, he was glad that he was out of high school. He definitely didn't want to study Greek and Latin.

Wiley looked around at the men. "I've carried on long enough," he said in a lowered voice. "Commander Sudner, we need to talk privately."

The two men moved away from the others and conferred for nearly five minutes. Then Wiley, accompanied by the bodyguards, walked out of the chamber and down the tunnel. Matt knew Wiley never stayed anywhere long, not with the federal government after him. They called him a murder suspect, but Matt knew that Dustin was trying to frame Wiley, to get him behind bars in an effort to stop Freedom Nation.

Sudner headed directly over to Matt. "Do you remember when I told you about a special mission?"

"Yes, I do. I've been waiting on it."

"Well, we're ready now. I'm sending you to Washington, D.C."

The news stunned him. He didn't know how to respond. "Washington? What am I going to do there, blow up Congress?"

Sudner didn't laugh. "You're going to make a delivery. Simple as that. I want you to take Jill with you. Tell her you are taking her to Las Vegas to get married. Do you understand?"

Matt frowned. "No, not really."

Sudner loomed in front of him, leaning into his face. "Just listen to me. Once you're out of town, you tell your bride-to-be that there's a change of plans, that you're making a delivery for me. You'll drive to Washington, drop off the package, then go back to Las Vegas, where you'll get married and spend four days at my expense."

Matt was confused. Marriage, delivering a package. He felt like he'd lost control of his life. He should've never gotten involved with Sudner's daughter. "I'm supposed to go to work, and I'm not sure I'm ready to get married."

"Then you should've left your dick in your pants. In case you don't know, Jill is pregnant. Now you do what I tell you, soldier."

He nodded, feeling numb and astonished, joyful, proud, and frightened all at once. "Yes, sir."

"Any questions?"

"What's the package and where do I take it? I don't know Washington, D.C."

"Meet me tomorrow at seven in the Denny's parking lot. I'll have the package and full instructions. Then you'll go get Jill and be on your way. If she gives you any trouble about the change in plans, you have her call me. Understood?"

He nodded again. "Yes, sir. But does Jill know about any of this?"

"Not yet. That's why you need to get out of here and go talk to her." After a moment, he added: "You do love her, don't you?"

"Yes, sir. Very much."

"Good. Then get going. One other thing. Don't worry about that job. Turn in your resignation on your way out of town tomorrow.

We've got a better job waiting for you when you get back. You're going to work for Freedom Nation.''

"Really? You mean it?" He caught himself, controlled his excitement. "Yes, sir."

He saluted and hurried off.

Seven

Camila sipped her coffee and took a couple of bites of her ice cream as she waited patiently for the president's speech. She had lost her appetite after her encounter with Howell and had merely picked at her chicken dinner. She tried to appear interested in the conversations around her, but her thoughts kept returning to the disturbing image of Howell dressed as a woman. What had possessed him to cross-dress for a presidential dinner? It just didn't make sense.

"I thought Vice President Mitchell gave a fine speech last night," said Marilyn Willis, first lady of Wyoming. "He's such a strong speaker."

"Yes, he is," Camila replied. "His speech hit all the major points of our new health care proposal. What did you think of it?"

As Willis launched into a lengthy reply, Camila reminded herself to check her messages immediately after the president's speech. She'd like to talk to Rollie Mitchell tonight, if possible. Maybe he and Darcy had made up already and she could simply dismiss it as a momentary spat that didn't deserve any attention.

When Colorado's Governor Harmon began his introductory comments, Camila glanced at the podium and then over to the head table where Dustin was sitting. She noticed the empty seat at the table and knew the name tag read Harvey Howell. She wondered if Howell had tried to reach the president before dinner. Somehow, she couldn't imagine the national security advisor discussing the futurist's comments with Dustin as he squeezed into his wife's gown.

Applause filled the room as Dustin ambled to the podium, his lean, six-foot-three frame moving at an unhurried pace. Even though she'd known him for nearly a decade, she still felt thrilled to work for him— for the president. Without a doubt, the office conferred a larger-than-life image upon whoever stepped into it.

While he projected a sense of strength and confidence, he also emanated warmth and understanding, and possessed a quirky side related to his belief in positive thinking and the untapped powers of the unconscious mind. Critics derided him as a feel-good, New Age president who was vulnerable to peculiar ideas and who quoted Carl Jung and Joseph Campbell more than Thomas Jefferson or Abraham Lincoln. She'd saved one cartoon, labeled "The Hero's Journey," that had shown him at the helm of a boat called *Synchronicity* after he'd told a reporter for *Time* magazine about the importance of seemingly coincidental events in his daily life.

"We in Washington are not the caretakers of the states," Dustin began. His speech focused on the administration's new initiative on the federal government's relationship to the states, which allowed the states more flexibility in how they spent federal money. The governors applauded on cue. "Yet, we want the United States of America to remain strong and powerful and we need the cooperation of the states to ensure our future as an international power."

Dustin was responding to the calls, especially from western states, for more independence from federal regulations and other forms of intervention. Some governors even seemed willing to take less money in exchange for less federal governance. Clearly, Gordon Maxwell's vision had drawn on such sentiments, but then carried them to the extreme.

She knew everything that Dustin would say in the prepared text and as he spoke she watched the reactions of the people around her. Dustin would be seeking reelection in two years and she tried to gauge the mood of elected officials. Their placid or agreeable expressions, regulated by the social surroundings of the moment, told her nothing.

But they couldn't hide the look in their eyes, which told her everything she needed to know. She saw agreement and support, even from elected members of the opposition. That seemed to confirm the president's solid standing in the polls.

She raised her gaze to the podium as Dustin paused near the end of his thirty-minute speech. He cocked his head to one side and she knew that he was about to launch into unprepared comments. Dustin's brief but provocative extemporaneous commentaries often attracted more attention than his prepared text. Just two weeks ago, while discussing welfare reform, he'd said that poverty would only be eliminated when people realized that we lived in an abundant universe, not one with limited, dwindling resources. That one had not gone over well with some environmentalists, and Dustin had later explained that he didn't advocate wasting resources.

His off-the-cuff comments had resulted in endless speculation about Dustin's unpresidential side, or his "daffy quotient." But pollsters repeatedly found that most people thought his ideas were refreshing and honest and every time he made one of his quirky remarks, his ratings seemed to rise a point or two.

"I understand that you were told by a futurist this afternoon that in five to ten years we may be losing a few stars from our flag when some of the states you represent secede from the nation." He paused again and smiled.

"Why are we feeling so divided? I wonder. If we were at war now, instead of in a relatively stable period, I doubt that we would be hearing such comments today. War, for all of its terrible aspects, unifies a nation against a common enemy. But let's take this matter a step further. What event would unite people all over the planet? What would help us recognize our commonalties rather than our differences?"

Uh-oh, Camila thought. She knew the answer to that one and hoped that Dustin didn't come off sounding like a lunatic. Greer would get his story, after all, and probably more than he'd expected.

"The answer is the arrival of visitors from another world. I'm not the first world leader to bring up this matter. Ronald Reagan and Mikhail Gorbachev both made references to how the world would be united if the planet was invaded. Prime Minister Gorbachev, back in 1990, said that he believed that the phenomenon of UFOs does exist and it must be treated seriously. Presidents Reagan and Carter said they had seen UFOs and were interested in the subject."

Great. Stop there. Go back to Maxwell and the unity of the nation, Camila thought.

But she had the uneasy feeling that wasn't going to happen.

"I'm going to take this opportunity to tell you about my own experience. In this case, my contact has arisen not by a sighting of a distant unknown craft, but as a closer encounter. I would call it mind-to-mind contact."

Oh, shit. Dustin had run the red light. She could see the headlines now—DUSTIN REPORTS ALIEN CONTACT—and it would be on the front page of the *Washington Post* and *New York Times,* not the tabloids. The editorialists would question his sanity. His opponents in Congress would call for his impeachment. Tomorrow's press conference would be a nightmare.

"First of all, there's no reason for concern," he said after a pause. "The entities who have contacted me have assured me that they are not interested in landing on the White House lawn, at least not in the foreseeable future."

That comment garnered a sprinkling of nervous laughter.

"But they are making themselves known in the hopes that with this new awareness, we will move forward toward becoming members of the galactic community. To take that step, we must first learn to live with one another."

With that, Dustin wrapped up his speech with a few more comments regarding his federal-state initiative. But it all sounded surreal after his comment on the galactic community. She could just imagine the questions she would soon face. How and when had the entities contacted the president? Were they coming back? What else had they said to him? Had he actually seen them? What had they looked like? On and on.

The seven hundred people assembled for the banquet responded to the speech with polite applause and baffled looks. Most stood up as

Dustin strode toward a side exit with several Secret Service agents. A quick escape. No hand-shaking or casual chitchat. Now he was headed for a four-day vacation on a ranch between Gunnison and Crested Butte owned by tennis professional Kyle Leslie. Annie, the First Lady, and their two sons were expected to join him in the morning.

Camila glimpsed Todd Waters, the president's corpulent chief of staff, disappearing out the same door Dustin had taken. She suspected that Waters was as confused by the ending of the speech as everyone else.

"What was he talking about, anyhow?" one of the women at the table asked. "Was he serious about the aliens?"

Camila smiled and shrugged. "I don't know. I mean . . ." She struggled for an explanation. "It was . . . I believe . . ." She shook her head. "I think he meant it as a metaphor, but . . ."

"Yes, that's it," Marilyn Willis chimed in. "A metaphor. A way of saying that we are all humans and very much alike."

Camila spotted reporters rushing toward the exits and decided to make a quick getaway herself. But a stout blonde blocked her way. "I had nothing to do with that," Sally Powers, the president's speechwriter, hissed in her ear. "Nothing."

"Take it easy, Sally. It was a metaphor. That's all. A botched metaphor."

"Goddamn, Camila. I hope so."

Eight

In the dream, Abraham Lincoln's decapitated head started to move. The features on the face shifted and suddenly Trent was staring at his old friend, Bobby Aimes. The mouth began to move. "Trent . . . Trent . . . Look what you did! You killed me! Now it's your turn. Die, Trent, die!"

The words struck him like a concussive blow. His body jerked back and forth in his sleep. The voice filled his head. The image zoomed closer and Aimes's features shifted into the face of a ticking clock.

"Trent, Trent, wake up! You've got to see this."

His eyes fluttered open, he looked around, startled, and realized that he was in a motel room in Denver, that he'd fallen asleep, that Doc had shaken him awake. She sat on the adjacent bed, and looked excited or nervous, or maybe both. She pointed at the television.

He rubbed his eyes with his palms, glanced at his watch, and realized he'd slept two hours. "What is it?"

He glimpsed a man with a long prominent jaw and graying hair and realized it was Gordon Maxwell. He stood at a podium, saying something about the future of the western states. The report ended and cut back to the newscaster. "This is just off the wire from that same conference . . . President Dustin in a speech this evening—"

Doc clicked off the television with a remote. "Can you believe it? He spoke at the governors conference this afternoon and made a prediction that the country was going to split apart in a few years.''

"He's about the last person I care to see on television or in person. Did he say anything about Washington blowing up early next week?'' Calloway hadn't meant to sound sarcastic, but it came out that way.

Doc shook her head. "Things are getting weird, Trent.''

He recalled his dream of a broken Bobby Aimes looking up at him. Maxwell's fault, he told himself. "Let's get going. It's time.''

They had driven all day and arrived on the outskirts of Denver, where they had gotten a room, at six. They'd realized that with the president speaking at the banquet, the hotel would be difficult to approach. So they'd decided to wait and try to contact Camila in the aftermath.

Doc frowned. "You still look tired. Maybe we should wait until morning.''

He shook his head. "I want to find her tonight. She may be gone in the morning.''

"All right,'' Doc responded. "But I'm going to stay here. I'm not going.''

"Doc, cut the crap,'' Calloway snapped. "I need you to confirm my story.''

Doc rubbed her arms as if she were cold. "You don't understand, Trent. There's going to be a lot of people in that hotel and I already feel a dull headache just from being on the outskirts of the city.''

"Look, Doc, I'd rather be sitting in my camp and drinking beer. I've deprived myself all day. So, I think you can handle a few people, and we'll stay away from the crowds.''

"Forget it, Calloway! You don't have a clue!''

Her eyes grew large and menacing, her fingers curled into fists. "It's like . . . it's like being crammed into a tiny room with the walls closing on you. Except the walls are transparent and a thousand pairs of eyes are staring at you, watching you slowly being crushed to death.''

"I get the picture. But I still want you to come with me. They might want me to work tonight and I need you as a monitor.''

She stood up. "I'm going home."

He bolted off the bed, stood in front of her. "No, you're not. You are going with me."

"Fuck you!" She kicked him in the shin, hurried to the bathroom, and slammed the door shut.

"Shit! Damn it, Doc." Calloway rubbed his shin and hopped on one foot. "Come out of there right now. You got me involved in this, now you follow through. Don't let me down."

Silence.

He leaned against the wall next to the bathroom, crossed his arms, and waited. After a minute, the door opened slowly. Doc stepped out, looked meekly at him. "I'm sorry for kicking you. But I can't do this. I told you that before we left. I just wanted to make sure that you got here. I'll drop you off downtown outside the hotel."

"Well guess what, Doc? I can't do this, either. Camila's not going to take my word. She's going to want proof and I'm not going to be able to give it to her or the Secret Service without you. Hell, she'll probably have me arrested for harassing her. I've never been any good without you monitoring me. I know that probably makes me sound like some kind of psychic wimp, but I don't care. That's the way it is."

"Damn you, Calloway." She gazed off as if distracted by an inner voice. "I've got one idea that might work, but don't count on it."

"What?"

"Your voice has a certain resonance that has always made me feel relaxed," Doc began. "I want you to take me slowly down an elevator and out into a tranquil setting by a pond. Then give me a suggestion that crowds won't affect me."

"That'll really work?"

"I worked with a hypnotist in Ouray for a while and it seemed to help, at least for a couple hours. But he left town a few weeks ago and I haven't done it since."

He nodded, glanced at his watch. "How about if we do it on the way. It's getting late. I'll drive and talk you down at the same time."

She frowned and he figured she would refuse. They'd spend another half hour here and arrive too late. "Okay, that'll work. I can lay the seat down and put Carlos Nakai on the CD player. That flute music helps me relax and so will the feel of the road."

Amazing, they'd agreed on something without coming to blows.

"Nice place," Calloway said as they walked into the lobby of the Brown Palace Hotel twenty-five minutes later. Even though it was ten-thirty, people crisscrossed the lobby and Calloway felt a buzz of energy that no doubt was linked with the row of media trucks parked outside.

"It's extraordinary." Doc gazed up to the eight-story atrium. Cast-iron balconies encircled each floor.

"How're you feeling?"

"Fine, so far. I think it worked. I went way down." She looked around, but he noticed she kept her gaze above the crowd. She wouldn't be much help finding Camila.

"Have you ever been here, Trent?"

"I think so, but not in person."

"What do you mean?"

He explained that one day Maxwell gave him a target that he described as a place in the future where they would meet. "I drew a triangular-shaped building with a huge atrium with iron balconies, just like this place. Except I didn't know it was an atrium or even a hotel, because I saw a bunch of cattle wandering around in it. I thought it was a barn of some sort, or a grain silo."

Doc peered up into the atrium again as several people moved past. "It's a very glamorous silo. Do you remember the date you were supposed to meet?"

He shook his head. "He gave me a suggestion that I wouldn't remember it so I wouldn't take any action either to avoid the meeting or try to make it happen."

"Interesting. Do you remember anything else?"

He thought a moment. "Yeah, there was one other thing. I got a number, fifty thousand. But it didn't help either of us. We couldn't figure out where I'd gone."

"I bet this was the place," she said. "The people are the cattle."

Except he was here looking for Camila, not Maxwell. His gaze slid across the lobby and drifted up to the mezzanine. He wondered if he would even recognize her after all these years, even if she walked right past him.

Then something else came back to him. "A week later, Maxwell gave me the same target. But that time I got something else altogether. I ended up in a place with a lot of boats and Maxwell was there himself sitting by one of the boats."

"That's sort of strange. What did Maxwell say about it?"

Calloway shook his head. "He was confused and disappointed, I guess, because it didn't make much sense to him."

Doc smiled. "He never liked ambiguities. He always wanted everything clear and easily understood."

A man who looked like he might belong to the hotel's security team patrolled slowly by. "I'll try calling Camila," Calloway said. "Maybe we'll catch her in her room."

Doc looked at the people now. "I'm starting to get a headache, Trent. That's the first sign."

"Here, read this while I'm on the phone." He handed her a brochure about the hotel.

He called from a house phone and as he waited to be connected, he tried to come up with a simple way of explaining the reason for his visit. Still at a loss for an answer, he listened to the phone ring. Then a generic recording clicked in, telling him to leave a message.

"Camila, it's Trent. Yeah, surprise. Ah, I'm in the hotel. In the lobby. It's ten-forty-five. I need to talk to you. It's important. Very important. You can leave a message for me at the front desk. I'll pick it up."

He shrugged. He probably sounded like an idiot or a maniac. He walked back over to Doc, who was still looking at the brochure.

"I left a message. You okay?"

She shrugged without looking up, then tapped her finger against the brochure. "Listen to this. Starting in 1945, cattle were displayed in the hotel's lobby and the prize steers were sold for fifty thousand dollars each—a record at that time.''

"Cool. Fifty thousand.'' He peered around the lobby again. "Except I was supposed to go to the future, not the past.''

"Maybe you were just establishing the location on your first try,'' she answered.

He didn't want to think about his work with Maxwell any longer. "Let's check the bar in case she's in there.''

"I hate bars. They're crowded and smoky and full of wandering eyes.''

"You want to wait here?''

"Hell no.'' She clutched his arm. "I'll just watch my feet. That's my favorite preoccupation in public these days.''

He guided her across the lobby toward the corridor. They reached the entrance to the Ship Tavern, then stepped into a cozy lounge with dark wood walls. He stopped, looked around, and noticed several model ships from the clipper era.

"Take a quick look before we go any further.''

Doc glanced up. "Your ships, Trent. Welcome to the future.''

"I guess.''

They moved into the lounge and he felt as if he were guiding a blind woman.

Doc let go of her arm. "I'm getting out of here. I can't stand it. I'll wait outside.''

He scanned the tables and bar a second time. "Okay. Hold on a minute.''

A woman who reminded him of Camila stood at the bar engaged in an animated conversation with two men. He moved a couple of steps closer. The woman turned, glanced in his direction. His heart pounded. Then he realized it wasn't her.

"Trent, I'm out of here.''

He grabbed her arm as she started to walk away. "Wait!''

"Let go of me.''

"I see him,'' he said.

Gordon Maxwell was perched on a corner stool talking to the

woman that he'd mistaken for Camila. Just above his head hung a model clipper. *Déjà vu.*

He had an urge to walk up to Maxwell and tell him what he thought of him, that he'd trusted him, that he'd once considered him a mentor, but that Maxwell had betrayed him in a terrible way. Maybe he'd turn to the woman and tell her that Maxwell had tricked him into killing someone, not just anyone but a man who had once been his best friend. But he knew he would sound demented. She wouldn't believe him. No one would, especially not when he explained how he'd killed Bobby Aimes.

Doc kept her back to the bar. "I don't want to see him. I don't want to be here."

He guided her back toward the door, but he took one look over his shoulder. For an instant, just before he moved out of sight, Maxwell peered his way.

"Yuck," Doc said as they reached the hallway. "I don't like being in the same room with him."

They moved into the lobby amid an unexpected rush of people moving one way or another, some carrying cameras. It looked like someone had hit a fire alarm, but no one knew where the door was.

"What the hell's going on?" Calloway muttered.

Doc placed her hands on either side of her head and winced. Then she rubbed her arms as she'd done in the hotel. Her face twisted in pain. Time to get her out of here. Several feet in front of him, a bright light illuminated a familiar-looking reporter with a microphone that said CNN on the side. A cameraman blocked their way out.

"Have space aliens invaded the White House? It's a strange question everyone here at the Denver Brown Palace Hotel seems to be asking in the aftermath of President Dustin's extraordinary comments."

The words didn't make sense. He couldn't quite grasp what he'd just heard. Then he no longer heard anything the reporter said. Camila Hidalgo stood at the railing of the mezzanine looking out over the confusion. She wore a shawl over her shoulders, and with her aquiline nose in profile she looked like a Native American princess, a vision from a mythical past.

Doc moaned. Her legs wobbled. She gasped for breath and started to sink to the floor, pulling Calloway with her. He grabbed her around her shoulders and tried to lift her. "Let's get out of here. I've got you. Here we go."

The security guard he'd seen earlier appeared and helped him guide Doc to the front entrance. "She just needs some air," he assured the man. "She'll be okay."

Calloway managed to glance back once toward the mezzanine, but Camila had vanished, gone like the Indians by the river.

SATURDAY

Nine

Everyone seemed in a jovial mood, no doubt inspired by alien jokes, Camila Hidalgo thought as she looked over the crowd of reporters. She began by spelling out the president's vacation schedule, acting as if everything were normal. Then she said that two hundred copies of the president's speech from the night before would be available at ten. A murmur rippled through the crowd.

"Also included will be an addendum to the speech, which clarifies his metaphorical comments near the end. We would hope that any mention of alien contact would include reference to the addendum material."

The *Denver Post* that morning included the metaphor explanation, which she'd issued in last night's press briefing. So did the *Washington Post* and *New York Times*. But the explanation didn't put much of a damper of the media's enthusiasm for a sensational story. The only one benefiting, as she saw it, was the vice president, whose marital tiff had ended up buried on the inside pages. The president's story, although short on details, had also overpowered Maxwell's forecast for secession in the western states. She figured that even if Howell had walked into the banquet in his wife's gown, Dustin's quirky comments would've played ahead of the cross-dressing national security advisor.

"When can we talk directly to the president?" someone shouted.

"He has no plans at this time for a press conference while he is vacationing.'' That could change of course, she thought, and it might be a good idea.

"How did the aliens contact the president?'' someone else called out.

"Metaphorically. Please raise your hands. Same rules in Denver as in the White House.'' Dustin had started off with a metaphor, but had never returned to it. That defined the problem in a nutshell. As long as she framed the issue that way, she could deal with it. She pointed to Barry Greer, whose hand had shot up from the second row.

"Metaphor or not, can you answer the question that's on everyone's mind,'' Greed asked in his resonant television voice. "Did the president encounter aliens?''

"I said it was a metaphor.''

"Couldn't it be both,'' he responded. "A metaphor and an actual encounter?''

"No, no such encounter took place.'' What else could she say? She'd just contradicted the president's comments, but if she sounded evasive, she would raise further suspicions.

And so it went for the next twenty-eight minutes. Once they'd dissected the alien matter as much as possible, questions about the vice president's marital status followed. Camila referred to a statement released by Darcy Mitchell that said she regretted her comments, that they'd resulted from a misunderstanding, and that she and the vice president had worked out their differences. At least that matter seemed settled.

A few questions that actually dealt with substantive policy matters on national and international issues followed. No one even mentioned Gordon Maxwell and his controversial prognostication until the final question. She pointed to a man in the rear wearing a string tie, who she guessed was a local reporter.

"Yesterday evening, General George Wiley, the Freedom Nation leader, issued a statement calling Gordon Maxwell's remarks about the future a clear possibility,'' the reporter began. "He said that the conditions were ripe for several western states to cut ties with the federal government and form a loose confederation. He added that the militias would be the backbone of the new independent nation. Could you respond to Wiley's remarks?''

''George Richard Wiley is a fugitive from justice wanted in connection to three murders. His comments about issues are irrelevant.''

That was the administration's position on all of Wiley's press releases. Wiley had been a one-star general with a promising future when he'd been drummed out of the army for sexual misconduct. He'd lost his career and held a grudge that had turned into a crusade against the federal government that had escalated into criminal acts. The man somehow had evaded capture for more than two years.

But today she decided to speak her mind on Wiley in the faint hope that it would shift the media's interest away from the president. ''Wiley can think whatever he wants,'' she added. ''Personally, I wouldn't want to live in a state run by amateur military organizations, especially ones that have been linked to white supremacy and a man accused of murder.''

With that, she left the podium. She hoped Wiley and his gang of racist creeps would respond. She would gladly deal with comments from a few angry secessionists rather than continue with alien nation and the galactic community.

She'd barely reached the door when her lanky young assistant Steve Watkins approached her. ''Howell wants to see you right away up in the staff lounge. I think he talked to the president.''

''Good. I'm on my way.'' She headed for the lounge. Watkins hurried after her.

''Wait. There's one other thing.''

She slowed her pace and glanced back at Watkins. ''So, what is it?''

''A man named Trent Calloway wants to talk to you.''

She slowed her pace. ''What was that, Steve?''

''Trent Calloway. He says he's your ex-husband.''

A couple of beats passed as she struggled to remain calm. ''Yeah, I know. Where is he?''

"Down in the lobby."

"Go tell him that I'm very busy. I'd love to say hi, but I don't have time."

"He said it deals with national security," Watkins responded, hurrying to catch up with her as she picked up her pace.

"Then you can refer him to either the Secret Service or the local FBI office."

"I suggested that already, but he said that it's a psychic thing and that you would understand."

She stopped, turned to Watkins. "He said that, that I would understand?" *The bastard.* "Go tell Harvey I'll be there in a couple of minutes. But don't say anything about this . . . this!—"

"Okay. Nothing about Mr. Calloway."

She nodded. "Yeah. Thanks."

What was she going to say to him? "Hi, how are you? How have you been?" Casual. Breezy. No. Better to be blunt, get right to the point. It made her angry that he'd shown up here. Especially today. She'd put the relationship behind her and she'd blocked out whatever curiosity she had about him and his life after the military.

She paused at the top of the wide staircase leading to the lobby. She spotted him standing a few feet away from a packed luggage cart in the busy lobby. The sight of him seemed to release some chemicals into her blood. She felt light-headed, nervous. Everything turned fuzzy around her. How long had it been since she'd seen him? Five, no, six years.

From a distance, he looked unchanged, but as she moved closer, she saw something different about him. The crisp military edge had vanished. He seemed distracted, almost otherworldly. He certainly wasn't part of her world.

As she approached, it suddenly occurred to her that his arrival might be directly related to the big news story. He wanted to remote view the president's aliens. She slowed down. She was about to turn around and get away before it was too late. But at that moment, he looked up and she couldn't make herself turn her back on him, even though that was what he'd done to her. She moved closer. He started to say something, but she interrupted him.

"This better not have anything to do with an alien threat that you just happened to pick up while remote viewing."

He looked confused. "I don't know anything about that. Hello, by the way. Good to see you."

His voice sounded tense, raspy. She had an urge to give him a hug, to apologize for her abruptness. But then she thought better of it.

"So what are you doing here, Trent?"

"I'm sorry to bother you. But . . . damn, you look good, Camila. I'm happy for you."

The familiar stranger stared at her. She moved forward, driven by a part of her that wouldn't listen to reason. She embraced him lightly, then stepped back. The fleeting contact triggered something inside her, a physical memory embedded in her cells. She suddenly felt unsteady on her feet, as if the floor were moving.

Her hands started shaking. She blinked away a tear. She bit her lower lip and commanded herself to relax. "How did you know I was here?"

"I heard Dustin was addressing the governors. I figured you'd be with him. I need your help."

"So what is it? I'm sorry, Trent, but I don't have much time."

"This isn't personal, Camila, if that's what you're concerned about. This is bigger than that."

Her mouth turned down. "There was a time when I thought our life together was important. But that got lost a long time ago. You were more dedicated to those psychic freaks than to me. And I wasn't involved with anyone, as you accused, but maybe I should've been. Your sudden departure would've made more sense to me."

There, she'd said it. She felt proud of herself for finally expressing to him what she'd held in for all these years.

"I take the blame, Camila. I'm sorry. I left because I didn't want to hurt you." He shrugged. "But I didn't come here to talk about the past. That's over."

"You bet it is, Trent. Does this have something to do with that ex-spook, Gordon Maxwell?"

He shook his head. "Not unless Maxwell is behind a scheme to blow up the capital. And I don't think he's the type."

"What are you talking about?"

"I'm talking about a powerful bomb," he hissed, "a nuclear bomb that's in a backpack and it's headed for the capital. Washington is going to blow in a couple of days—Monday or Tuesday."

The words literally knocked the wind out of her. She forgot the personal stuff. "What do you know about it?"

He hesitated. "I saw it happening."

"Saw it?" she repeated. "Psychically, right?"

"Yes."

She closed her eyes a moment, trying to get her bearings. She had an urge to tell him to take his goddamn fantasies to the *Enquirer*. But what if he were right? She saw two familiar faces, Secret Service agents, carrying their luggage across the lobby. She knew instantly what she had to do.

"Okay, are you ready to tell the Secret Service what you just told me, and explain how you got the information?"

"Yes, of course."

"Well, get ready." She signaled the two agents.

They veered over toward her. The older of the two, a man in his late forties who had once told her that he'd worked under four presidents, addressed her. "Yes, ma'am. How can we help you?"

"Sam, this gentleman's name is Trent Calloway. He's just informed me about a bomb that he says is going to blow up the capital."

The agent touched something on his wrist that must have set off a silent alarm. The other one instantly scanned the lobby. "Mr. Calloway, we're going to take you to a room where we can speak in private," Agent Sam said in a firm voice.

"That's fine with me."

Just then a stout woman with an open, friendly face moved their way. "I can verify what he's going to tell you," the woman said in a confident voice. "Hello, Camila. We met once, but you probably don't remember me. I used to work with Trent."

Camila looked closely at her. "Doc?"

The woman nodded. She smiled, but her lips quivered. She looked tense, worried.

Two other Secret Service agents joined their colleagues, a few words were exchanged, and then the group, all but Camila, moved across the lobby and toward the bank of elevators. She stared after them and her hands started shaking again. What if Calloway were right? What if a nuclear bomb was set to go off in the capital in a couple of days?

Just then she spotted Gordon Maxwell standing at the end of a line, waiting to check out. Harvey Howell could wait a couple more minutes, she thought, and headed toward him.

Ten

The agents hustled them up to the third floor in different elevators and placed them in separate rooms of a suite that looked as if it had been the Secret Service's temporary communications center. Telephones and computers and other electronic gear was strewn around on tables and counters. Boxes and cases lay on the floor and wires dangled everywhere. The agents apparently had been packing the gear when the call had been received.

No one said anything to Calloway for several minutes, then one of the agents joined him at a table, while a second one remained standing near the door as if he might depart for another crisis at any moment. "My name is Sam Clarke. My partner is Nick Tyler."

Someone turned on a radio behind the closed door. "Are they going to listen to music over there, or is that just to cover up my screams when you break my fingers," Calloway asked.

"We don't want either of you overhearing what the other says. Just a precaution."

"Doc and I aren't making up anything. We don't need to get our stories straight."

Clarke nodded. "So tell me about yourself."

Calloway told him about his background in the air force, emphasizing his years as a psychic spy. He explained how he'd glimpsed the six-digit number and what had happened when Doc monitored him. He went on to explain that he had decided to come to Denver to tell Camila about it.

"So you think a young man named Matthew is delivering a nuclear bomb to Washington, where it will destroy the city on Monday or Tuesday. And you think Matthew's mission might be sponsored by some sort of group. That's not much to go on, Mr. Calloway."

"I know. But I think I can get more."

Clarke nodded noncommittally. "You and your friend were observed in the hotel last night after the president's speech. Did you meet with Gordon Maxwell?"

"No. I saw him in the bar, but I didn't talk to him."

"Why not? You used to work closely with him, didn't you?" Clarke asked.

He felt a dangerous urge to tell Clarke all about it. To confess to murder. No, he wasn't a murderer. *Stay focused.* "He was talking to some other people, and besides, I was looking for Camila, not him."

"But you left last night before finding her," Clarke said.

"Doc didn't feel well. She has a problem with crowds. So we left." He glanced toward the door to the adjacent room. Calloway had suggested she stay at their hotel this morning, but this time she had insisted on going with him. So he'd relaxed her again en route from their hotel.

"In fact, I hope she's okay in there."

"I'll check on her in a minute," Clarke said. "Did you know ahead of time that Maxwell would be speaking at the conference?"

"No. I haven't been in contact with him for four years."

"Please wait here." Clarke stood up and disappeared into the next room.

Calloway felt frustrated and vaguely disappointed in Camila. She'd simply turned him over to the Secret Service and then gone about her business.

Agent Tyler strolled over toward Calloway. "Sam believes that stuff you're talking about. I'm more skeptical."

Even though Tyler wore a suit, Calloway could tell by his thick, muscular neck that he probably spent his spare time in a gym bench-pressing four or five hundred pounds.

"So what is it? You don't believe it's possible to remote view, or you just haven't looked into it?"

He shrugged. "I've got to see it before I believe it. That's just how I am."

"You remind me of myself before I got hit by lightning and got my brain rewired."

"You were hit by lightning?" Tyler sounded shocked.

He nodded. "Sixteen years ago now. It hit me just below my collarbone."

"What happened?"

"At first, I couldn't walk or use my arms. My voice slurred. The doctors thought that I might regain the use of his arms, but I'd never walk again."

"But you recovered," Tyler said.

"Slowly."

First his voice, then his arms. Within two months, he was hobbling on crutches. But his brain was never quite the same. He knew things before they happened and saw things that happened elsewhere. He was tested and retested by air force psychologists. Then one day he got a telegram from Colonel Gordon Maxwell. The next morning he was on his way to Colorado Spring for more tests and that led to his involvement in Eagle's Nest.

Tyler nodded when he finished. "I was at Maxwell's talk yesterday."

Calloway stared out the window toward the parking lot and at that moment the sun reflected off the windshield of a moving vehicle. He blinked and suddenly saw Tyler standing on ice.

He turned to the agent. "Did you used to play ice hockey?"

Tyler frowned. "I haven't done it since I was a kid. I wasn't very good. Why do you ask?"

"Sometimes I get impressions about people. I just saw ice around you and you were excited about it, like you were going to play hockey or maybe go ice fishing."

He shook his head. "Never gone ice fishing and I don't plan to. Sorry about that."

"It might be something else related to ice, because you were wearing a suit, the same one you've got on now. I saw you pointing at the ice. You know something about it."

"What do you mean that you saw me? How does that work?"

Calloway smiled. "Don't you ever have impressions, hunches about something that's about to happen?"

Tyler shrugged. "Not that I know of. If I do, they're based on something I see or hear. Like someone looking very sullen and tense while everyone else is laughing at a joke the president just told."

"But how do you find someone like that in a crowd?" Calloway asked. "The president attracts big crowds."

"I use my eyes, my physical senses. I don't get any psychic visions or hunches. Even if I did get one, I wouldn't tell anyone about them. I want to keep my job."

Calloway was surprised that Tyler had turned out to be so talkative. "So I guess you don't take what I said about the bomb very seriously."

"I didn't say that." Calloway heard a sharp edge in his tone. "We take all threats to the president seriously, no matter what the source."

"That's good. Because you need to take this one real serious."

"We'll evaluate it and decide how to proceed," Tyler replied.

"How would *you* proceed on this one?"

"It's not up to me."

The door between the rooms opened. Camila stepped into the room, smiled. He watched her closely, forgetting all about Tyler. Just being near her activated a part of him that he'd suppressed. He realized that he missed her. Or maybe he missed the person she had once been. The person in front of him, he reminded himself, wasn't his wife, not even the memory that he called his ex-wife. Something had changed in her.

She looked at Tyler. "Sam would like to talk to you."

The agent nodded and moved into the other room.

Alone with her. "I've been getting grilled by your buddies."

"Not my buddies. They work for the president. They're here talking to you because what you've told them could endanger the president."

So precise. Smooth. Friendly, but professional. More poised than when they'd first talked. Was it really her, the girl who liked to dance in the nightclubs, stay up late, smoke a little pot? "So what's the verdict?"

"First, I want to tell you that Doc has taken ill. Sam Clarke told me about her phobia."

He stood up. "Where is she?"

Camila held up a hand. "She's been taken to another room and a doctor has been called. She said it wasn't serious, but I insisted that a doctor look in on her."

"Thanks. I guess I'll see her in a while."

"Next, I want to assure you that your impressions are being taken seriously, and we need to try to get more information."

"Good."

Ironic, he thought. His work in Eagle's Nest had destroyed their marriage and now, because he had remote viewed again, she had reappeared in his life. He felt none of the impatience that he'd felt with Clarke. He wanted to watch her, to talk to her, to know more about who she was now. Did she still retain some of the same old memories as he did? Did she ever think about him? He had always suspected that he would see her again. He just hadn't known when or under what circumstances.

"Would you be willing to remote view for the Secret Service agents and myself?"

"Of course. I'm ready. Except, one problem. Doc is my monitor."

"That's no problem." Gordon Maxwell stepped into the doorway and into view. "I'll monitor you."

Calloway just stared at him as he approached. Maxwell's hooded eyes met his gaze. He extended a hand and smiled. Calloway crossed his arms over his chest. "What are you doing here?"

"I asked him to join us," Camila said. "He gave you an excellent reference. He told the Secret Service agents that they should take what you say very seriously.''

Maxwell glanced at her. "I'd like to talk to Trent alone, if you wouldn't mind, Camila."

She nodded. "But please don't keep us waiting."

"It's good to see you again, Trent," Maxwell said as the door closed.

"Is it?"

Maxwell ignored the sarcastic comment. "I told everyone that you were the best remote viewer that I've ever worked with and that if you had psychically seen a bomb heading for Washington, they'd damn well better pay close attention. That's why they want to see what else you can get."

"Thanks for your help. But I'll wait for Doc," he answered firmly. "She's my monitor."

"Trent, these guys are busy," Maxwell explained. "They were on their way out. They're anxious to get going. You've got to do it now to convince them. You can find the perpetrators and alter that future event before it's too late."

"At least, now I know why Doc took ill," Calloway said sullenly. "I have the feeling that when you arrived, the room suddenly became very crowded."

"I'm sorry that she has a problem being around people," he responded, blandly. "Now can we get started?"

"Look, Max. Doc and I both know about the drug we were given, the one that we absorbed through our skin when our blood pressures were taken. You probably know by now that it created some adverse side effects, like Doc's problem with crowds."

Calloway expected Maxwell to deny knowing what he was talking about, but Maxwell surprised him. "That drug was a light hypnotic, that helped you relax and focus, nothing more. There were no side effects."

"If it was so innocuous, why didn't you tell us about it?" Calloway persisted.

"I didn't want you guys thinking that your abilities were dependent or even related to a drug. If you got that into your heads, you wouldn't function well when you didn't receive it."

His answer sounded pat, Calloway thought, as if he'd thought it all out—a defense strategy.

"But that's old stuff, Trent. They're waiting for us. Are you going to do it or not?"

"No, I told you four years ago that I'd never remote view for you again. Not after what you did to Bobby Aimes. And I'm keeping that promise."

Maxwell tensed at the mention of Aimes. His eyes narrowed. "I wonder how many people are alive today because Bobby Aimes is dead. Just think if someone could've pushed one of Hitler's guards into killing him. Look at the bloodshed that could've been prevented."

"You fucker. How dare you compare the two. Bobby was no monster and you know it."

"And you know what he was doing and why he was a target." He shrugged. "Regardless of what you think about me, you're not working for me now. This one's for the future of the country. Let's show these guys what remote viewers can do."

"Not this lifetime, Max. Not with you monitoring me." Calloway walked past Maxwell, tapped on the door to the other room, and opened it.

Camila looked up from a table where she was sitting with several others. "Well, are you ready?"

"I want to talk to Doc. Give me five minutes with her."

Camila glanced at her watch, then nodded toward Tyler, who led Calloway out of the room. As they headed down the hall, he told Tyler that he needed a tape recorder because Doc wasn't going to monitor him in a crowded room.

"I can do better than that. I'll set up a remote mike in the room so we can listen from the other room." Tyler rapped on the door and looked around restlessly as they waited.

"I hope she's not asleep," Calloway said.

The door opened. Doc peered out, then smiled when she saw Calloway. "Come in. You just missed the doctor."

Tyler said he'd wait in the hall and Calloway stepped inside. Doc's short hair was mussed, but she looked better than the night before when he'd walked her out of the hotel.

"Do you know who's down there?" Doc asked.

"Maxwell. I talked to him."

"He pushed me right over the edge. I had to get out of there. I'm sorry."

"It's okay," Calloway assured her. "What did the doctor say?"

She shrugged. "He said I should have some tests. All the stuff I've already done. They never found anything to account for what happens to me."

He told her about his conversation with Maxwell. Doc scowled. "He changed his story. When I asked him about the drug the day he approached me at the bookstore, he denied it completely."

"I think he's scrambling. He knows we're on to him. Do you feel up to monitoring me?"

She rubbed her arms and took a step back. Her words ran together. "I can't, Trent. Not with Maxwell and the rest of them looking on. No thank you. I just can't do it. I'm sorry."

"It'll be just you and me, right here." He explained his plan.

She thought a moment. "I'll do it as long as no one else is in the room."

"Great. I'll get things rolling."

A few minutes later, they were wired and ready to start.

"I don't want to use your numbers this time, Trent," Doc began. "If you see the event again, that could be construed as simply your memory of the earlier remote viewing experience. It also doesn't add anything new. So I'm going to try another approach."

"Go ahead. Surprise me."

He took several deep breaths and slowly sank down into his zone. No music accompanied him. He let his thoughts drop away and focused on his breathing.

"I'm going to begin talking and I want you to just follow my voice awhile. With each word you will go deeper into that place where remote viewing works for you. Keep in mind, Trent, that from what we know, remote viewers just keep getting better and better. Beginners describe form, shape, color, and maybe texture, but experienced viewers, like yourself, are capable of much more. You can describe feelings, the function of objects, and obtain meaning from a situation. If you have to, you know that you can go inside your subject and pick up his thoughts and maybe even nudge him to do something.''

The idea of going into another person again and affecting the person's behavior disturbed him, but he let it pass. He drifted deeper, only half listening to Doc's idle patter. Like old times, he thought.

''Okay, Trent, let's go to a person instead of a place,'' she continued. ''Find the person named Matthew, the one you mentioned the last time. You might have caught a fleeting glimpse of him before. Now you will see him much more clearly. You will know who he is, what he is doing, and where he is going.''

Images were already appearing to him. When Doc finally stopped talking, he began describing them. ''I see a very rugged landscape. No trees, just rocks. Like the moon. I'm seeing the landscape moving past me. I see it through Matthew's eyes.''

''Can you see Matthew?''

Calloway was surprised to find himself peering through the windshield of a vehicle at a driver. ''He's young, still a teenager. I can tell that he's vulnerable, under the influence of others. His mind is pliable, but there is a part of him that stands back and quietly examines everything.''

''Can you tell me what kind of vehicle he's driving?'' Doc asked.

He shook his head. ''I don't know. It might be a pickup.''

''For the time being, let's not worry about the vehicle. Where is Matthew headed?''

Calloway remained silent for several seconds. ''I'm not sure. It's confusing. I see a huge white thing, a creature. It looks like a dinosaur. I also see a large man, as big or bigger than the dinosaur, and I see a building nearby.''

''Don't try to analyze too much, Trent,'' she said in a soft voice. ''Just describe what you see.''

Doc's comment annoyed him. He knew that he could describe

scenes in detail without being distracted or confused by analytical overlays. "I'm seeing something that resembles a dinosaur. I didn't say it
was one."

"Let's go on. What's Matthew doing there?"

Calloway closed his eyes again, returning to his target. "He's concerned about something in the building. He has some connection with
this place. He might work there."

"Go inside the building and describe what you see," Maxwell said.

It took a minute for Calloway to refocus. "I see a room with lots
of small objects on shelves and a counter."

"Move back now out of the building and look down on the entire
scene. Sketch what you see."

He opened his eyes and began drawing on his pad. He felt like he
was working again on a target supplied by the CIA. Just like the old
days. The images remained clear in his mind. First, he drew a two-
dimensional rectangle that he interpreted as a parking lot. Next to it he
quickly sketched the tall man and also two poles with a rectangle on
it . . . a billboard. He outlined the dinosaur nearby and then drew the
building.

Behind the building, he added a path. Along the path, he scrawled
images of people. But they were like the dinosaur—immobile and
merely lifeless images. Like statues, he thought. He drew a black hole
at the end of the trail to represent an underground entrance. To one
side, he sketched a rough schematic of what he saw underground.

"There are some sort of tunnels and caverns here. I see walkways
and frost on the walls. It's like a big refrigerator. It's cold and icy.
People wear coats in here."

"Who goes in there?"

"Visitors. But . . . I sense people with guns, too. They go into the
off-limits area."

"Who are they?

Calloway took a couple of breaths as he tried to reach deep into
the caverns. "Militia. That's the word I get. The kid has something to
do with them."

He remained aware of being both at the target and in the room.

But suddenly, he felt another presence, as if someone had joined him and Doc. Disturbed, he pulled back from the target. He felt the intruder close by, seemingly sharing his body. Then his hand started rapidly scrawling words across the bottom of the page. He neither looked at nor sensed what he was writing.

A loud rap at the door interrupted him. His pen jumped from the page and the sense of the other disappeared. The door opened and Tyler stepped inside. "Sorry to disturb you," he said in an excited voice. "But I've got to tell you, I know where that place is."

Calloway opened his eyes.

"I've been there," Tyler continued. "That's the Shoshone Ice Caves near Shoshone, Idaho. I grew up in Boise. There's a big white dinosaur and a big Indian—Chief Somebody—in front of the place."

Calloway rubbed his face as he returned fully to the room.

"Let's stop right here," Doc said and turned to Tyler. "Now you've got something to go on. The kid has some connection to the place and a connection to a militia group."

Camila followed Tyler into the room. "That was impressive, Trent. Have you ever toured those caves?"

"Nope. Didn't even know they existed."

She nodded. "You know, I never saw you do it. Not once."

"You still haven't. You heard me do it."

"You're right. Well, I've got to go, but I'd like you and Doc to stay right here in this suite for at least one night at Uncle Sam's expense, including meals. We may need a follow-up."

"That's fine with me, especially the meals." Calloway turned to Doc, who nodded in agreement.

She left and Tyler collected the two cordless remote mikes that he'd clipped onto their collars and packed away the electronic gizmos into a black metal box. Calloway could tell that Tyler was still mulling over what had just happened. "Ice. You were right. I did know something about it. On the other hand, it didn't have a damn thing to do with ice fishing."

"I guess I was the one fishing. Let's hope we hooked into a big one."

"Yeah, let's hope."

"Was Maxwell in the other room?" Calloway asked.

Tyler nodded. "He stayed to interpret what was going on in here, but frankly I'm still confused."

"Why?" Calloway asked.

"Because it shouldn't be possible."

"But it is," Doc said.

"Okay, think of it this way," Calloway said. "This ability seems to go against the laws of nature. But some scientists involved in quantum physics now talk about what they call the non-local mind. It's a part of us that's not limited to our physical bodies, that's connected with everything in the universe."

"How come I'm not aware of my non-local mind?" Tyler asked.

"Good question." Calloway gathered his thoughts. "Normally, our minds are busy with a lot of noisy distractions, a continual chatter. But remote viewers have found that by relaxing, quieting their minds, and focusing, they can become aware of the non-local mind and perceive in ways that extend beyond ordinary perception."

Tyler frowned, nodded. "I get it. Sort of."

"That was very good," Doc said after Tyler left. "I remember you were one of the best instructors of the new people joining Eagle's Nest."

"That was a while back. I had to dig for it."

Then he remembered the presence of the other, and that he'd been scribbling something when Tyler had barged in. He picked up the notebook.

"What the hell?"

"What is it?" Doc asked.

He handed the notepad to Doc. "I had no idea what I was writing at the time."

Doc read it aloud: *"Calloway—your non-local mind is going to explode if you don't stop sticking it where it doesn't belong."*

Eleven

Matt held his long, muscular arms out like an airplane and weaved back and forth as he ran across the parking lot. The wind caressed his face and ruffled his thick, sandy hair. He looked up at the statue of Chief Wasakie, who guarded the lot, and yelled up to him. "Good-bye, Chief! I just quit! I ain't guidin' no more tours. I'm a free bird!"

He continued on, arms extended, turning, pivoting until he landed at the door of the camper. "We are outa . . . here!"

His voice dropped on the last word. He stared through the open window to the empty passenger seat. His arms collapsed, lifeless at his side. He felt as if the plane had just crashed. He'd been gone no longer than ten minutes. Maybe she'd changed her mind, just walked away, and caught a ride back to town.

He heard a tap on the rear window of the cab and saw Jill, all freckles and flowing red hair, stick her tongue out at him and make a face. Her shoulders were bare, her T-shirt gone. Then she turned and pressed her butt against the window. No jeans, no panties.

"Christ!"

He laughed and ran around the back of the camper, opened the lift gate and climbed in. He already felt himself getting hard. Jill lay sprawled on the bed, staring at the bulge in his pants as he wriggled out of his jeans.

She reached up for him and he climbed onto her, kissing and groping. She felt so damned good. It always happened so fast. He felt her hips grinding against him, driving him crazy. Sometimes he didn't even make it inside her. He could only imagine what it would be like if he could hold himself back. His body shuddered and he collapsed, gulping for air.

"You're like a bunny rabbit, Matt," Jill whispered in his ear. "You gotta slow down. When we're married, no one's gonna care. We'll have lots of time and we'll be in our own bed."

"That'll be great. A real bed."

Matt tried to stretch his arms overhead, but banged a hand against the front wall of the eight-year-old camper. He sat up, shook his hand, then pulled on his clothes. "We better get on the road. We've got a lot of driving ahead of us."

More than she realized. He wasn't looking forward to telling her the truth. The longer he held off, the better.

Jill picked up her T-shirt, then reached under the bed. He felt a ripple of panic. "Here, let me help you."

He dropped down and peered under the bed. He saw her jeans and panties and Jill's hand patting the floor just inches from the backpack containing the bomb. He grabbed her clothes just in time and handed them to her.

He watched in fascination as she performed a reverse strip. He'd never seen her get dressed, at least not in the light. He noticed how she stepped into her panties, pulled them into place, and the way she wriggled into her jeans and pulled up the zipper. He liked the way she looked in jeans with nothing on top. She reminded him of pictures in *Playboy.*

"Matt?"

"Yeah."

"I was wondering where we're going to stay tonight."

"I don't know. Depends how far we get," he answered.

"No, that's not what I mean. Are we going to sleep back here at a roadside rest?"

"Or a campground," he said. "That's what I was thinking."

"I like your camper and all, but it would be fun and really sexy to get a motel room tonight. You know, we could stay up late watching TV and messing around.''

He shrugged. ''I suppose we could try.''

''Try? What do you mean, try? Do you think we're too young to get a room on our own?''

''I didn't say that.''

''But you were thinking it.''

''No, I was thinking that they always ask for credit cards and I don't have one.''

''I've got one,'' she answered with a smile. ''We'll use mine.''

''I thought your dad gave it to you for Las Vegas.''

''He did. But it works outside of Las Vegas, too, you know. You said that we might be gone for up to two weeks. So we'll need the card.''

''I guess. I've got cash, too, from your dad. A wedding present. We'll be all right.'' Her father had given him an envelope containing three thousand dollars in hundreds, more money than Matt had ever seen at one time. He'd stuffed the envelope under the front seat.

''He gave you cash?'' She shook here head. ''I don't get it. Two days ago, he was really mad at me, at you, too, especially you for getting me pregnant. Then he gives me a credit card and you cash.''

''I guess he got over it. He was kind of stern with me, but he gave us his blessings.'' And a bomb to deliver, he thought.

''Two weeks on the Strip in Las Vegas is a long time. Were you thinking of going somewhere else, too?''

The question surprised him. ''Why do you ask? Did your father say something to you?''

''Matt Hennig, you're hiding something from me. Now tell me what it is. How are we going to be married if you're already keeping secrets?''

He started to deny that he was keeping a secret from her, but stopped. ''Jill, your father and I are involved in the Idaho Supreme Militia, which is affiliated with Freedom Nation.''

''So what?''

"So there are going to be times when I can't tell you everything we do."

"That's bullshit!"

"No, it's not," he replied, firmly. "We're patriots of the new order and we're getting closer to making a new country out here."

She didn't say anything for several seconds. "Sometimes I think it's all just a game that men like to play, a way to get away from their wives and kids for a while. But other times, when I hear Dad talking, I realize there's more to it, that you guys are serious."

"We are serious and there is something that I've got to do on this trip. I was gonna tell you tonight, but I guess now is as good as later."

"No, wait. Let's start driving, Matt. I've got the feeling that I'm not going to like what you've got to say. But if we're on our way to Las Vegas to get married, it won't be so bad."

They climbed out the back, got into the truck, and left Chief Wasakie, the white dinosaur, and the ice caves behind. He turned onto Highway 75 and accelerated.

"What did Mr. Cavanaugh say about you quitting?"

"The old geezer said we should stay here and get married in the caves. He said he'd even give me more hours—thirty-two a week."

"Get married in that underground icebox?" She laughed. "No way. Las Vegas, here we come!"

"I told Mr. Cavanaugh that I'd come back after our trip and tell him about it, but I don't think I will."

"Why not?"

"By then he might've found out that we used the caves last night without telling him. He'll be mad about that because when he told me about that other entrance to the closed section, I said I wouldn't tell anyone about it. I didn't keep my word."

"Are you gonna miss your job?"

"Not really. It wasn't much of a job. It was like walking around in a big refrigerator all day and saying the same things over and over to different people. About the only thing interesting about it was trying to guess what question they would ask first."

"Like what?"

"They mostly wanted to know who discovered the caves. They always ask that one just before I get around to telling them."

"So who did discover them?" Jill asked.

"I don't need to answer that question anymore. But for old times, I'll tell you and that'll be the end of it."

"Good. Who was it?"

"Chief Wasakie."

"Does he count?"

"That's another question I hear a lot. I guess people don't think Indians count."

Jill looked over at him curiously. "What do ya tell 'em?"

He shrugged. "I say we gotta big statue of the chief out front. So he must count for something."

She patted him on the shoulder. "Now you don't have to ever talk about it again. So what's this thing you gotta do now? Does it have anything to do with the new job you're getting?"

"Sort of. I don't know much about the job yet. But I know that working for Freedom Nation will be a helluva lot better than being a tour guide back there." After a moment, he added, "I'll know more after we get back."

"You sure you want that job? A lot of people say that Freedom Nation is an outlaw organization. I mean its leader is wanted for murder. It's kind of like getting a job with the Mafia or something."

He hit the heel of his hand against the steering wheel. He couldn't believe what she'd just said. "Jill, your father is associated with Freedom Nation. It's the umbrella organization for the militias. There's nothing illegal about it. What's illegal is the way the federal government is sucking us dry, trying to take away our guns, telling us what to do and not to do. The bastards in Washington are trying to run our lives. They're a foreign power. It's not my government."

"What about your brother? He fought in the Gulf War and died."

"Leave him out of it. I'm proud of Jimmy. He did what he had to do. It was important for him. But it was a mistake. We can all see that now, the way the government lied to us about what was going on over there with the chemical weapons.''

Jill didn't respond.

"The thing is, about this new job.'' He paused, trying to figure out how to put it. "I'm sort of being tested now to see if I make the grade. That's what I was going to talk to you about. Your dad didn't want me to mention it right away, because he wanted to make sure that you didn't tell anyone.''

She frowned. "I wouldn't tell anyone anything. Why does Dad always think I'm such a blabbermouth? If the militia people were smart, they'd get women involved.''

"There's been talk of that,'' he said uneasily.

Most of the men thought it was a bad idea. Some said they'd even quit if women got involved. Others, like Gary Burke, said that women could build morale, but they were only good for one thing. He didn't tell her any of that.

"So what is it, anyhow? Where else are we going and what are we doing?''

"Washington, D.C.''

"What? Washington?'' Her face crumpled. "You mean the whole goddamn thing is a lie? We're not going to Vegas?''

"Yes, we are. It's not a lie. Calm down. We've just got to take this side trip first. It won't be bad.''

"Side trip? What are you talking about? That's all the way across the damn country. Do you know how long that's going to take?''

"We can do it in three days. We get there by Tuesday and we leave the same day.'' The words rushed excitedly out of him now. "We can get to Las Vegas by late Friday. That's the first night of our reservation at the Sands. We'll get married Saturday or Sunday at the latest.''

She didn't say a word for nearly a minute. He focused on the road as the stark, rocky landscape blurred by. "Okay. But if I'm going on this so-called side trip, I want to know what we're doing. No secrets. It's only fair.''

"Jill, I can't tell you. I promised your father. You've got to go along with me on this."

"See, you're already putting the militia ahead of me. I don't like it. Turn around and take me home. I'm not playing this stupid game."

Matt thought about the consequences of what she was saying. "Damn, you are stubborn, Jill Sudner." He pulled over to the side of the road and turned the engine off.

She crossed her arms and stared ahead. If she insisted on going home, and he thought she would, he'd lose everything. His girl, his standing in the militia, his new job. Everything. The only thing to do was tell her. After all, she said she wouldn't talk.

"Okay, but you can't say a word to anyone about this. No matter what happens."

"Of course I won't."

"Not even your father. Especially not him. He won't trust me if he finds out I told you."

"Don't worry about it. I won't say a word."

"Okay, when we get to Washington, I'm going over to a closed elementary school. The windows are boarded up, but there's a loose one. I'm going to drop a backpack inside the window. That's all."

"Wait a minute." Jill frowned and shook her head. "You lost me. What backpack?"

"It's in the camper, under the bed."

"What's in it, anyhow?"

"I don't know. Some stuff, I guess," he said, uneasily.

"C'mon, Matt. You know what it is," Jill responded.

"You don't need to know that."

"Bullcrap, Matt Hennig. If we're traveling across the country with it, I want to know what it is."

"It's a bomb, but—"

"A bomb!" She jabbed a finger toward the rear of the truck. "There's a bomb back there and we just screwed on top of it? Are you crazy?"

He held up his hands. "Don't worry. It won't go off. Somebody in Washington is going to detonate it. We'll be long gone by then."

"What's the point of blowing up some old elementary school? It don't make no sense."

"Your father says it's like pounding a fist on a table. No one's gonna get hurt, but it'll get their attention. They'll know we're damn serious about getting the federal government off our backs."

She shook her head. "They'll just say you're all criminals. It won't help the cause none."

"Don't you remember studying the American Revolution, how the revolutionaries messed up the British, dumped the tea in the harbor and all that? They blew up things, too. It's like that."

"Great. Dad and General Wiley can sit back and call themselves revolutionaries, but what about us? What if somebody slams into the back of the truck? Won't the bomb go off and kill us?"

"Look, your father said it can't explode, not even if we drove off a cliff. I'm sure he wouldn't put you in any kind of danger like that."

She thought a moment. "I'm not so sure of that. Not at all. My mother's biggest complaint about Dad is that he puts his militia above his family. And it's true, too. He's trying to use me in his goddamn plan without even telling me. I won't do it. That's it."

"Oh, knock it off, Jill. Let's get going. It'll be over before you know it, and we'll be free birds."

"No. N-O. I'm not doing it."

Matt stared glumly ahead. He conceded that it wasn't going to work. But it was Sudner's fault as much as his own. Neither of them had figured on Jill's insistence to know all the details. He started the engine. "All right. I'll take you home."

"No. Let's go. Drive. All the way to Washington."

"Forget it. I'm not going to listen to you complaining the entire way. Let's go back."

"No. I said, let's go."

He looked at her, exasperated. "Are you sure?"

She shrugged. "I guess so."

He reached for her hand. "Tell me the truth. If you want to go back, I'll take you home."

"I don't want to mess it up for you, Matt."

"I'll deliver the damned thing myself."

"No way. I want to marry you, and if it takes blowing up a god-damn school, then I'll do it with you. Just don't leave me out and don't ever hide anything from me. Never."

He pulled her to him and hugged her tightly. He wasn't sure what he was getting into any more than Jill. But at least they had each other. Right now that mattered more than anything.

Matt heard a noise and looked in the rearview mirror to see a flashing red light. "We got company. A cop."

Jill paled and sucked in her breath. She ran a hand through her mussed red hair. "Oh no, Matt. What are we going to do if they want to look in the back?"

He kept his eye on the mirror. "Stay calm. He's got no reason to search us. He probably just wants to know if we need any help."

"I hope you're right."

The door opened. A deputy with a bald head and sunglasses stepped out. Matt smiled. "Hell, that's Gary Burke."

"Gary? Oh, thank God. He knows my dad real well."

Matt rolled down the window. "Hi, Gary. What's up?"

Burke leaned down and looked into the cab of the pickup. "Aren't you two supposed to be heading out of town?"

"Yeah, we're going to Las Vegas to get married, if we ever get moving," Jill said. "Did Daddy tell you about it?"

Burke smiled. "I know all about it." He looked at Matt, lost his smile. "There's been a change in plans."

Matt's heart started to pound. They'd been watching him, testing him, and knew he'd been playing around in the camper rather than heading out of town. They thought he wasn't up to the job. Too much of a kid, just like Burke said. He'd lost his chance and he'd already quit his job.

"You need to drop over to the post office," Burke said in a low voice.

"Why, what's over there?"

"A new red Cherokee. Courtesy of General Wiley. A wedding present."

"You're kidding!" Matt exclaimed.

"No way!" Jill shouted.

"Boy, am I glad you found us," Matt said.

Burke seemed to glare at him and Matt wondered if he were jealous. "You don't know the half of it, Hennig. Now you two get moving. Pick up that Cherokee and don't forget to take everything you got with you." He patted the hood. "We'll take care of this baby for you."

"Thanks, Gary."

"Don't forget to leave the keys."

"Got it!" Matt slapped Jill on the thigh. "Let's go."

Twelve

While Doc called room service, Calloway tuned into a noon news program broadcast from a Denver station. A perky anchorwoman, named Jessica Parks, flashed a toothy smile and launched into the top story.

"In national news, our top story comes out of Crested Butte, where President David Dustin is vacationing at the estate of tennis pro Kyle Leslie. In the aftermath of the president's extraordinary comments about alien contact last night, the media have gathered outside of Leslie's property and are awaiting further developments. Let's go to WTVF's Martin Cole."

Calloway leaned forward and Doc's phone conversation with the kitchen faded away. A mob scene of reporters and camera crews appeared on the screen against the backdrop of a wooded entryway and distant mountain peaks. "Jessica, as you can see, the media is out in full force and the atmosphere here is buoyant and almost giddy as most reporters here are taking the president's comments about his contact with aliens with a grain of salt. I spoke with one state trooper here earlier who told me that no reports of aliens or UFOs have been filed in Gunnison County since the president's arrival in Crested Butte last night."

"Marty, in spite of the atmosphere, it seems the media is taking this story seriously enough to stand in the road and wait for the next word," the anchorwoman commented.

"That's true, Jessica. The unanswered questions are piling up. If the president did encounter aliens in the White House, how did they get past security? Did Mrs. Dustin also encounter them? On the other hand, if there were no aliens, as his own spokespeople are saying, the tough question now being asked, especially by opponents of the administration, is whether or not the president remains sound of mind. If not, they say, he must step down from office. In any event, we are here until the president gives us an update or the aliens land with news from afar."

"Thank you, Jason." Parks smiled, shook her head, then spoke to the camera. "Let's take a look at exactly what the president said last night at the Brown Palace Hotel."

Doc sat down next to Trent as Dustin appeared at a podium. He looked serious, earnest, and concerned as he spoke of his encounter and its meaning. The comments were edited into three segments of five or six seconds each. The editing left the viewer thinking that aliens were about to land, but there was also something dream-like about the entire scenario, Calloway thought.

Parks returned and gave the camera a long, thoughtful look as if she were attempting to figure out what was going on. "Here now is White House spokesperson Camila Hidalgo, speaking to reporters at the Brown Palace Hotel this morning."

Calloway watched Camila respond to a shouted question about aliens. He admired her poise, how she remained unflustered and calmly emphasized that the comments were a metaphor. But seeing her on the job made him realize how out of touch he'd been, not only with her personally, but with events surrounding her life that were public knowledge. He had no idea that she'd become the White House spokesperson, that she appeared regularly on television. A far cry from his temporary work guiding rafts on the San Juan.

"Now let's see what Denver thinks about the president's comments," Parks said at the end of the brief slice of the press conference. The scene shifted to an interior of a restaurant to a table of diners.

Calloway heard a knock and turned off the television. He opened the door to see Nick Tyler. "Let me guess, the suite comes with a catch and you're it."

The Secret Service agent didn't laugh. He stepped inside. "We've got word back from the sheriff's office in Shoshone."

"Yeah, and . . . ?"

"And nothing."

"Nothing!" Doc said. "What do you mean?"

"The sheriff's office sent a deputy out to the ice caves. There's no one named Matthew working there and nothing at all unusual going on."

"It's got to be a mistake." Calloway shook his head. "That kid had some connection with that place. I felt it."

"What you felt didn't translate to the real world," Tyler responded. "Not in this case. The bottom line, Mr. Calloway, is that we don't have anything and there's no reason to continue the investigation. Period."

After a moment, he added. "But, of course, you can stay here and check out in the morning."

"Wait a minute!" Doc raised her voice and moved over to Tyler. "You guys haven't given Trent half a chance."

"I'll take care of this, Doc," Calloway interrupted, then turned to Tyler. "We're not going to stay here unless we're making use of our time. This isn't a vacation. We'll try again. We'll come up with something new, something you can put your hands on."

Tyler looked grimly at him.

"You can observe firsthand this time," Calloway added.

"If you can come up with anything specific and verifiable, I'll check it out."

"Good. Let me relax a minute and then we'll get started," Calloway said, and flopped down in one of the chairs.

"I'm ready when you are," Doc said.

He tried to settle down, but Tyler's report disturbed him. Maybe he'd misread the images he'd gotten of the kid at the ice caves. Maybe the entire scenario had been his imagination, his mind's way of making up a story to fill his need for something to say.

No. He pushed away the thought. Everything he'd gotten felt right. In fact, he sensed that his abilities were improving, that he might even be better than when he'd worked daily as a remote viewer.

On a whim, he reached for the telephone. He ignored the questioning looks from Doc and Tyler and dialed the long-distance operator. He tapped the number for the Shoshone Ice Caves and waited. A woman answered on the second ring.

"Is Matthew working today?"

"Matthew? I don't believe we have any Matthew working here."

"Are you sure?"

He felt a sinking sensation in his stomach and was about to hang up when he heard a second voice in the background say, "Who's looking for Matt?"

"Oh, wait, you mean Matt, one of our tour guides," the woman said. "Just a minute. Let me put Mr. Cavanaugh on."

Calloway was greeted by a crisp but wary voice. "Hello, who am I speaking to, please?"

"My name is Joe, Joe Williams. I took a tour there a couple of weeks ago and got to talking to Matt. I'm a river rafting guide on the San Juan River in Bluff, Utah, and I told him I'd send him a brochure."

"Oh, so you were trading guiding stories." The man's wariness vanished. "I'm sure Matt would love to get the brochure, but he's not here and I'm not sure when I'll see him again. He quit this morning."

"Oh, does he have a new job?"

"Actually, I don't know. He was heading to Las Vegas with his girlfriend. They're getting married."

"Oh, really. He didn't mention he was getting married to me," Calloway replied.

"I think it was a spur-of-the-moment decision. I told him that I thought he was kind of young. But maybe it'll work out. You never know."

"That's true. You never know. Do you have his home address so I can send him the brochure?"

"Why don't you just send it here and I'll get it too him. Shoshone's a small town. I'll see him around if he doesn't stop by."

"That's fine. What's Matt's last name?"

"Matt Hennig. Do you need our address?"

"Nope. I've got it," Calloway said as he jotted the name on a notepad by the phone. "Thanks for your time, Mr. Cavanaugh."

Calloway hung up, tore the page off the pad, and handed it to Tyler. "Guess that sheriff's deputy didn't do a very thorough investigation up in Shoshone."

"Maybe the cop didn't want to help the feds find a local boy," Doc said after Calloway related what he'd just heard.

"We'll run his name through the DMV computer for the state of Idaho and find out what he's driving," Tyler said. "We'll put out an APB and figure out how far they could've driven today. If he's heading to Las Vegas, or even to Washington, we shouldn't have too much trouble locating him."

Tyler started for the door, but hesitated. "You didn't say anything before about him getting married. If you were really in his mind, I'd think that would be a big deal."

"I was focused on the kid's connection with the bomb, not his personal life. The girl could've been right there in the truck with him and I wouldn't have seen her."

Tyler frowned. "I guess I still don't understand what you do."

"I've been trained to remain focused on the target, not to get caught up in the surrounding distractions. The more images you get, the more confusing it becomes."

"So that's it," Tyler said.

As soon as the Secret Service agent left, Calloway turned to Doc. "Let's go after the girl. I want to see what she knows."

"What about lunch? Don't you ever get hungry?"

"We'll take a break when it arrives," he assured her. "Let's get started."

He moved back over to the comfortable chair and sank into it. He breathed deeply, slowly expanding and contracting his diaphragm with each breath. He pushed aside his concerns about his accuracy. Let it go, he told himself. He relaxed and sank deeper, his breath now shallow, barely perceptible. The flow of thoughts slowed to a trickle. His mind stilled and the first images appeared.

A blur of light and movement. Cars and landscape raced by him as if he were on a wild ride. Strapped in. The smell of leather seats. Comfortable, smooth. Different from before . . . a different vehicle.

Then he became aware of the girl and under Doc's guidance moved closer into her awareness. Outwardly, she projected a sense of confidence, but it belied her inner turmoil. He could hear her talking with Matt, but he couldn't understand what she was saying. She sounded happy, in love. But just below the surface, a cauldron of dark emotions slowly simmered. She felt manipulated. Not by Matt. Someone else close to her and close to Matt. Her father.

"She hopes that Matt really wants to marry her, but she knows that he has another agenda. This trip was her father's idea. She's angry about that. It's just a cover-up for the other thing—the bomb. Matt's just too damn loyal. A good soldier. Just the kind of person her father likes around him."

"Is her father the one who's behind the bomb?"

"One of the people. There's someone higher who's giving him orders."

"Who is it?"

His head buzzed with static. "I'm getting blocked. Or maybe she doesn't know."

"Where are you now?" Doc asked when he didn't say anything further.

"I'm seeing, no, feeling her life." He opened his eyes, fully aware of being in the hotel.

"What's her name?"

He felt the motion of the vehicle and knew he was still with her. "I don't know. Let me see if she'll tell me. Don't guide me on this. Let me drop in a little deeper."

He took a couple of breaths, closed his eyes again. He moved closer to the girl, settled into her awareness. This time he let her know he was there. He asked her name, posing the question silently to her subconscious. If her conscious mind heard him, she would sense him as a thought, a whim, an imaginary companion.

"I'm Jill. Who wants to know?"

"Just a friendly visitor."

"Why are you here?"

"I'm concerned about something you're carrying."

"I know. I don't like it, either."

"Where are you taking it?"

"Washington, D.C. I don't really want to go. But it'll be nice driving across the country with Matt. I'll see a lot of states, places I've never been."

"Is this Matt's vehicle?"

"No, we changed. It's a Jeep Cherokee. A nice red one."

"Where did you get it?"

"In Shoshone."

"Whose car is it?"

"Don't ask so many questions."

"Did your father get you the car?"

"No! Leave him out of this."

"Back off, Calloway! Leave her alone!"

Calloway felt a blow, like a hand lightly slapping his forehead. He abruptly pulled away from Jill and back into the room. Moments before the intruder had spoken, he'd felt a presence, like someone reading a newspaper over his shoulder. The same creepy feeling as before, he thought.

The intruder wasn't just peeking in on him now, he was making himself known, showing his power. There was a certain familiarity in the presence, but he couldn't quite match the voice to a face or a name. He reached out, searching for the intruder.

"Show yourself. I know you. Let me see who you are."

He sensed the intruder nearby. He momentarily glimpsed a singular figure, but instantly it turned plural, like an image reflected between two mirrors. It pressed forward for an instant, then blurred and receded. He opened his eyes and rubbed his forehead where he'd felt the contact.

He smelled food. A waiter in a white jacket transferred platters to the table. Calloway had been so far out there that he hadn't even heard him arrive.

Doc handed the slender young man a couple of dollars. He started to push the cart toward the door. But he stopped halfway there, hesitated, then slowly turned toward Calloway.

"You want to see me. Here I am." The waiter let loose with a burst of sharp, mean-spirited laughter. "Better watch yourself, Calloway. Both of you. You're poking into the wrong places. Back off if you know what's good for you."

"Who are you? What are you saying?" Doc demanded. She grabbed the waiter's shoulder and shook him.

The man looked around stunned, confused. "Jeez, I'm sorry. I'm really sorry." He held up his hands. "I don't know what got into me. It was like someone else talking. That wasn't me. I don't understand."

Calloway stood up. He touched the man's arm. "It's okay. Just calm down. It's over now. You'll be all right."

The man gave him a frightened look and hurried away.

"What was that?" Doc asked as the door closed.

Astonished, Calloway just shook his head. "I was impressed with the automatic writing earlier. But this . . . this manipulation of vocal cords, of speech, that was a show of strength."

"Who is it?"

"It's the others, Maxwell's gang," he said. "They're tracking us and the bastards are strong. Real strong."

Thirteen

The eight-passenger corporate jet descended for a landing, but Camila could only see mountains and forest.

"There's the ranch, right below us," Harvey Howell said. "Oh, just take a look at all those vehicles lined up on the road." He patted her knee and chuckled. "All your people, all just waiting to hear the latest from you."

Camila didn't bother to lean over Howell to look. "No, they're waiting for the president to talk." The plane seemed to skim the trees, a landing field came into view, and the craft touched down.

"Welcome to Crested Butte," the pilot said over the intercom. "I hope you've had a comfortable flight. There will be a car to pick you up."

"Nice little spread," Howell said. "Two thousand acres complete with landing strip. Not bad."

"I bet the house is nice, too," Camila added.

"I'm sure it's splendid. All earned by hitting a little ball over a net. I should've worked more on my serve when I was young."

Camila glanced over at him as she held her nose and tried to clear her ears from the change in pressure. "I didn't know you played tennis, Harvey."

"I'm not bad. But I stick to doubles now."

The plane taxied along the runway, turned, and headed back in the other direction. Now that she was on the ground, Camila braced herself for the inevitable encounter with Todd Waters, the president's chief of staff. Waters would be incensed about their tardiness. He would demand an explanation and he wouldn't like it when he heard it.

Howell leaned toward her, but didn't look at her as he spoke. "Listen, Camila, about last night in the room, I've been meaning to tell you that I'm really sorry about that."

She'd wondered if he would mention it again and waited for him to continue.

"I just want to make sure that you know it was just a joke. That was why I invited you to the room. Just to see your reaction."

"A joke?" Camila frowned. "I didn't laugh."

"No kidding." Howell chuckled and watched her closely. "Actually, you looked really shocked. I could hardly keep from laughing. Can you imagine what would've happened if I had gone down to dinner like that?"

"Not really. You seemed kind of confused about what you were doing."

Howell glanced over at Secret Service Agent Sam Clarke, who had accompanied them on the flight, then lowered his voice. "I wasn't a bit confused. That's what I'm telling you, it was an act."

"You fooled me."

"Listen, I'd prefer if we just kept my silly little caper between ourselves."

The plane taxied to a stop. She didn't believe Howell's version of events. For whatever reason, he had temporarily lost control of his faculties. A cross-dressing public official, especially one in charge of national security, didn't exactly engender her confidence, and now he was lying to her as well.

"Look Harvey, we both work for the president. Considering his own problems, he doesn't need to hear about your preference in evening attire, joking or otherwise. I don't know what the hell that was about, but I'm willing to shelf it. Let's go help the president."

A Land Rover waited outside. "Any verification yet on what Calloway told us?" Camila asked Clarke as the vehicle headed to the main house.

She tried to make the comment sound as matter of fact as possible, but she had to struggle to control her voice. She still hadn't fully recovered from the sudden appearance of her ex-husband, much less from the message that he'd brought with him. In retrospect, she felt he was sincere in his concern, that he had tuned in to something. But she hoped he was dead wrong about the bomb and the intent of the bombers. They didn't need another crisis, especially not now.

"It's confusing," Clarke said. "The local cops couldn't tell us anything helpful, but then Calloway called the ice caves himself." He told her what had transpired.

"We ran a check on Matthew Hennig and got an APB out on his pickup-camper. But then Calloway did another session and said that Hennig and his girlfriend switched vehicles and are now driving a Jeep Cherokee and heading for Washington with the bomb."

"Jesus Christ," Howell said. "Did he get the license plate number?"

"His abilities don't seem to be that specific. We're checking with the dealers in the area."

"Tell me frankly, Sam, what's your assessment on Calloway?" Howell asked. "Is there anything solid here or are we chasing fairies?"

Camila bit her lower lip, stared straight ahead.

"Calloway has been just accurate enough to keep us interested," Clarke responded. "But until we verify that Hennig switched vehicles and we get a license plate number on it, there's not much we can do."

Hearing the two men discuss her former husband brought back memories, some good, some not so good, and a few that were very strange. She'd never forgotten the time he'd come home after getting inside the mind of some murderous dictator or drug dealer. She couldn't remember which. He'd actually looked and acted like a different person, one who frightened her. She'd rushed out of the house and called Gordon Maxwell for help.

"Who's behind the bomb? Where did it come from? Howell persisted.

"We don't know if there is a bomb," Clarke said, patiently. "But the implication is that a militia group is involved and that could mean a connection to George Wiley and Freedom Nation. Wiley has the means to obtain a backpack nuke."

Camila recalled that just a few weeks ago a backpack nuclear weapon, traced back to Russia, was confiscated at the U.S.-Canadian border. If one had reached the border, another might have gotten through.

As they approached the front gate to the ranch, she pushed away the thoughts and surveyed the horde of reporters, several times the number who usually followed the president on a vacation trip. Clarke flashed his badge at a state trooper and the gate opened.

"Mr. Waters asked me to take you both directly to the guesthouse when you arrived," the trooper said.

After they parked, another trooper guided them along a walkway that wound around the house and into a courtyard that connected to another house. They entered a library and Camila's feet sank so deeply into the thick carpeting that she wanted to take off her shoes. Cherry-wood bookcases grew out of the walls and were lined with thousands of volumes. Three inviting reading chairs with footrests filled the floor space on one side of the library, complemented on the other side by a mahogany table with six chairs around it.

Camila eyed the comfortable chairs, but took a seat at the table. Howell sat across from her. "We better tell Todd about your ex-husband," Howell said. "He'll need to know about it."

She didn't like the way he'd said it, as if this new annoyance was her fault. "Yeah, I suppose if somebody's planning to blow up Washington, D.C., the chief of staff would probably want to know about it." He'd probably also be very interested in the national security advisor's evening gown, too, she thought.

The door opened and Todd Waters, a soft-sided human tank, trudged into the library. Balding and bespectacled, Waters's round face looked flushed, as if he'd been arguing with someone. "What did you two do, stay for the brunch so I could sweat it out here myself?"

He stood over them, hands on his hips. "Did you see that CNN has already labeled this thing as the 'President's Alien Affair.' It's only going to get worse. All they want to do is exploit, exploit, exploit."

"As soon as we're done here, I'll go out and calm things down," Camila said.

"You already talked to them this morning," he snapped. "They're not going to let this go until the president addresses the nation on the issue. That's the bottom line."

She knew that Waters occasionally seemed on the verge of losing control, but he rarely let his emotions get the better of him. He could be shouting angrily one moment at a staff member who needed reprimanding, then turn and calmly talk to someone else as if nothing unusual had just occurred.

"Then he should do it as soon as possible," Howell said, turning up his hands.

Waters glared at him. "Harvey, you don't know what you're talking about. You haven't heard the full story."

"Then let's hear it," Howell replied.

"I'm not sure how much more you should know," Waters said. "In fact, I don't think you should know anything more about it."

Camila understood perfectly. The president's comments had certainly aroused her curiosity, but from a professional standpoint, it might be easier for her to maintain the administration's position if she didn't know any more details.

"Nonsense, I need to know," Howell insisted. "We're talking about a matter that could affect national security."

Camila knew that Waters was about to ask her to leave, so she quickly redirected the conversation. "We've got something we need to report to you, Todd. It's about a possible nuclear threat."

Waters took a seat. He suddenly appeared calm. "Lay it on me."

She looked to Howell, but he demurred to her. She realized that talking about her ex-husband to Waters was going to be harder than

she thought. "Do you remember the speaker at the luncheon yesterday?"

"Of course I do. That was a mistake and I told Jon Harmon about
it, too," he groused. "So what does Maxwell have to do with a nuclear
threat? Is he making it or predicting it?"

"Neither. My ex-husband, Trent Calloway, used to be a remote
viewer for the CIA when he was in the air force. He worked for Gordon
Maxwell."

Waters crossed his arms and waited for her to continue. She told
him what she knew.

"But you're saying this is all a vision, that there's no concrete
evidence of the existence of a backpack nuke yet."

"No direct evidence. Not yet."

"The FBI is working on it," Howell said. "We heard that the kid
who supposedly has the bomb was on his way to Las Vegas to get
married, but Calloway thinks that's a cover story."

"Stop!" Waters held up his hands. "I've got a million and one
things on my mind and I've had my fill of weirdness already. I don't
need this. But I want *you* to stay on top of it, Harvey. And, for chrissake, don't say anything to . . ."

The door opened. Two Secret Service agents preceded the president
into the room. David Dustin wore a lightweight jogging outfit and running shoes and towered over her as she stood up. He gave her a friendly
hug, something he did on occasion when he hadn't seen her for a while
or wanted to congratulate her.

He shook hands with Howell and nodded to his chief of staff.
"Please sit down. I'm sorry for interrupting your meeting, Todd, but I
want to take advantage of this opportunity to personally fill in Howard
and Camila on what's been going on."

"Sir, are you sure about this?" Waters interrupted. "I thought we
were going to keep the details under close wraps. I don't think that
Camila, in particular, should be here."

"I trust Camila to handle this matter with utmost sensitivity," Dustin said.

"But she doesn't need to know," Waters protested.

She'd never seen Waters go up against the president so forcefully.

"I understand your position, Todd, but I want Camila to have the full background," Dustin responded.

Well, here it comes, she thought. She glanced at Waters, who now stared ahead glassy-eyed, his cheeks glowing burnt red.

"Let me begin by saying that what you've heard is only the tip of the iceberg, and the story I'm going to tell you is both strange and awesome. Please keep an open mind. You know, the skeptics always asked, if there were aliens, then why don't they land on the White House lawn? Well, they did better than that—they landed in my bedroom."

Oh, shit, Camila thought.

He paused, collecting his thoughts. "It began six weeks ago. I was awakened during the night by a brilliant flash of light that was accompanied by a turbulence. It felt as if I were lying on a waterbed and suddenly someone had jumped on one end of it. Annie woke up too, but she didn't remember the flash or the turbulence. That was all that happened on the first night."

Camila noticed how Waters watched the president as if he were analyzing his delivery of the State of the Union the night before the address. He was hearing the story for at least the second time and was probably checking on the consistency of details.

"That turned out to be the precursor," Dustin continued. "Two weeks later, I woke up in the middle of the night and found myself floating above my bed."

"Floating?" Howell looked as if he were waiting for Dustin to say it was all a joke.

"That's right."

"Did Annie see you?" Camila asked.

"She was sound asleep. It was just them and me."

"Them," Howell repeated. "The aliens?"

"That's right. I felt terrified. I couldn't see them, but I knew they were there, watching. One of them even tried to comfort me. He spoke to me telepathically and said there was nothing to fear, nothing bad was going to happen to me. But he warned me that they would be back and the next time they would take me with them on a trip to the stars."

Camila didn't know what to say. No one, much less the president of the United States, had ever calmly told her about being abducted by aliens. Was Dustin really going to say next that he'd left the planet? If so, it was worse than she'd thought.

"Why didn't you say something?" Howell asked. "Did you tell anyone?"

"Just Annie. She convinced me that it was a nightmare, even though I swore that I was awake. I wanted movement sensors put in the bedroom, but she wouldn't hear of it. She just wanted the whole thing to go away and who could blame her for that. Nearly a month went by. Nothing happened and I was beginning to think that Annie was right, that it had been a nightmare."

Camila waited for the proverbial other shoe to drop.

"Then three nights ago, they came back and took me out of the White House and onto their ship."

Howell leaned forward. "How . . . how did they do that, sir?"

In Howell's eyes, she saw the reflection of her own greatest fears, that the president had lost it, flipped out, gone berserk.

"I was levitated up from my bed, but this time I was caught in a bright beam of light that lifted me right through the ceiling and into their craft." Camila felt baffled and disturbed by the casual way he said this; he might have been describing the clothes he'd worn to dinner the night before.

If there had been a vessel hovering above the White House, it would've been blasted out of the sky before the aliens had a chance to penetrate the president's bedroom, she thought. Certainly, he must have considered that, as well as the matter of how he'd moved through the ceiling. But she kept her counsel and listened.

Dustin smiled at her. "Camila, you look like you're in shock. I know this is upsetting and you probably are thinking that I've lost my marbles, but you need to hear this. So please bear with me."

"Yes, sir. I'm just surprised. Very surprised."

Dustin folded his hands and continued. "Keep in mind that we are dealing with entities far more advanced than we are. They have ways of disassembling and reassembling matter that we don't comprehend at this time. They can apparently not only block radar but create a shield of invisibility around their crafts.''

Camila fought back tears.

"So I found myself inside a small circular room about ten feet in diameter," he continued. "There was no furniture whatsoever. Nothing and no one. I wandered around this room feeling the smooth curving walls and looking for a door. But there were no seams anywhere. I panicked. I pounded on the walls. I shouted, but no one answered.

"Then a door that I hadn't detected slid open. I couldn't see anything but light in the doorway. Several seconds passed and a figure appeared—a woman. She was tall with shoulder-length hair and looked human except for her eyes, which were too large and very dark." He paused and held up his hand. "Her fingers were extremely long. Out to here. She wore a light, filamentous robe that changed colors in the light. She walked up to me and the robe fell away. She was naked and very much a woman, but she also frightened me.''

Camila glanced at Howell, who seemed transfixed by the story. Waters stared at the table. She couldn't even guess what he was thinking.

"The floor opened behind me and a piece of furniture rose up. It looked like a huge egg shell with an opening on the side. She took my hand and my fears started to evaporate. She led me into the egg and I knew I couldn't resist her. The egg bed was soft, so soft that I seemed to sink down through the floor with the woman embracing me.''

Dustin stopped, glanced at Camila, then the others. "I know you might be thinking that I was just experiencing some sort of science fiction wet dream, that I was asleep the entire time. That's what Annie and Todd have suggested. But it was real. I was as awake during that experience as I am right now.''

"Did the woman talk to you?" Howell asked.

Dustin nodded. "Yes, she did. Again, it was telepathic. She told me that she would carry my child, who would travel among the stars and live on another world.''

"What?" Camila interrupted. "What child?"

No one said anything, but they all looked at her as though the answer were obvious. Dustin believed he'd had sex with the alien.

"Why did she want you as a father?" Howell asked.

"She told me the child would carry genetic material that would help seed a new world that was an experiment of the galactic community."

"But they didn't take you there?" Howell asked.

"No, not yet. But let me get back to this world. There was a reason I spoke up last night. An important one. We are reaching a point in our development as a race—and of course I mean the human race—in which we will either exterminate ourselves or move into the galactic community and into a new way of understanding who we are."

"Who are we?" Howell asked.

Camila wished that Howell would shut up. His questions just allowed the president to expand on his fantasies, and that was what she was convinced they were.

"Harvey, we are extraordinary beings who are more—much more—than we seem. We transcend the physical. We transcend time. We are a part of something larger and parts of us exist in many worlds—both physical and nonphysical."

"That's interesting," Howell said. "But how would that apply to, say, national security?"

"You haven't been listening to me, Harvey. This is an unprecedented opportunity to move beyond nationalistic concerns and into a galactic mainframe. We're talking about dropping all disputes between nations because very soon they will be meaningless. We can pursue higher ambitions."

Howell nodded and grew quiet.

"Any questions, Camila?" Dustin asked.

She wanted to know if he'd seen anyone else in that craft besides the woman. But she thought better of it. "I don't think so."

Waters cleared his throat and spoke up for the first time since Dustin had begun telling his story. "As I said before, Mr. President, we've got to face some basic facts. There is no physical evidence of these events and without it going public would be a mistake.''

"On the other hand, going public with a full explanation might result in further contact being established," Dustin said.

"I've been thinking about this," Waters said. "Do we really want them here?''

"That's a reasonable concern, Todd," Dustin responded. "Eventually, I hope that I will be able to address the nation on this entire matter in a forthright manner. But for now, I think you are right on the mark. We need to take a reasonable approach that won't frighten people. We should maintain that my statement was a metaphor."

"That's good," Howell said. "Metaphors carry their own weight."

Camila felt relieved. "I think that's the best way to go, Mr. President. There'll be controversy for a few days, maybe even a week or two, but we can overcome it. We'll just keep telling them that the president is busy governing the nation."

Dustin nodded. "I hope I'm making the right decision."

"Of course you are," Waters told him.

Dustin stood and they all came to their feet. He turned to Camila. "Alert the press that I'm going for a jog. I'll swing by the front gate for photos, but I won't answer any questions."

He smiled, then turned and left.

She looked from Howell to Waters as the door closed. "I admire him," she said. "He's incredibly resilient."

"But do you think he's well?" Howell asked.

Camila recalled something that Steve Watkins, her assistant, had said the night before in the aftermath of the president's speech. "I understand that most people who claim to have been abducted by aliens test normal on psychological profile. In other words, they're not deranged.''

Waters supplicated the sky, but said nothing.

"He never told us how long he was up there with his lady friend, or who was controlling the ship," Howell said.

Waters smiled and placed a hand lightly on Howell's back. "He told me. But I'm keeping it to myself."

Fourteen

Gordon Maxwell pushed through the swinging doors of the old bar in the corner of the Strater Hotel in downtown Durango. The Strater maintained its nineteenth-century flavor with the barmaids dressed in brightly colored long, frilly dresses and bartenders with bowlers, vests, and handlebar mustaches. Maxwell found a corner table, a momentary refuge from his mounting worries.

He glanced at his watch. Ten to three. Steve Ritter would come down from his room in exactly ten minutes. No sooner. No later. He always required one mug of beer in the bar before he would invite Maxwell up to his room to begin the session. If Maxwell didn't follow the routine, Ritter simply refused to work.

If he wasn't so damn good, Maxwell wouldn't bother with him. About two years ago, Ritter had started refusing to work over the phone and he wouldn't fly or drive to Denver. He'd become a recluse, rarely going out except for his weekly trip to Silverton and back on the old steam-powered train. So Maxwell had been forced to deal with him in Durango.

Fortunately, Maxwell enjoyed driving his new Corvette and visiting the historic town, especially since he'd started seeing Marlys Simms, a barmaid at the Strater. He watched Marlys as she moved about in the purple, low-cut dress that reached her ankles and her auburn wig with its abundant, flowing curls.

A decade younger than him, she had maintained herself well, and carried a youthful air about her. Separated from her husband, she'd made it clear she wasn't looking for a new one, which was fine with him. Pursuing Marlys gave him something to do between sessions with Ritter, and it helped him deal with the male menopause thing. He'd even created fantasies about reversing the process.

The muffled ring of his cell phone caught his attention and he reached into his leather briefcase. He fumbled for the phone and answered on the third ring. "You want to talk to him? Take down this number," a raspy voice said.

He jotted down the area code and phone number. "Got it. I'll call in twenty minutes."

At least George Wiley had returned to his cautious approach in communicating with him. As the hunt for Wiley intensified, Maxwell had gotten more and more concerned. If the FBI ever found out that Wiley employed remote viewers to protect him, Maxwell's rising star would crash hard, especially if Wiley was linked to the plan to nuke Washington as he suspected. It was one thing to provide protection for the recalcitrant general, who'd become a folk hero in the West. But he certainly wouldn't stick with him if he planned to single-handedly destroy the country.

"A beer there, guy?" Marlys asked.

Maxwell looked up and smiled as he slipped his phone back into the briefcase. "I'll wait for Ritter. How ya doing?"

"I'm fine, but your friend . . ." She shook her head and pointed toward the ceiling. "He gets weirder and weirder all the time."

Marlys knew that Maxwell called himself a futurist and that he visited Ritter to obtain psychic impressions. Other than once asking about Ritter's accuracy, she expressed no interest in finding out about what he predicted. She had enough to deal with in the present, she said.

"What did he do now?"

"After eating all of his meals in his room for the past two months, he started coming down for lunch last week. But instead of getting his own table, he would sit right down with strangers and start telling them about their lives as if he'd known them forever. He scared people, so the manager told him to stop it or we wouldn't serve him anymore."

"Was he accurate?" He smiled, thinking that he was asking Marlys the same thing she'd asked him about Ritter.

She considered his question. "I heard one of the waitresses say that he picked up on everyone's secrets, things they thought no one else knew, and that's what he told them."

Maxwell was convinced that virtually anyone who made the effort and practiced could learn to remote view to some degree. But Ritter possessed something extra. A natural psychic, born with the talent, he could not only work remote targets, like other trained remote viewers, but he could read people as if he'd known them all their lives, as if he knew their futures.

Marlys looked up. "Oops, here he comes now. I'll go get the beers."

Maxwell glanced at his watch. Exactly three o'clock. He heard the annoying clatter of Ritter's steel taps scraping against the tile floor. Ritter, thin and angular with bulging eyes and the gaunt face of an ascetic, approached the table. As usual, he wore black corduroy pants and a black shirt. He extended a hand with spidery fingers and greeted Maxwell.

"I saw you on CNN, Max. Very impressive." He sat down next to him and leaned toward him. Too close. Too intense. "Glad to see you had the guts to stand up there and tell the bastards that their old world wasn't going to last. They listened to you, too. They listened good."

"Thanks, Steve."

Maxwell leaned back and wondered what the comments prefaced. Ritter rarely offered a compliment without following it up with some sort of criticism.

"You *better* thank me. After all, I nudged the governor into inviting you to speak. Harmon finds your work very interesting, but without me he would never had made the effort. Never."

He hated the way Ritter repeated himself, like a goddamn verbal hiccup.

"You did your part. But why did Dustin spill his gut last night? We've been working on him for weeks without him saying anything. Why then? Why not tomorrow or next week?"

Ritter grinned. "Because I pushed him, too. I pushed hard."

"You what? I hope you're joking."

"Nope. I did it because your head is getting too fucking big. You don't understand the consequences, colonel. The consequences."

He felt like strangling the bastard. "What are you talking about?"

"I took a peek into your future, something you don't like to do because you're so goddamned afraid of getting old and impotent. If you would've gotten all the publicity you wanted, you would've paid a big price. You would've been linked to Wiley in no time, and you wouldn't like the results. You both would've gotten nailed. Yeah, nailed."

Maxwell considered what he'd just heard. Maybe Ritter was right. Or maybe he just didn't want to see him gaining wide recognition and becoming independent of Wiley. Ritter, in his own way, admired Wiley, sympathized with him and his cause, and liked working for him.

Ritter watched Maxwell for several seconds as if he were studying a strange bug through a magnifying glass. "You know, you work closely with General Wiley, but I don't get any sense that you really favor Wiley's goals. Why is that, Max? Why?"

"We're not part of his army, Steve. You know that. We work on a project-by-project basis."

Ritter grinned. "Ah, like merrr-cen-arrr-ies."

"My interests are different than Wiley's. I'm a scientist. I'm interested in man's relationship with his future, how he can predict it and how he can alter it, and George Wiley has given me a great opportunity to test that hypothesis."

"And a chance to make a lot of money. A whole lot of loot."

"That helps," Maxwell responded. "And I pay you and the others well."

Two mugs of beer arrived and when Marlys moved away, Ritter rephrased his question. "Just by the act of working for Wiley you, Colonel, are involved in helping create Wiley's version of the future."

"I think it's pretty well understood now that the experimenter always affects the data by simply carrying out the experiment. But Wiley is helping me, too. He's allowing us to explore the far reaches of remote viewing and the results, as you well know, have been phenomenal."

Ritter smiled and flashed his uneven row of teeth. "I'm glad you noticed, Max. Glad you noticed. When me and the boys put our heads together, we can go far. Real far."

Maxwell glanced at his watch, remembering that he'd promised Wiley he'd call him. "Let's drink up. I've got a call to make before we start."

"What is it tonight, another Wiley job?"

"Not exactly." He wished Ritter wouldn't use Wiley's name in public. "I don't want to tell you any more about it."

Ritter gazed off. "You don't have to." He laughed. "You're going to send me to Wiley, right into him." He nodded, telling himself that he was right. "That's an interesting twist, Max. I like it, like it a lot. You're such a control freak."

"You're not always right, Steve. I'm going to call him, that's all."

Ritter sipped his beer and watched Maxwell over the rim of the mug. "So you have something else to worry about now, something besides your boring preoccupation with getting old."

Maxwell ignored the comment. He finished his beer, put a ten-dollar bill on the table, then slung the strap on his leather briefcase over his shoulder. He crossed his arms and waited.

Ritter got the hint, finished his beer. They trudged through the bar toward the hotel lobby. Maxwell waved to Marlys and signaled her that he would see her later. They climbed the stairs to the fourth floor and walked down the hall to the room. Ritter unlocked the door and they moved into the room.

Maxwell wouldn't care to stay in the room more than a night or two, but he'd given up asking Ritter why he didn't move into an apartment or a house. Other than a few books and his clothes strewn about, the room lacked any personal touches. Maxwell didn't like to think of his own past very much—his failed marriage, his son who never spoke to him—but Ritter appeared to have no past. No pictures, no memorabilia, the guy could pack up and leave in ten minutes. Except he preferred to stay here, as if it were a permanent residence.

He'd come to realize that all his viewers had developed quirks, odd patterns of behavior that might be related to their work, or to the Z-Factor, the hypnotic drug that had enhanced their abilities, or to both. He didn't know anything about the side effects when he'd first begun discreetly administering the drug. But he conceded that the remote viewers had changed. They'd gotten better, amazingly better. Meanwhile, they'd all slipped into a realm that made them borderline sociopaths.

Even the three outsiders. He'd known about Calloway's obsessiveness, his instability, and Eduardo Perez's burrowing paranoia, and now he'd found out about Doc's crippling fear of crowds. The three remained unwilling to work with him, so they'd have to pay. He couldn't allow any loose cannons to remain at large. Especially not since they were all so closely linked together and that link seemed to be intensifying along with their abilities.

But right now he faced a more pressing matter. He sat on the edge of Ritter's bed and called the number that Wiley had given him. The general answered on the second ring. "What is it, Max?"

He told Wiley about Calloway and what had happened at the Brown Palace Hotel. When he finished, the silence stretched out so long that Maxwell asked if Wiley was still there.

"I'm here. What you say is interesting. But it's pure fiction, Max. If anyone associated with Freedom Nation were involved in such a deadly matter, I'd definitely be aware of it. This Calloway fellow sounds out of control, Max. He's picking up on his own fantasies."

"So there's nothing to it?" Stunned, Maxwell couldn't think of anything else to say.

"Absolutely not."

Maxwell nervously adjusted the phone. "What about the dinosaur and the ice caves?"

"What about it? Calloway probably stopped there once on his travels. That's no proof of anything."

Maxwell didn't believe him, but he didn't know why Wiley would lie to him.

"Don't call me with any more wild conjecture, Max. Don't call me at all unless you're responding to my call, or you have something of substance and extreme importance. Do you understand?"

"Yes, sir." He hadn't meant to call Wiley "sir," as if he were one of his troops, but the word had just spilled out.

"By the way, nice job at the conference." Wiley's voice softened. "But what do you make of this alien stuff?"

Maxwell smiled to himself. "I don't know what to think about it. Maybe he's losing his mind."

"It sounds like it. You don't have anything to do with any of it, do you?"

"Me?" Maxwell laughed. "Not a thing."

Several seconds passed. "No, of course not." With that, Wiley hung up.

Let him keep wondering. Maxwell had planned to tell Wiley about his little experiments with the president as soon as they produced results. But now that Wiley was lying to him, he didn't feel compelled to tell him anything about his own projects, even though some of them worked to Wiley's advantage.

Ritter watched him from a comfortable chair in the corner of the room where he'd listened to one side of the conversation. He grinned and saluted. "Yes, sir." He grinned. "I liked that. Like it a lot."

Maxwell ignored him. He had planned to send Ritter after Calloway, to interfere, if necessary, with his remote viewing. But now he wanted to confirm that Wiley was lying. He'd send Ritter into him. Ironically, it was exactly what Ritter had said he would do.

Without another word, Ritter put on a headphone set and pressed the play button on a tape recorder. He liked to listen to electronic sound waves that moved him quickly into a receptive state. Maxwell sat down at the small table a few feet away and prepared to record the session. A couple of minutes later, Ritter took off his headphones, letting Maxwell know he was ready.

"Okay, I'm giving you a target that I'm identifying by the following numbers 540-921. Your target is a person. You'll be going inside."

Ritter sighed. Thirty seconds passed. "I smell food. I'm in a kitchen."

"What are you eating? How does it taste?"

Maxwell didn't care what the target was eating, but he wanted to affirm that Ritter had dropped into Wiley rather than simply observing the scene. In years past, it had taken hours of repeated efforts to reach the point of merging with a target, but Ritter now moved easily into his subject.

"Not eating. Just drinking coffee."

"Identify yourself?"

"George Wiley, of course."

"Can you tell me what I want to know?"

"All about the bomb."

Maxwell wished that he hadn't called Wiley from the room. If he were performing a scientific test on Ritter, the entire session would be seriously tainted. But Ritter had proved himself over and over again. It shouldn't matter that he'd heard him questioning Wiley about the bomb, he decided. Especially since Wiley had denied any knowledge of it.

"What do you know about it?"

He answered in a monotone, speaking from Wiley's point of view. "I want it delivered. We're going to speed things up now. We'll put the federal government out of business. It's the only way to stop them from destroying us. We need to get Freedom Nation established."

"When will the bomb arrive in Washington?"

"Less than seventy-two hours now."

"Where's the weak point in the mission?"

Ritter's silence extended so long that Maxwell figured that Wiley had refused to divulge anything further. Finally, he spoke, his tone surprisingly angry. "One of my commanders wants to call off the fucking mission, but I'm standing firm. We're going through with it."

"Why does he want to call it off?"

"The Secret Service is on to it, and they've got the FBI looking for the kids. One of them is his daughter. But I just reminded him that they switched vehicles. The feds don't know what they're driving. Now he's concerned about what will happen to his daughter after it's over. I told him not to worry, we'll take care of her and the boyfriend. They'll get new identities, if necessary. But I'm getting tired of his whining. He may have to disappear soon. Real soon. I don't like his insubordination. It's not the first time.''

Maxwell felt as if he'd just stepped into a cold shower. After all he'd done for Wiley, the bastard didn't trust him. "Steve, move outside of the target now, but stay with him.''

Ritter raised a finger. "Okay. Watching now.''

"Can you tell if any other remote viewer has been there ahead of you?''

"You mean, Calloway? Let me clean house. I'll check for his droppings.''

Ritter remained quiet for nearly two minutes. "No sign of Trent. He hasn't been here, either inside the target or in the safe house.''

"Are you sure?''

"He's busy looking for the bomb. But he'll come after Wiley in no time. No time at all. Count on it. I'm hooked in with him. Hooked in good.'' Ritter laughed.

A shudder rippled through Maxwell. Once Calloway got to Wiley, he'd find out everything. They had to deal with him. Doc too. Just like they'd dealt with a couple of the FBI agents on Wiley's trail.

"Okay. Come back now. Leave him alone.''

Ritter took a couple of breaths, blinked his eyes. "Wow! He's really going to nuke Washington!''

"We've got to stop them.''

Ritter frowned. "Hey, who's side are you on?''

"I don't want to see Washington destroyed. I wouldn't want to live with the result, and I don't think you would, either.''

Ritter snorted. "I could do without the big Washington shithouse.''

"You're on the government dole, Ritter. So am I.''

Ritter grinned. "Who needs it.''

"The point is that bomb will never make it to its destination.''

"Why not? You think our old buddy Calloway is going to find it?" Ritter asked.

"No, you are. You and the boys. We'll get the bomb, then deal with Calloway and company."

"Sounds like fun," Ritter said with a smirk. "We get the nuke, then the kook."

Fifteen

The green, illuminated highway sign, indicating the approach to I-80, stood out against the purple evening sky. If he remained on I-84, they would hit Salt Lake City in no time, and continuing south, they would head right into Las Vegas. Jackpot!

Can't do it. Not now. Hell, maybe they'd never get there. Matt pushed away the thought, fighting off the gloom that slowly descended over him. Of course they would go to Las Vegas, as soon as they made their delivery. They'd get married, have a good time in the casinos with the extra money Jill's father had provided, then they'd go home. In a couple of weeks, he would start his new job with Freedom Nation and embark on a new life. But first he had to pass his trial and that meant delivering the bomb.

He switched lanes and flowed into the traffic that followed the curving entrance to I-80. He felt tired, but they had a long, long drive ahead—two and a half more days—and that was driving day and night, stopping only to eat and sleep for short stints at rest areas.

Jill stirred next to him as he nudged the Cherokee into the curve. She'd fallen asleep half an hour ago. "Where are we now?" she murmured, trying to get comfortable in the seat that she'd folded back.

"We're just turning onto I-84, heading east. We're gonna be on this road all the way to Ohio. That's a long haul."

"If we make it that far."

"Why do you say that?" The gloom started to creep over him again.

"I had a dream, a kind of scary one. We were driving and driving, and we couldn't stop. Then suddenly, a big hole in the road opened up and we drove right into it and disappeared. It just swallowed us."

"That's just a fucking dream, Jill. It's nothing."

She hugged her arms. "I don't mind telling you that I'm scared, Matt. I don't like carrying that bomb around with us, even if it can't blow up, like you say. What if we were stopped? The cops'll look at this brand-new Cherokee and want proof that you own it, and you don't."

"I've got the temporary registration. The owner just loaned it to me. The cops can call him." He didn't know who's name was on the registration. Probably a dead person.

"Yeah, and meanwhile they'd snoop around and search the back and guess what—they'll find a little ole bomb."

"It'll never happen, Jill. Don't worry. We're stickin' right with the speed limit. As long as we don't do anything weird to draw attention to us, we don't have any problem."

"I'm hungry. Let's stop somewhere," she said, stretching.

No, keep driving.

"Let's get some more miles under our belts," he responded.

"Matt, we've been on the road for hours. All we've eaten is crap from machines. I want a meal."

He glanced over at her. "You're not wearing your seat belt."

"Oh, shut up. Look, two restaurants at the next exit."

"Burger King and a truck stop. Let's keep going. We'll find something better further on."

"Hello, is that you, Matt? Since when are you picky about food? You eat at Burger King all the time."

He drove past the exit. "Let's see what else is coming up."

She slid down in her seat. "Shit. The next exit isn't for another twenty-two miles. I don't want to wait that long."

"We'll be there in no time. When you're on the road, you know, the miles click by fast. You start to count them by the hundreds."

"How do you know? You've never been more than a couple of hundred miles from home."

Tell her to can it.

"Fuck off, Jill. Just fuck off. I don't have to listen to your lip."

She looked sharply at him. "Don't talk to me that way. Maybe that's how your jailbird dad talked to you, but don't do it to me. Not if you want to marry me."

His hand curled into a fist. *Smack her good.*

He raised his hand, leaned toward her, and waved his fist, threatening to backhand her across the face. She shouted as the Cherokee swerved into the left lane, cutting off a tractor-trailer. Bright lights impaled Matt from behind, followed by the deafening blast of an air horn. He swung the wheel hard to the right and weaved back into his lane.

"Fuck that guy," he snapped. "Can't he use his brakes instead of his horn."

"Are you crazy, Matt Hennig? Were you going to hit me? I can't believe you."

"Okay. I'm sorry. I don't know what got into me. But don't talk about my father that way. I told you what he did. He sold army weapons to the militia and he got caught. That's not such a bad thing." When she didn't answer, he added: "I said I'm sorry. I'd never hit you. You know that."

She dropped her head into her hands and began to cry softly. "I don't know that. Not anymore." He reached over, touched her shoulder, but she shrugged his hand away.

He glanced into the rearview mirror and spotted a highway patrol car, lights flashing, coming up on him in the left lane.

"Shit, shit, shit!"

He touched his brakes, dropping back to sixty-five, and held his breath.

"What's wrong?" Jill asked.

"Cop! Stop crying. Act normal."

The flashing lights from the Highway Patrol vehicle momentarily illuminated the inside of the Cherokee. Then, the patrol car zipped past at eight-five or ninety.

"Thank God," Jill uttered.

"That was close."

What the hell was wrong with him, anyhow? He'd attracted attention to himself, exactly what he'd wanted to avoid. He'd just been lucky that the cop had something more pressing on his mind than stopping him.

"Do you realize what would've happened if that truck had slammed into us?" Jill whined. "We'd be dead and that damn bomb . . . who knows what would've happened. I don't believe that it's not dangerous. I'm sorry, but I just can't believe that."

Chuck the fucking bomb. Chuck it.

"I'm tired of hearing about that bomb," Matt said in a low voice. "I'm really tired of that. I'm not going to listen to that for two thousand miles. You better believe it."

"Tough," she answered.

Chuck the bomb! That'll show her.

Matt stepped on the brake and eased over to the shoulder.

"What are you doing now?" Jill asked.

He didn't answer. He drove at thirty miles an hour, then slowed to twenty as an overpass came into sight. He stopped under the bridge and stared straight ahead, the engine still running.

"What is it, Matt? Tell me."

Without a word, he popped open the back gate, got out and walked around to the back. He lifted the gate and moved aside Jill's suitcase. He carefully pulled out the backpack and hooked the strap over his shoulder. It weighed about fifty pounds. Not too heavy. Probably enough to blow up the bridge, though, if it exploded, he figured.

Chuck the damned thing. Don't waste your time. Just go to Vegas.

He walked along the passenger side and stopped by the window that Jill had rolled down. "Stay here. I'll be right back."

She looked at him, a mystified expression on her face. "What are you doing?"

"Chucking it."

He climbed up the underside of the bridge. He leaned forward, trying to keep his feet from slipping, slowly working his way up. He reached a three-foot wide ledge near the top and lowered the backpack to the concrete. He caught his breath.

Get out of there now. Fast. Move it.

That voice in his head almost seemed as if it were separate from him. He turned away and loped down to the bottom of the bridge.

Jill stood near the passenger door. "Matt, do you know what you're doing? Why did you put it up there, anyhow?"

"Because . . ." He looked back toward the darkened underside of the bridge, frowned, momentarily confused. *Who the fuck needs it? Let's go.*

". . . Because we don't need it. C'mon. Let's go to Las Vegas. The hell with it. Let's go get married and have a good time."

"To Las Vegas? Now?"

"Why the fuck not?"

Jill hugged him. "That's great, but what about Dad? What about the militia and General Wiley and your new job? If you disobey Dad, you're out. He won't have anything to do with you anymore."

Who cares? Who cares? None of it matters anymore.

He waved a hand, then opened the door. "Forget about it. And stop asking questions. Let's go."

She shook her head and climbed in the vehicle. "You amaze me, Matt Hennig. You really do. Fuck the bomb. You're right. But what about the Cherokee? Won't Wiley want it back?"

He won't get it back.

"It's ours now. And we got some cash, too. We're on our own."

"Damn, Matt. I can't believe you. If Wiley and Dad don't like it, tough. We'll make it. I know we can do it."

"Hell, yes!" He started the engine, turned up the sound on the radio, filling the vehicle with a throbbing wall of sound.

Turn around. Right here. Go to Vegas.

He pulled out, crossed two lanes, making a U-turn.

Jill shouted. "Matt, what the fuck are you doing? Wrong way!"

She grabbed for the wheel, but he pushed her back, and accelerated toward the lights.

A car, its horn blaring, whizzed by.

"Get off the road. Quick!" Jill yelled.

Keep going! Keep going! Into the bright lights!

What the hell was wrong with her? "We're going to Vegas!"

Another car flew past them. A tractor-trailer filled the lane, its lights shining into the windshield. Jill screamed.

Moments before the impact, Matt felt a presence lift from his mind. His confusion cleared. Too late he realized what he'd done. "Oh, shit!"

He slammed on the brakes, skidded sideways and slammed hard into the oncoming truck.

SUNDAY

Sixteen

Calloway rolled over, reached for the phone, and answered on the second ring. He heard Doc's sleepy voice as she picked up at the same time.

"Good morning," a crisp voice said. "This is Clarke. You can both stay on the line." For a moment, Calloway couldn't place the name. Then he remembered the Secret Service agent, Tyler's partner. He looked at the clock. Six-forty.

"Morning." Calloway cleared his throat and threw his legs over the side of the bed. "Thanks for the wake-up call. What happened to Tyler? We never heard anything from him after he left."

"Agent Tyler has been sent to another location," Clarke said, cryptically. "I want to thank you two for your help. We won't be needing you any longer."

"Did you catch them?" Calloway asked, sitting up. "Did you find the bomb?"

"We found a man named Matt Hennig and a young woman named Jill Sudner. Both are dead," Clarke said in a matter-of-fact voice. "Highway fatalities. There was no bomb in their vehicle."

"What?" Calloway came wide awake.

"Where did this happen?" Doc asked.

"The accident occurred about forty miles northeast of Salt Lake City on I-80. The girl's parents verified that she and Hennig were planning on getting married. They must have realized they'd taken the wrong turn onto I-80 and were trying to go back at the time of the accident.''

"Why do you say that?" Calloway asked.

"Because they were driving down the interstate in the wrong direction."

"In the wrong direction!" Doc exclaimed. "You mean the wrong side of the interstate?"

"That's right."

"That doesn't make sense," Calloway said.

"Very little of this entire scenario makes much sense, Mr. Calloway. But, as I said, there was no bomb in the vehicle. The highway patrol is investigating the accident."

"But you haven't found the bomb," Calloway said. "It could be anywhere."

"Or maybe there is no bomb," Clarke responded. "We still don't have any evidence it ever existed."

"On the other hand, it could be on its way to Washington in another vehicle." Doc sounded just as annoyed as he was by Clarke's dismissive attitude. Her anger flared. "I thought you were the guy who believed in this stuff. It sounds to me like you're rejecting everything that Trent has picked up as if it were some sort of wild fantasy. I got news for you, Mr. Clarke. Trent gave you that kid's name and the vehicle. Why would he be wrong about the bomb?"

As she spoke, Calloway glimpsed a vague form. He reached for a notepad and pen on the bedstand, closed his eyes. The image remained obscure, but he quickly sketched its essence—four parallel lines and another line that arched over the others. It was a skeletal view of . . . of something.

Then he turned his attention back to what Clarke was saying. ". . . but it's out of my jurisdiction. I'm going to give you a number where you can contact special agent Lewis Fielding of the FBI."

"Does he know about the bomb?" Calloway asked.

"He's aware of the bomb threat and he's looking into the possibility of a connection with George Wiley. In fact, he is in charge of the Wiley investigation. Also, Ms. Hidalgo asked me to give you a number where you can reach her while she's in Colorado."

Calloway jotted down the numbers, then examined the abstract sketch again. He realized the four lines represented a roadway. The arching line that crossed over the others was a bridge or overpass. "Did anyone look for the bomb underneath that bridge?"

"What bridge?" Clarke asked.

He closed his eyes again, focused. Still relaxed from his night's sleep, images and impressions flooded over him. He knew that he'd hit upon something important. "The overpass near where they turned around."

Clarke remained silent for several seconds. "How do you know they turned around near an overpass?"

Calloway ignored the question. "You better get someone on it fast. Someone's picking up the bomb. It might already be gone."

"I'll contact the Highway Patrol. We'll check it out immediately," Clarke said and hung up.

Gordon Maxwell's shoulder muscles twitched. He squeezed the steering wheel, fighting the urge to shove the accelerator on the Corvette to the floor. He needed to wait for the right moment. Then he'd shake the damn black Suburban that had followed him off two exit ramps and back onto the interstate again.

No doubt about it. Wiley's men had found him. He'd gotten to the bomb first, because he'd known right where the kid had put it. But they'd shown up, probably tipped off by someone in the highway patrol. They must've spotted him pulling away from the overpass, and trailed him into the city.

Shit. What a mistake. Wiley would kill him for the bomb. He should've kept his nose out of it, and anonymously tipped off the authorities. Then he and the boys could've taken care of Calloway before he looked any closer. Too late now.

He flashed past the first exit to Salt Lake City. He could easily outrun the Suburban. No problem. But he might pick up the highway patrol and no matter how fast he drove the cops would be waiting for him as soon as he left the interstate. He definitely didn't want to get stopped with a nuke in the trunk.

But he needed to do something. Something soon.

He moved into the left lane, accelerated. The Suburban picked up its pace, but stayed in the middle lane. He hit a hundred and five. The Suburban shifted to the left lane to avoid traffic and came up fast. One mile to the exit.

One-ten, one-fifteen. The early-morning sun flashed off the rear windshields of the cars he passed. Half a mile. In spite of his speed, everything seemed to move in slow motion. A quarter mile. He glanced once more into the rearview mirror. Now.

He swerved into the center lane, then the right lane. Hit the brake. Skidded. Every muscle in his body tense. He gritted his teeth, knuckled the steering wheel. Came up on two wheels.

"Shit!"

The 'Vette dropped back down. And shot out the exit. Still braking, gasping for breath, Maxwell looked into the mirror just in time to see the Suburban fly past the exit.

Christ. He'd almost killed himself. But he'd shaken Wiley's gang. Now he needed to ditch the bomb. He pulled into a Holiday Inn and drove around to the side of the building. He noticed a shed at the back of the property near a set of Dumpsters and eased over to it. He got out and saw the lock on the door. He was about to put the bomb into one of the Dumpsters when he noticed a large sewer pipe wedged between the shed and a high concrete wall.

A better choice. He could pick it up later without worrying about the Dumpsters being emptied. He hurried over to the car and opened the trunk. He couldn't help staring in amazement at the green backpack. A fucking nuclear bomb stuffed in the trunk of a 'Vette. In-fucking-credible. He lifted out the pack and carried it over to the sewer pipe. After finding the bomb just before dawn following an all-night drive, he'd considered burying the weapon somewhere out in the salt flats. But when the Suburban had latched onto him, he'd nixed the idea.

He climbed back into the Corvette and drove off. Stay off the interstate, he told himself. Wiley's men would be watching for him.

He drove across town until he noticed a ma-and-pa motel with parking at the rear. Perfect. He checked in as Charles Simms and used one of Marlys's credit cards. He quickly found the room, took off his shirt and shoes, and lay on the bed.

He would rest a few hours, then call Wiley. He'd reason with him, tell him exactly why he took the bomb. Wiley might be angry, but he understood power, and through him, Wiley had access to unusual power. The power to see, the power to manipulate, the power to kill without leaving a trace of evidence.

Maxwell closed his eyes. Yeah, Wiley would understand.

Doc stood in the doorway between rooms, her hands on her hips. She wore a voluminous Colorado Rockies T-shirt that reached her knees. "Out of his jurisdiction. Can you believe that? If Washington blows, he won't have a jurisdiction."

Calloway sat on the edge of the bed in gym shorts and a sleeveless T-shirt. "Take it easy, Doc. I think he'll follow up on what I said. He can't ignore it."

"But why would the kids dump the bomb, make a U-turn, and drive into traffic? Tell me that, Trent."

"It sounds like something unexpected happened in that vehicle."

She didn't respond right away and seemed to be holding her breath. "Do you know what it feels like to me?"

Calloway nodded. "I think I do. Someone turned the driver into a puppet, a self-destructing one."

"Exactly. Max's boys."

"When Clarke was talking about what happened, I could almost feel them out there, working on those kids as it happened."

"I felt it, too. I just didn't want to believe it."

Calloway crossed his arms over his chest. "Should we congratulate Maxwell and his gang for saving Washington or should we turn him in for killing those two kids?"

"Either way, Maxwell would just laugh it off. He wouldn't admit to killing anyone and there's no way he could be convicted."

He thought a moment. "Let's assume they forced Hennig to ditch the bomb. What was their reasoning? Why didn't Maxwell just leave it in the Cherokee?"

"Maybe he thought the bomb might explode," she responded.

"Or maybe he wanted it for himself."

Doc frowned. "I can't imagine why he would want a nuclear bomb, Trent."

"Maybe he wants to sell it back to Wiley. I wouldn't put it past him."

"That would be very cynical and dangerous."

Calloway shrugged. "Maybe. But what if he's working for him, what if he was following orders?"

Doc frowned. "But why stop the bomb?"

"Maybe Wiley changed plans and wanted the bomb back and the kids eliminated."

"I suppose that's a possibility," Doc replied.

"Have you been following the FBI's search for Wiley in the news?" Calloway asked.

"I hear about it now and then."

"Well, the first two FBI agents in charge of the case died accidentally. One was killed in a car crash like those two kids. The other had a massive heart attack." Calloway walked over to the window, gazed out over downtown Denver. "If Maxwell's behind their deaths, how many people do you think could actually figure out what's going on?"

Doc picked up the thread. "They look like accidents. The investigators would never even consider the possibility that remote viewers were involved. And even if it did occur to them, how could they prove it or even stop the real perpetrators?"

"They couldn't. But we can track down a remote killer," Calloway said. "We could not only expose what's going on, but we could see what's being planned."

"Of course this is all speculation," Doc said. "We don't really know that Maxwell is involved in anything illegal."

Calloway rubbed the back of his neck. "Is it? I think we do know,

Doc. We're both picking up on the others and their involvement."

"And they're picking up on us, too," she said.

Doc slumped into the thick upholstered chair where he'd remote viewed. She closed her eyes and he knew that she was sinking into her zone. Although Doc preferred to monitor others, from time to time she and Calloway had reversed roles, and he knew her abilities were substantial. She raised, then lowered her right hand, indicating that he could direct her to a target.

"What's Maxwell doing?"

"Sweating and sweating it out. He's afraid things have gotten out of hand. Way out of hand."

"Because of Wiley?" Calloway realized too late that he was leading her. But Doc didn't follow him.

"Wiley, yes, but also the net."

"What do you mean?"

"The net. All of us. Everyone who took the drug. We're all bound together in a big, invisible fishnet. When one part of the net moves, the others feel it."

"Tell me more about the net."

"It's expanding beyond what Maxwell thought possible. He wants to control and manipulate, but he's afraid that it's out of control."

"You mean us. He's afraid of us?"

"All of us. You, me, and Eduardo Perez, in particular. But he's concerned about the others, too. He doesn't want to believe that they're out of his control, but deep inside he knows that something is wrong."

Calloway realized that Maxwell had carried on the experiment that he'd begun with Bobby Aimes as a target. He'd thought Calloway would be pleased to kill Aimes, because his old friend had stolen his girlfriend and turned into a drug pilot. But Calloway had been tricked and forced into the act, and Maxwell had lost his best remote viewer.

Calloway snapped out of his momentary reverie as he heard Doc groan. Her face was twisted in pain. She slid off the chair, dropped to her knees. Her hands clasped her head. Her eyes bulged. She gasped for breath.

"Doc! What's wrong?"

Her mouth moved, but she couldn't speak.

He took her by the arms, tried to lift her off the floor. As soon as he made contact, he catapulted instantly into his own zone. He felt the others crowded around Doc, pushing, pressing in. He pushed back. He heard the same sharp cackle rattle inside his head. *Calloway, get ready to be dead. Real dead.*

Then they were gone. Calloway found himself lying on the floor, depleted. A few feet away, Doc gasped for breath.

"They wanted to crush me, to squeeze off the blood to my brain," she whispered between breaths. "I think they could've done it, but you distracted them."

Seventeen

An hour later, Calloway and Doc headed out of Denver with plans to meet Eduardo Perez, the only other person who could not only grasp what was happening to them, but might help them overcome Maxwell's invasive gang of remote viewers.

As they headed west on State Road 6, Doc paged through the complimentary copy of the *Rocky Mountain News* that had arrived with breakfast. She held up the paper for him. "Did you see this?"

The headline running across the top of the page shouted: *Dustin-alien mystery deepens*.

"I'm getting tired of it already. What's the big deal now?"

"Nothing that I can see. It's just that the idea of the president being abducted by aliens is just too juicy to leave alone. Even if it isn't true."

Calloway had glanced at articles and seen snatches of television news reports. He was vaguely aware of upcoming specials and a renewed focus on all that was alien. But he remained preoccupied with the bomb and now wondered again if the FBI had found it yet. He allowed his gaze to stray to the distant mountain peaks. He had a bad feeling that someone else had gotten there first.

"Listen to this," Doc said, interrupting his thoughts. "This is what the Senate majority leader says. 'If the president truly wants to run the country, and as he says, get on with the business of government, then he must come clean. He must address the nation on his so-called alien encounters. He must tell us what it's about and why he made those comments. Otherwise, his presidency will be terminally ill, weighed down by questions and doubts about the president's ability to govern and lead the nation.' ''

She looked over at him. ''The bastards are definitely after blood. I mean it was a metaphor, wasn't it? He didn't mean it literally. Unless he really did have an encounter.''

Calloway shook his head. ''No, I doubt that.''

''Oh, why not? We used to remote view UFOs for Maxwell.'' Her voice trailed off.

''Interesting that you mention that,'' he answered.

Calloway recalled that when Maxwell began targeting UFOs, a variety of scenarios had resulted—aliens that looked like reptiles, others that looked tall, blond, and Nordic. But gradually the remote viewers started only seeing one type of alien—the thin gray ones with large heads and black eyes that looked like wraparound sunglasses. According to the information they'd gathered, the Grays were from an advanced society that was dying because they were losing their ability to reproduce themselves. As a result, they were using genetic materials from humans to revive their species and they felt they had the right to do it. The reason they picked on humans and felt they were justified was because they were us—vastly advanced and mutated humans residing on Earth thousands of years in the future. Essentially, they looked at their relationship to us as we looked at our relationship to apes.

Calloway had always withheld judgment on the alien targets. While Maxwell felt he had solved the puzzle, Calloway had never been completely convinced that their interpretations were accurate. He sensed it was more complicated, a multidimensional puzzle that would continue to perplex and baffle for a long time to come.

''What are you thinking?'' Doc asked.

''That I've got to talk to Camila again. If Maxwell and his gang can kill those kids and raise havoc with our heads, they could damn well put aliens in the president's head.''

"That thought just occurred to me, too," she replied. "They could also push the vice president's wife into saying she's going to divorce her husband. They could cause all kinds of outrageous behavior."

As they continued along the road in the bright morning sunshine, Calloway's thoughts drifted back to the river, the highway of the ancients. He realized that he missed his rafting trips and, yes, he missed his quiet evenings with his beer and his radio. A part of him wished that Doc had never turned up, never pushed him into going after that target.

How about stopping for a beer right now?

He pushed the stray thought away. He had a six-pack of O'Douls in the cooler in the back, if he really wanted one. He thought about his last trip on the river and wondered if the software guys had complained to Ed Miller about him, about how he'd shoved Art out of the raft. If that was the case, he wouldn't have a job to return to when this odd journey was over.

Calloway, I made you push him. You're under my thumb. Now how about that beer? Yeah, a beer.

"What's wrong?" Doc asked. "You just tensed up."

"They're here again. Right with us." He heard the familiar cackle in his head. Then he recognized its source.

"It's Steve Ritter. He's their front man."

Good guess, guy. But I'm not alone.

"Maybe you should pull over and stop," Doc suggested.

Sure, why not!

The Explorer suddenly swerved to the shoulder, spewing stones and dust. Calloway struggled with the wheel, trying to steer back onto the road, but the Explorer edged closer to a steep slope. Doc lunged over, grabbed the wheel. The instant their hands touched, Calloway felt the presence release. He braked, eased over to the side of the road, and slumped over the wheel.

"Are you okay, Trent?"

"They almost did us in, Doc." He raised his head and wiped the perspiration from his brow. "They're strong, stronger than I imagined."

"But they let go as soon as I grabbed the wheel."

"I noticed," Calloway said, dryly.

"When we get Eduardo with us, we should be able to hold them off and find out what they're up to."

"Let's hope so."

But Calloway had the feeling that Ritter and the gang were just playing with them, like big cats with glowing eyes and deadly claws toying with a couple of mice before the kill.

The rest of the drive unraveled without incident. After lunch at a roadside diner, they turned south on 82. An hour or so later, Crested Butte Mountain came into view. "Let's stop in town," Doc said. "I told Eduardo I'd warn him when we got here."

She sounded uneasy and he wondered why. "Fine with me. I'll try Lewis Fielding again, and give Camila a call, too," Calloway said.

They parked in front of a café on the main street of the old mining town. He found a pay phone and called Fielding first. As earlier, an answering service took his name. This time he left Perez's number, then left it again when he tried to reach Camila.

"Let's hope we get to Eduardo's place before he gets calls from an FBI agent and the president's press secretary," Calloway said with a laugh as Doc handed in a cup of coffee in a Styrofoam cup.

Doc looked stunned. "You gave them Perez's number? How did you get the number?"

"You wrote it on the notepad by the phone. I picked it up before we left. What's the big deal?"

"Well, I didn't want to discourage you from driving here, so I didn't tell you that when I talked to Eduardo from the hotel he didn't exactly sound accommodating. He wouldn't tell me how to get to the house."

"Great. Now you tell me. What did he say this time?"

She frowned.

"You did get the directions, didn't you?"

She gave him a guilty look. "Not exactly. I tried to get him to come here and meet us."

"And?"

"He wouldn't do that either."

"Wonderful. So we just wasted our day."

She smiled, held up a napkin with some scribbling on it. "Nope. I got lucky. I asked the waitress if she knew anything about an underground mansion and it turned out her husband did some work on it. She gave me directions."

"Let's go. This should be interesting," Calloway said.

"I know. We've got to convince him that he needs us as much as we need him. Otherwise, he's not going to open his door."

They followed the waitress's map and within minutes were traveling on a two-lane road that wound through the countryside. After several miles the pavement ran out and Doc consulted the napkin again.

"Keep going one point six miles, then turn right into his drive. It's marked with a stake that's painted red on top."

"I guess he doesn't like neighbors," Calloway said, peering around at the sloping landscape. "I haven't seen any houses for a couple of miles."

"I think we can safely say that Perez is ensconced in what the real estate folks would call a true mountain hideaway."

Calloway laughed. "That sounds about right."

They came to the red-topped marker and turned onto a rutted single lane. No mailbox, no sign. He wondered how the hell Perez found the place at night. They bounced along the road for a quarter mile before they came to a compact reddish brown, wood-frame building with a sloping roof that backed against a modest rocky butte. As they moved closer, Calloway saw the front wall was actually two garage doors.

They stopped and stepped outside. Crested Butte Mountain, majestic and solemn, pulled his gaze. "If I lived here, I would've built a house with a wide-angle, picture-window view of the mountain," Calloway said. "But I guess Eduardo had other ideas."

They walked to the building and found a door on the right side. Doc gave Calloway a puzzled look. "Do you think this really is where he lives? Maybe it's the wrong place."

Calloway pointed to a rectangular-shaped piece of wood above the door where the words "Yaro Lu" had been inscribed.

Doc smiled. "That's right. That's the name he heard when he was trying to remote view the winning lottery numbers."

Calloway started to knock when a disembodied voice spoke up. "I told you, Doc, that you two are not welcome here. Please leave right now."

Calloway looked around for a camera, but didn't see any. They must have triggered hidden sensors that had alerted Perez to their presence. "Eduardo, you've got to listen to us," he said. "We're all in danger. You can't hide in your cave against them. We've got to work together."

"They can't do anything to me. I'm protected."

Calloway turned to Doc, shrugged.

"Eduardo, damn you!" Doc shouted. "You came to me. You found out about the drug. I let you in my house. Now you don't have the courtesy to do the same for me?"

"Go away," the voice firmly replied.

Calloway touched her arm. "Let's go."

Doc slammed her fist against the door. "You coward. You fucking coward, Eduardo, hiding in your hole, shaking and sweating, waiting for the big asteroid to hit. That's some life, Eduardo. Enjoy it."

They turned and headed for the Explorer. "I guess it's you and me, Doc."

"I guess so," she muttered in disgust. "That bastard."

Calloway started to open the door when Perez's voice boomed at them through a loudspeaker. "The door is open. Come in, walk to the back, and push the buzzer."

Calloway exchanged a look with Doc. He shrugged, baffled by the sudden change in Perez's position. They walked back to the building.

"Maybe he didn't like being called a coward," Doc whispered.

Calloway wondered if they should've just driven off. Perez seemed

unstable as well as paranoid. He placed his hand on the doorknob.
"You sure about this?"

"We don't have any choice," she said under her breath.

He opened the door and they stepped into a three-car garage with
a Range Rover, a pickup with oversized tires and a snowplow, and an
old Toyota that looked out of place. In addition to the vehicles, the
building included a workshop and a storage area. They moved past the
workshop and found a fortified steel door.

"That one would take a tank to break down," Calloway said as
Doc hit the buzzer.

Nothing happened for several seconds, then a recorded woman's
voice requested them to enter. Calloway pulled open the door only to
reveal an elevator door. "A door within a door. Now what?"

Doc reached out and pressed a square button. The doors instantly
whispered apart. They stepped inside and saw a panel that indicated
there were three levels below them. "So, where are we going, Eduardo?" Doc asked.

"Press number three," Perez's voice answered through an intercom.

The elevator slowly descended. Calloway turned to Doc and
smiled. "Deeper and deeper we go."

"And where we come out, no one knows," she answered as the
elevator stopped. The door slid open and they stepped out into an entryway dominated by tall columns that looked as if they'd been carved
out of the gray stone wall.

Calloway lowered his gaze from the columns. He barely recognized
Perez, who stood off to one side, his arms crossed. The onetime Cuban
refugee looked lean and muscular, not a bit pudgy as he remembered
him. His hair was close-cropped and he wore a short goatee. His brown
eyes fell on Calloway, then Doc, as if he were seeing them for the first
time.

"So, what is this all about?" he asked in a suspicious voice.

No hellos, no greetings of any kind. It was as if they'd just returned
from lunch and were continuing an earlier conversation.

"It's been a long time," Calloway said.

"So long that I still do not understand what brings you here."
Perez spoke in a faintly accented English that always sounded too formal to Calloway because he rarely used contractions.

Calloway had gotten along with Perez, but they'd never been close
during the three or four years when they both worked in Eagle's Nest.
But right now he felt as if he'd never worked with him, never even
known him.

"Can we come in and sit down?" Doc asked with a smile.

Perez stared at them as if he considered sending them on their way
again. "First, I will tell you the reason I let you in. I realized they were
here, pushing me, urging me to turn you away. They most definitely
do not want us together."

"So you really didn't want to let us in?" Calloway asked.

"No, I did not. But when I realized how much they feared us
together, I knew I had to open the door."

They followed him further into the underground abode. "This
looks like quite a place, Eduardo," Doc said. "I'm very impressed."

"It took a big piece of my fortune," he responded. "But it is worth
it."

"I didn't see any neighbors around," Calloway said. "Isn't it sort
of lonely."

"Lonely?" he responded in a dismissive tone. "No. I have more
than a hundred and forty-five acres. It is not a prison. I can go out into
the world anytime I want, but mostly I prefer to stay right here."

No doubt, Calloway thought.

They moved into an enormous room that looked like the interior
of a lodge with walls made of treated logs that glistened. An oversized
fireplace with a dark mantel dominated one wall and a flag-stone floor
gave the place a sense of sturdiness and impenetrability.

The walls curved inward, rising up toward a skylight high overhead. Calloway gazed up, noticed that the atrium had been blasted out
of solid rock. Walkways at the two higher levels circled the atrium.
"It's not the Brown Palace Hotel, but it's pretty damned impressive,
Eduardo," Doc said.

"I wanted a secure home, not a palace."

"If the idea here is protection, doesn't this atrium leave you vulnerable," Calloway asked. "I'd think someone could smash the glass and drop a hand grenade on you."

Perez laughed. "No. There are two layers of a very thick coated plastic that are five feet apart. You could smash an ax against it and it would just bounce off. But that is not all. By pressing a button I can seal off the top with a three-inch plate of steel. It takes eight seconds to close electrically and about twenty by hand."

"I take that back. It looks as if you're prepared for about any catastrophe," Calloway commented.

Perez nodded solemnly. "As soon as I became rich, I also became obsessed with survival. I needed to know that I was going to live long enough to enjoy the money."

Calloway knew all about obsessions. "Are you enjoying it now?"

Perez smiled at Calloway. "I am feeling very secure, at least secure from physical changes in the environment."

"Like an asteroid strike?" Calloway asked.

"I would hope so."

Calloway wondered if they were just going to stand around or if Perez would offer them a seat in his house. Doc didn't wait to find out. "Eduardo, do you think we could sit down and tell you about what's been going on over the last couple of days?"

"I'm not used to having guests, especially ones who so willfully impose themselves on my privacy," he said, coolly.

He reached into his shirt pocket and took out a black, rectangular object not much thicker than a card. He spoke softly into it, requesting a pitcher of iced tea. Then he pointed at a black leather couch. Calloway and Doc sat down, but Perez remained on his feet, moving nervously about.

"The asteroid scenario is one possibility that concerned me when I began work on this project six years ago," he said, glancing at Calloway. "But now I'm more concerned about solar flares. We have entered solar cycle number twenty-three, and there already has been an increase of solar activity, X class flares, the largest we know of. An enormous flare could send enough radiation, X rays, and gamma to destroy most of the life on earth.''

''Why would you want to survive something like that?'' Doc asked.

''I do not think the devastation is going to be total. Some people will survive, but life will be different. I want to be around to help with the post-cataclysmic reconstruction. I think my talents—our talents—will be very useful.''

''You mean remote viewing?'' Calloway asked.

''Of course. You see, I believe other forms of intelligent life will make themselves known to us. Some will be helpful, others will not. Those of us with our skills will be able to distinguish which ones we can trust.''

''You mean like the ones supposedly talking with the president?'' Doc asked.

''I heard about that,'' Perez said slowly. ''My feeling is that he is making a very big mistake. Those are not friendly entities. They have wrongly invaded his life. They are manipulative and they have probably even influenced his thinking.''

''So you believe he was actually contacted?'' Doc asked.

''It was not a dream. I think he is in trouble. Very big trouble.''

''That's what the politicians are saying,'' Calloway said.

''I do not mean political trouble. I think his life is in danger. These creatures are holding him hostage, some sort of mental hostage.'' He tapped his temple.

Calloway agreed with what he'd said about Dustin's encounters, except he didn't think the creatures came from a distant planet. He wondered if Perez had gotten lost in his fantasies, whether they were about dangerous aliens or a worldwide cataclysm. The underground mansion, in fact, was a monument to Perez's paranoia. Certainly, what he said about the solar flares represented one possible future. But Calloway had also peered into the future world and he had never sensed any dramatic planetary changes happening in his lifetime.

Perez's preoccupation with disaster gave Calloway an opening to turn the conversation in the direction he and Doc wanted to pursue. "Eduardo, what do you think about Gordon Maxwell's projections about several western states breaking off from the union in the next few years?"

"Maxwell? Why would I pay any attention to him? He is not a visionary. He is an exploiter. He sells his services to the highest bidder. He tried to get me to join the others again to remote view by telephone. He said I could travel the world without leaving my house, and he told me I could work on a special project, something that would help keep the federal government from infringing on my freedom."

Perez snorted. "I told him to go fuck himself and that he was the one trying to infringe on my freedom."

"Maxwell approached me, too," Doc said.

Perez looked distracted. "Excuse me. Let me see what's taking Sarah so long."

Doc sidled closer to Calloway on the couch after Perez walked away. "So what do you think?" she asked in a low voice.

"I think that if I stayed here a couple of days, I could get very paranoid about the outside world."

She smiled. "But you'd be comfortable."

Perez returned, followed by a pretty blond woman who carried a tray with a pitcher and glasses and an assortment of cookies. Perez introduced her as Sarah, his housekeeper, and mentioned that she was from Denmark and was spending a year in the States. Calloway recalled the old Toyota in the garage and guessed it belonged to her. What an introduction to America, he thought.

Sarah greeted him and Doc, and set down the tray. She and Doc exchanged a few more comments, then she moved off and disappeared into another room.

Calloway took a sip of tea, then set his glass down. He wished Perez would've offered him a beer. He pushed the thought away and turned to the reluctant host. "So, Doc and I have been doing some work together. We've been tracking a nuclear bomb."

Perez sat down on a reclining chair, crossed his arms, and listened as Calloway proceeded to summarize all that had happened since he'd seen the numbers by the river. He detailed the search for the bomb, the attacks they'd encountered, and finished by speculating on the deadly acts possibly committed by Maxwell's remote viewers in defense of Wiley.''

Perez dropped his head back and stared up into the atrium. ''I've protected myself from the dangers of the outer world, but now I face an attack through the inner world. I hope that I am prepared for it. Maybe the Z-Factor made me a little paranoid, but then there are good reasons to be that way.''

''The what?'' Calloway asked.

''That's the code name for the drug that Maxwell used on us. Let me show you something.'' Perez abruptly stood and walked off. He returned less than a minute later with a file folder.

''I want you both to read this. It is a fifteen-page monograph that Maxwell wrote six years ago. There were only twelve copies of it published. It circulated privately in the intelligence community and this copy was passed to me just three weeks ago.''

Calloway glimpsed a top-secret classification stamp on the cover. He started to move closer to read over her shoulder, but Perez held up a hand. ''Let Doc read first. You need to call a Camila Hidalgo. Who is she?''

''She works for the president. She helped us out.''

Perez didn't seem impressed. ''You also should call Lewis Fielding, an FBI agent. I have their numbers for you.''

''When did they call?''

''Before you arrived. One after another. Come. You can use my study.''

Calloway stood up. ''Damn it, Eduardo. It would've been nice if you had told me a little sooner.''

Perez's eyes narrowed. He pointed a finger at Calloway. ''And it would have been nice if you would not give my telephone number out to government agents.''

''I'm sorry. But I'm concerned about that bomb.''

They moved into a study with built-in bookcases, another fireplace and expensive mahogany furnishings. He took the phone Perez handed him and settled down into what he immediately recognized as the most comfortable leather chair he'd ever sat in.

He waited until Perez left the room, then dialed the first number on Perez's notepad and asked for Camila. He felt unexpectedly nervous. This time she answered right away. "I hope I'm not interrupting you."

"Don't apologize for calling me, Trent. Just get to the point."

She sounded frazzled. Things were not going well in her world. "First, do you know if they found the bomb under the bridge?"

"Clarke told me there was no bomb."

"It was there. I'm sure of it. Someone picked it up."

"Trent, is there anything else? I'm really under pressure right now. If you've read the headlines, you can understand."

"Wait a minute. I know this sounds weird, but I think there might be a link, a direct connection between the bomb and Dustin's alien contact."

No reply.

"Camila, did you hear me?"

"Trent, there was no bomb. In all likelihood, there are no aliens, either. So in that sense, yes, they are connected."

"That's not what I mean." He felt his head pounding again and rubbed a finger between his eyes. "I'm almost certain there's a group of remote viewers who are imposing on the president's mind, and now I think they've got the bomb."

"Trent, I'm sorry. I've got to go. I've got a meeting in five minutes. But if you've got anything substantial, talk to the FBI."

He felt a sinking feeling as he hung up. He had hoped that she would congratulate him for locating the bomb, for saving Washington. He wanted her to believe his explanation about the aliens and to ask him to help protect the president from more psychic assaults. But of course, it didn't work out that way.

He remained seated for nearly a minute. Then he slowly stood up. Disappointment spread through him like a virus. His legs felt leaden, his head pounded. If Camila didn't believe him, then who would? Not Clarke or Tyler. Not Fielding, the FBI agent. He felt his doubts returning. Why should they believe him? Maybe there really was no bomb.

Stop. That was exactly what Maxwell and the others wanted him to believe. They wanted him to give up and go back to Bluff, to drown himself in his drinking, and maybe one day his body would be found floating down the river, and of course it would look like an accident.

He walked back out to the spacious central room where Doc, the monograph in her lap, talked with Perez. They looked up as he approached.

"Trent, you've got to read this document," Doc said, excitedly. This proves what Eduardo told me before and what we've been thinking."

Calloway sat down on the couch, took the monograph. "Proves what?"

"It proves not only that the Z-Factor enhanced our remote viewing skills, but linked us all together into a psychic web."

Perez picked up a sketch pad from a nearby table and scrawled something on it. "So, we are the three from the old group who are not playing the game and we are caught in Maxwell's psychic net like flies in a spiderweb. If we buzz and shake our wings, the spiders will descend upon us."

He dropped his sketch pad on the coffee table. He'd drawn a spider's web, and at the center of it he'd written: PSI NET. He leaned over and made a diagonal slash between the two words.

PSI/NET.

"We are all linked, but divided," he said, and tossed the pencil on the table. "Maxwell must remove us from the web and the only way he can do that is to eliminate us. We are in big shit trouble."

"You mean deep shit trouble," Calloway corrected.

Perez nodded solemnly. "Deep shit is right."

Eighteen

The window air conditioner groaned and rumbled, but it wasn't cooling the room. Maxwell had awakened drenched in sweat after several hours of restless sleep. He opened the door a few inches and felt a blast of warm air. Close to ninety, he figured. He cautiously opened the door wider and looked around the deserted parking lot.

In his frenzy to find an inconspicuous spot to rest, Maxwell had ended up in a hotel with no phone in the room. He needed to call Wiley right away, to make a deal, to get things moving. He crossed the parking lot to the pay phone outside the office. An out-of-order sign hung on it. Great. Just get the fuck out of here. He had his cell phone with him, but he didn't want to take any chances, not even for a quick contact call as he'd done in Durango.

But he would use the cell phone to check up on Ritter. He went back to the room, called the hotel, and was connected to Ritter's room. "Steve, I got it."

"Right where I told you, wasn't it."

"Yeah. But now I need your help again. I'm going to face off with Wiley and I want you to keep checking on me. If you sense I'm in trouble, you've got to put the squeeze on him. Don't kill him, just let him know that he's going to pay if he harms me."

"Sure, Max. Gotcha covered. Gotcha good."

"We'll go after Calloway when I get back."

"We already took a peek. They're on the road. Heading to Perez's place. But they almost fell off the mountain." Ritter laughed and Maxwell pulled the phone away from his ear to avoid his grating chortle. "Me and the boys will get 'em next time. Don't worry, Max. We'll get Perez, too. Can't wait."

A warning light flashed in Maxwell's head. Ritter was going out on his own without his guidance. Not a good idea. But it wasn't the right time to confront him. "Don't do anything more for now," he said, firmly. "Just watch my back."

A few minutes later, after taking a cool shower, he dropped the room key on the bed and walked to the rear of the building. So far, so good, he muttered when he saw the Corvette right where he'd left it. He clicked off the alarm and drove away in search of a phone booth. He wanted a cup of coffee and something to eat, but he needed to find a phone booth first, somewhere in a comfortable setting without a lot of traffic noise or people standing around, where he could wait for a return call.

He'd driven a couple of miles when he stopped for a red light near a shopping center with a supermarket, a Starbucks, and a pay phone outside. Perfect.

He turned as he saw an attractive blonde motioning to him from the passenger side of a dark blue Town Car. He rolled down his window. The woman smiled at him. "Sir, did you know that there's something underneath your car?"

His smile vanished. "What do you mean?"

"I mean, Mr. Maxwell, that you've got a locator attached to your pretty Corvette. You can't get away from us."

"Who are you?"

Stupid question. He knew it must be one of Wiley's women. The general's appetite for women hadn't diminished since his army years. Ritter had picked up on that.

The woman's tone darkened. She pointed to the shopping center as the light changed. "Pull in there and park. Don't try to run. It won't do any good."

He did as he was told and tried to stay calm. At least he'd gotten rid of the bomb. That gave him some leverage, and if they tried to torture him to get the location, they might be in for a surprise. But now that the threat was actually materializing, he wondered how reliable Ritter would be. Without a monitor, his mind might be literally off in space. For a moment, Maxwell imagined Ritter in the restaurant giving unwanted impromptu readings to diners while a thug with a pliers methodically pulled out his fingernails.

He pushed the image away and parked near the front of the lot, next to a handicapped space. If he were dragged away screaming, people would see him. Someone would report it. He kept the car running and the air conditioning on.

He tried to relax, wondering how long he would have to wait. He looked around for the Town Car, but didn't see it. He'd known all along that he'd been taking a chance working with George Wiley. But at least the general would now realize that he was a player, not just someone on the sidelines waiting to be told what to do next. Tough talk. But realistically, how long could he hold up against Wiley's thugs? He suddenly found himself dependent on Ritter and the others, more dependent than he cared for.

He blamed the idiots in Congress for his present predicament. They'd possessed a tool that could defend the nation in ways that could hardly be imagined. But the shortsighted bastards had banished remote viewing from the government's agenda and dismissed the finest group of psychics ever assembled.

A tap against his rear window broke his reverie. He turned, saw a man dressed in shorts and a T-shirt move alongside the Corvette. "Get out and walk over to the black Suburban two rows over."

He stepped out and locked the doors. He noticed the man peering into the vehicle as if looking for the bomb. He walked around to the trunk and opened it. "Take a good look. Nothing here."

The man grunted and walked away, moving toward the supermarket. Maxwell ambled over to the Suburban and saw it was the one that had followed him earlier in the day. He couldn't see anything through the darkened windows. He tried the back door. Locked. He moved to the front passenger door and opened it.

"Get in," a gruff voice ordered. A brawny man with a thick, stubby neck sat behind the wheel.

"Where are we going?"

"Get in and close the door."

Maxwell slid into the seat. The Suburban pulled out of the lot and they drove around in a winding pattern. Ten minutes after leaving the shopping center, he saw it again. "Do you know where you're going?"

No answer. He'd read somewhere that people who were following orders to kill typically didn't look their victim in the eye or treat the person as a human. So far the driver fit the profile.

He sent out a silent emergency message to Ritter and waited for an inkling of some sort, an impression that he'd been heard. Nothing. But then maybe he just didn't sense Ritter's presence. His own psychic abilities weren't very well developed. He'd once hoped to be a psychic spy, but his talents were judged to be minimal and he'd ended up as an administrator. Initially, he'd been disappointed. But, of course, he'd learned to take advantage of his unusual position.

The Suburban eased into a gas station across the street from the shopping center and stopped at a pump. The driver turned to him. "Go to the men's room."

He got out and slowly walked around the side of the station. Light and shadow flickered over him as he moved through the sultry afternoon, the sun filtering through a majestic cottonwood. He silently called out to Ritter again as if he were praying to some god. He stopped in front of the door. He considered running, but then noticed someone standing near the rear of the station watching him.

He opened the door. Before his eyes had a chance to adjust to the dimly lit bathroom, hands reached out, grabbed him, and pulled him inside. The door closed. Two men he'd never seen before ran their hands roughly over his body.

"He's clean," one of them said. Both men abruptly left.

George Wiley leaned against the sink, his arms crossed. "You can sit on the toilet seat, if you want."

"Can't we go somewhere else?" Maxwell asked. "This place stinks."

Wiley, dressed in dark slacks and a pressed button-down shirt, looked trim, fit, and suave, as always. Only now his new features seemed more predatory than the old face. He stared darkly at Maxwell. "This place is just fine. Our meeting won't last long. Where's the bomb?"

"My team found it. I picked it up and put it somewhere safe."

"Did your team kill those kids, too?"

Maxwell hesitated, made up his mind. "I did it because they were going to be caught with the bomb and they would've exposed your plan. You would be in much deeper trouble than you already are. You wouldn't be a folk hero anymore. You'd be considered a maniac, the Unibomber a hundred fold."

Wiley considered what he'd heard. "So you took it upon yourself to save the bomb and knock off the kids."

"I couldn't very well tell you about it, because you denied that you had any connection to the bomb."

"I didn't trust you. I'm still not sure that I do. What do you want?"

He wanted leverage, power, influence, respect. That for beginners. "I want you to drop this idea. Don't use the bomb."

Wiley smiled. "Do you know what interests me about this Calloway's vision? He saw the future and Washington, D.C, wasn't there. That leads me to think that I will succeed. Whether you know it or not, you've already carried out the necessary acts that will make that vision a reality."

That's not the way Maxwell saw it. Calloway had glimpsed a blueprint of the future, but now the elements had changed and that would alter the perceived future. He could turn over the bomb to Wiley, which he would do, but the general still had to get it to Washington.

Wiley reached down and pulled a .38 from an ankle holster. "So where is it, Max? If you don't tell me in ten seconds, you're going to be an early casualty of the new civil war."

Okay, Ritter, where are you? Help me, Steve.

He watched Wiley for some sign that Ritter and the others were working on him. But he didn't appear in any anguish.

"Wait, hang on." He held up his hands. *C'mon, Steve.* "Take it easy, George. I've got it hidden in a good spot. No one will find it.'' It suddenly occurred to him that Calloway could find it. He might already have pinpointed it.

Wiley pressed the gun against his temple. "Stop stalling. Where is it? Last chance, Max. What do you say?''

Nothing from Ritter. The bastard.

"Okay. I'll make a deal with you. I'll tell you where it is if you take care of a little problem.''

"What problem?''

"We've got three renegades on our hands. Remote viewers who aren't playing by our rules.''

"Three? You said two—Calloway and the woman.''

"There's one more. He's been quiet, but I don't trust him. If the three of them get together, which I think is exactly what's going on, they can cause big problems.''

"So you're asking me to whack them?'' Wiley laughed. "Why don't you just take care of them the way you did those kids and the two FBI agents?''

"I need your men as a backup, just in case something goes wrong.''

To Maxwell's relief, Wiley put away his gun. He leaned over the sink, turned the water on, and splashed his face as if nothing unusual was going on. "Maybe you underestimate the abilities of your team. From what I've seen they're pretty damn potent.''

"So are the other three. It's not child's play with them. They know the score and they can fight back. But your men could serve as a distraction. I know where they're hiding. It's isolated. A nice easy target for your militia.''

Wiley wiped his face with a paper towel. "We'll go after your freaks. But I want you to deal with this new agent, Fielding. The same as the others. Get on it. But first point me to the bomb.''

Nineteen

For the second time in two days, Camila found herself waiting for a meeting in Kyle Leslie's library. She moved along the rows of bookshelves casually examining the titles. But her thoughts were elsewhere. This time she and the president would be alone, which would give her a better chance to talk to him about the topic that now dominated the news media and which threatened to short-circuit the government's efforts to carry on its business.

The incident had been compared to the infamous "War of the Worlds" broadcast, but with the president of the United States, instead of Orson Welles, behind the microphone. The *New York Times* had already called Dustin's comments the most bizarre forty-five seconds in the history of presidential speeches. The staid *Wall Street Journal* had suggested that sexual misconduct in the Oval Office was more acceptable than an encounter with aliens in the presidential bedroom.

Even more startling, a Harris Poll had found that 61 percent of Americans believed that Dustin was in contact with aliens, while 22 percent were undecided, and only 17 percent didn't believe him. To her astonishment, eight out of ten of those who believed the president was in contact with aliens also accepted the metaphor explanation.

Her thoughts drifted to Calloway as she moved on along the bookshelves. She felt bad about the way she'd treated him on the phone. But what else could she do? She had her hands full, more than full.

The FBI would certainly follow up on the case, but she couldn't put any more time into it. Oddly enough, she couldn't stop thinking about his comments suggesting a psychic-related conspiracy against the president. What if it were true? Even though it sounded absurd, it clearly wasn't any more so than the president's own contentions.

The door opened and Dustin entered the room. He wore khakis and a pale blue work shirt. He looked surprisingly relaxed as he greeted her.

She stepped over to the table and smiled. "Good afternoon, sir."

He motioned for her to sit down. No hug this time. Although he often confided to her when they were alone, he kept a physical distance between them. After a couple of affairs as a senator that had nearly ruined his political career, Dustin apparently had left his lecherous days behind. That might be one of the reasons the media had latched on to the alien affair with such fervor.

"Camila, I'm sorry this sensitive matter came about while you're still getting used to your new position." He paused and looked across the table at her. "You look tired. How are you holding up?"

"I'm doing fine, Mr. President. It's just that along with everything else my ex-husband showed up in Denver," she blurted.

"Trent?"

Like most successful politicians, Dustin had a knack for remembering names. But then his one encounter with Calloway had been an unusual experience, one not likely to be quickly forgotten.

"You know, after all these years, I still clearly recall that cocktail party when he met my challenge. That was no trick, was it?"

"No, sir. That was just Trent doing his thing."

Dustin, who was a senator at the time, had asked Calloway to describe where he would be at 3 P.M. the next day. But instead of waiting until the appointed time, Calloway said that he'd view the site immediately. He'd disappeared into a quiet room and twenty minutes later emerged with a folded piece of paper. He asked Dustin not to look at it until after his appointment.

"I remember how he described a tunnel leading into a mountain and a network of corridors. He even made a diagram of the place and included a sketch of a laser drilling machine that was used to cut the tunnels, and an underground people mover. It was all there, including the location. But you remember what really impressed me? My plans changed that day. When he did the remote viewing, I thought I would be about twenty-thousand feet in the air heading to Washington. Instead, I ended up in Cheyenne Mountain meeting with several other members of Congress and ranking military officers."

"I remember you saying that," Camila said.

"So he couldn't have been reading my mind." He shook his head. "He actually saw a future event. Is he still doing the remote viewing?"

Suddenly, Camila realized that she'd made a mistake mentioning Calloway. Todd Waters had asked her not to say anything about the bomb scenario to Dustin, that he didn't need to know about it. But now if she didn't tell him and he found out about it later—which was a good possibility—he would know that she'd lied to him.

"Yes, he is. In fact, that's why he came to Denver. He saw something."

"Oh? Go on. I'd like to hear about it."

She nodded, then proceeded to tell him about Calloway's apocalyptic vision and the remote viewing sessions that had followed. She described the events in a matter-of-fact tone, sounding neither supportive of Calloway nor disapproving.

Dustin listened carefully. "So the couple in the crash were definitely identified as the same ones who Trent had seen with the bomb."

"That's right. But, as I said, there was no bomb in the vehicle."

He frowned. "Did you ask Trent to look for the bomb? Maybe it was transferred to another vehicle before the accident."

"Someone from the FBI was going to contact him. But, to be truthful, Mr. President, the sentiments here among Clarke and the others seems to be that Trent was mistaken about the bomb. You know, the CIA dropped the remote viewing program in '95 because the accuracy rate didn't justify continuing it."

"Camila, we're talking about the very future of the country here. We know that Wiley is well financed, that the purchase of such a weapon is within his means. So what if Trent is right? What if the bomb is still out there? I want to know if Trent has given the FBI any new leads. Please, keep me apprised on this, Camila. I want regular updates on everything related to the matter. Is that clear?''

Oh shit.

''Yes, sir. I'll contact Trent as soon as we're finished here.''

He nodded. ''Okay. I'll be brief. First, I want to apologize again for what I've put you through.''

''There's no need for that, Mr. President. I'm just concerned about what's going to happen next. The press isn't going to let up anytime soon.''

''I know. That's why I called you here. I'd like you to make a strategic leak to one or two influential reporters.''

During her short stint as press spokesman, Dustin had never made such a request. He complained about leaks when the information was damaging to the administration, but now she realized he played the same game as other leakers.

''What would you like me to say?''

He thought a moment. ''Let's just make it one reporter. What about Greer?''

''Barry Greer? Okay.''

''CNN will get it out fast. Let it slip that Dustin actually communicated with aliens and that their message is one of peace.'' He watched her closely as she wrestled with the revelation.

She'd gotten used to him speaking about himself in third person, but she knew he usually did it when he wanted to distance himself from an issue. ''Sir, I don't understand. You want me to go against our own position? Won't that just further exasperate the situation?''

Dustin seemed unperturbed. ''Officially, we stick with the metaphor story, at least for now. At the same time, we must also tell the world that there is something very important going on, and that we are not being threatened.''

She considered her options. ''Do you want me to inform Todd or Harvey before I make the call?''

''No, they don't need to know the source of the leak.'' He considered the matter another moment. "Actually, I'll talk to them. Otherwise, they'll suspect each other."

She wanted to tell the president that he was making a mistake. Instead she asked if she could wait until morning. After a night's sleep, he might change his mind.

"No, I've thought this over carefully. I want this out tonight."

"Yes, sir."

He stood up and she did the same. "Call Trent first. Get him working on that bomb."

She started to leave when Dustin called after her. "Camila, do you believe in alien life?"

She dropped her hand from the doorknob. "In theory, sir, I do. I believe it's possible, even probable. But I'd prefer if they'd stay home in their own worlds."

"Why is that?"

"Because they don't seem to know how to make proper introductions."

Dustin smiled. "So you believe they are here."

She hesitated. "I can't say for sure. David, could I ask you a question?"

"Of course. What is it?"

"Did you really encounter these aliens?"

He walked over toward her. "Without a doubt, Camila. And I believe they'll be back. Maybe even tonight or tomorrow. I feel they're coming back before I return to the White House. There's something decisive coming."

"Do they look human, like the woman you described to us?"

"I don't think she was human, not totally. She was just one of three distinct species that I've encountered—the human-like ones, the thin little Grays, and others that looked like oversized teddy bears, but without any hair."

"I find this all very overwhelming."

He touched her on the back. "I understand. It is overwhelming, amazing, and transforming."

She left the room and all that was amazing and transforming van-

ished, replaced by a feeling of being burdened, confused, and de-
pressed. If she'd known that within two weeks of taking on her new
job she would be confronted with both aliens and a potential nuclear
holocaust, she might've resigned and taken a long vacation somewhere
far, far away.

That vacation might not be far off. After Waters found out about
her leak and that she told Dustin about Calloway's bomb, she might
very well be cleaning out her office in the West Wing when they returned to the White House.

She walked back to the room she was sharing with Sally Powers.
She was relieved that the speechwriter wasn't in the room. She picked
up the phone to call Calloway. On top of everything else, she felt torn
between her old feelings of distrust and a renewed interest in him. She
punched the number. A woman with a Scandinavian accent answered
and said she'd get Calloway. Where the hell was he staying, anyhow,
in a bed and breakfast?

"Hello, Camila?"

"Hi, Trent. Sorry to bother you, but your name came up in my
meeting and I ended up telling David everything, all about the bomb."

Calloway sounded surprised. "You mean no one had told the president about it?"

"With everything else going on, it didn't seem like a good idea.
There wasn't really time."

"I guess I shouldn't be surprised," Calloway replied. "No one
there seems to take the threat very seriously."

"Well, he knows now, and he wants you to look again to see if
you can locate it. He believes in you. He still remembers that underground base you saw him visiting."

"Your request comes a tad late, Camila," he replied. "We already
did it. Three of us here worked on it."

"Three? Where are you?"

He explained briefly about Perez and his underground home.

"So what happened?"

"We located it in a sewer pipe behind a small building outside a
Holiday Inn in Salt Lake City."

"That's pretty damn specific, Trent. There can't be too many Holiday Inns in Salt Lake City."

"I called Agent Fielding and told him about it."

She could tell by the confident tone in his voice that he was holding something back. "And?"

"Glad you asked. I got a call back about ten minutes ago. They found it right where we said it would be."

"That's great, Trent." She felt not only relieved, but glad that Calloway had proven himself. "The president is going to be very pleased."

"Good. Too bad Fielding doesn't feel that way."

She frowned. "Why do you say that?"

"The guy's suspicious. He acts like I planted the damn thing there myself. He wants to question me tomorrow, but Eduardo doesn't want an FBI agent here. He's sort of a hermit. So I'm going to meet Fielding in town."

"I'll speak up for you, Trent. You can count on that. I'm sure that Fielding is just doing his job. But you deserve some recognition, too. Maybe dinner at the White House, and I think you should definitely be paid for your services."

"I'd settle for lunch with you sometime when you have time."

She laughed, nervously. "That's a deal. I better go. Thanks again, and it was good seeing you."

"Yeah, same here."

She was about to hang up when a thought occurred to her. "Trent, about what you said before, you know, about the president's situation. Who are these psychics you think are behind it?"

"Ex-government remote viewers working with Gordon Maxwell."

"That's a strong accusation. Why would Maxwell create aliens in the president's head?"

"It's not about politics. He would do it just to prove that he could and to see how much he could affect the future through a mind-control experiment. But he also might be working for George Wiley."

"I can't believe he spoke to the governors," she said.

"It does seem odd that he got that far. But maybe his psychic pals had something to do with that."

"You mean they could actually push someone like the governor of Colorado to select Maxwell as a luncheon speaker?"

"Back four years ago, I would say it might be possible. Now, definitely. They can do it."

"I'm sorry, but I still have a hard time believing this stuff is possible."

"Me, too," he responded.

"Trent, what do you think about remote viewing the president's aliens?"

"I was wondering if you were going to ask. I would be interested in seeing what turns up."

"I'll talk to David about it. After he hears about your success finding the bomb, he might be open to it. Let's tentatively plan for something around lunchtime tomorrow."

Calloway hesitated. "That's when I'm supposed to talk to Fielding."

She thought a moment. "I'll tell you what. I'll call Fielding. He can interview you right here later in the afternoon after you're done with the president's request. How would that be?"

"Great."

"Trent, one more thing. I'd appreciate it if you would kept this quiet. Just tell Doc and Eduardo that you're coming here for lunch with me and for the interview with Fielding."

Calloway hesitated. "That's a problem. I'd like to bring Doc along to monitor me. I need her help."

"Don't say anything to her yet. I'll call you later."

She hung up, feeling hopeful for the first time since Dustin made his comments on the aliens. But her levity was short-lived. She needed to leak a story to Barry Greer, a story that she didn't believe.

MONDAY

Twenty

His preference would've been to bring Doc along to monitor him. But Camila had told him that the president's chief of staff had insisted that he come alone. That, of course, was fine with Perez, who wouldn't have gone even if he'd received an engraved invitation signed by the president. Calloway worried, though, that without Doc his abilities might be considerably weaker.

Now, as he neared the ranch between Crested Butte and Gunnison, he thought about asking Camila to monitor him. He'd never made such a request while they were together, because he didn't want to bring his work home and she was busy with her own career. Besides, Maxwell had always insisted that the spouses not be told anything about their targets. Looking back now, he realized that he should've tried some experiments with her, if only to let her observe how he worked and what he did.

Perez had generously offered him use of his Range Rover and Calloway had taken up the offer. He didn't mind traveling in comfort to his meeting with the president, not at all. He liked the new-car smell of the vehicle and the soft leather seats. He thought about his battered pickup back in Buff, ten years old, a hundred and fifty thousand miles on the odometer, and in need of new tires. He and Perez had followed far different paths after Eagle's Nest. Oddly enough, they had come together again and he felt he knew him better now than he had in the years they'd worked together. He turned on the radio and let the receiver automatically roam the channels. When he heard a news report beginning, he locked in the station. The first story dealt with Dustin and the aliens. An anonymous source close to the president supposedly had confided to CNN that Dustin firmly believed that he had been contacted by aliens and that their intentions were benevolent. Meanwhile, Chief of Staff Todd Waters, responding to the story, called the revelation baseless and said that the president "had simply intended to show that in spite of our differences in race, nationality, and beliefs, we were all more alike than different."

Sounded like a confused situation, Calloway thought. If Waters was telling the truth, then why would Dustin want him to remote view a metaphor?

"Just off the wire, we have a story from Salt Lake City where the FBI reports that a disarmed backpack nuclear bomb was discovered in the parking lot of a Holiday Inn." Calloway turned up the volume. "Information remains sketchy at this time, but apparently investigators are looking into a possible link with the radical Freedom Nation organization. An FBI source said that the bomb had apparently entered the country from Russia by way of Canada, but emphasized that it lacked plutonium and could not have been detonated. More on that story as information becomes available."

He reached into the glove compartment, took out the cell phone, and called Perez. "Hey, that bomb was disarmed. What do you think that means?"

"I don't like it," Perez answered after a few moments. "Something's wrong."

"We'll talk about it later." Calloway started to put the cell phone away, when it occurred to him that he hadn't talked to Ed Miller since he'd left Bluff. He thought a moment, recalled the number, dialed it. He got Miller's recording.

"Ed, I'm in Crested Butte. I think I'm going to be here a couple more days. I hope that's not a big problem for you. I'll tell you about it later." Then again, maybe he wouldn't tell him anything.

He followed Camila's directions and had no trouble finding the ranch. When he saw the entrance surrounded by media vehicles and reporters, he knew he'd arrived. As he slowly moved toward the gate, reporters closed in on the vehicle, trying to see who was inside. Some of them trailed behind, jotting down the license plate number.

"Oh, great. Just great." Perez no doubt would have a fit if he knew reporters were taking down his license plate, and he'd go ballistic if even one of them showed up at his door.

A state trooper walked up to his window. He told him his name and showed his driver's license. The trooper, apparently expecting him, opened the gate. He drove to the parking area and was surprised when Agent Tyler walked up to the Range Rover and opened the door for him. The agent glanced inside, then closed the door.

"Good morning, Mr. Calloway. Nice to see you again."

Tyler sounded businesslike and it quickly became clear that he wasn't here to chat. "Sorry, but I need to quickly scan you." He ran a handheld metal detector over his body, then motioned for Calloway to follow him. He led the way into the house to a formal sitting room to one side of the entryway.

"Ms. Hidalgo will be right with you." Tyler looked down as if he were examining his shiny, wing-tipped shoes, then raised his gaze to Calloway. "By the way, congratulations on the bomb. Very impressive."

With that, he left the room.

Camila had told him the luncheon would be casual, to wear anything he liked. Sarah had laundered and pressed his clothes for him, but he still felt out of place in jeans and an open-collared shirt. He felt more like he was waiting for a root canal in a dentist office than a casual lunch.

"Trent, sorry to keep you waiting."

He stood up as Camila entered the room. She wore jeans that hugged her slender hips and a sweater. He embraced her lightly. "Good to see you again."

"There's been a little change in plans. The president is going to be busy this afternoon. So we were wondering if you could do the remote viewing right away before lunch."

He shrugged. "I suppose."

"David would appreciate it." She smiled. "We'll have lunch afterwards."

"So I get my wish, after all."

"Trent, I would've gone to lunch with you anytime, if you would've asked. You didn't need to prove anything to me."

"I guess I never really thought we'd cross paths again, and I didn't see any point in revisiting the past."

"Do you think it's different now, that fate has brought us together or something?"

He laughed. "I don't know about fate, but here we are. Purpose has brought us together. I needed to do something and I knew you could help."

"And vice versa. You're here because I thought you could help me, the president, and the country."

"So it's a utilitarian relationship. Is that it?"

"Except it's one-sided," she responded. "We're utilizing you."

"Well, I'd like to utilize you," he answered.

Her voice turned wary. "Oh, what do you mean by that?"

"I need a monitor, someone to guide me since Doc's not here. Will you do it?"

She hesitated. "What would I do?"

"Not much. I just need direction, help in staying focused. That's all. It's easy."

She shrugged. "Okay. I'll try. But before we go into the library I want to go over the ground rules."

"Which are?"

"That this session is private and confidential, that you will not talk about it, that you will not even admit to remote viewing for the president."

"I've got no problem with that."

She handed him a long envelope. "I'd like you to read over this statement to that effect and sign it. Your check is also enclosed. I hope you find it acceptable."

"Jeez, I didn't know this was going to turn into *Mission Impos-*

sible.'' He sat down again, opened the envelope, and read the brief statement that reiterated what Camila had just told him. He noted that he was being paid for a "special consultation not to exceed two hours."

He raised his gaze over the document. "Can I ask you a couple of question before I sign this?"

"Go ahead."

"I guess I should've thought of this last night, but you caught me off-guard. Can I assume that, in spite of the metaphor explanation, that the president does indeed believe that he is being visited?"

She considered the question a moment. "You can assume that."

"Second question. If I pick up on another source, besides aliens, do I tell the president?"

"Of course. He can handle it. It's better to get it out, to clear the air. Besides, to my way of thinking, a human source might be the best option. At least it's something we can get a better grasp on."

He understood what she meant. If there were aliens in the White House, that was a problem. But if the president is hallucinating them, then he was the problem. But outside intervention—even a psychic one—would at least provide an explanation that avoided all the pitfalls and baggage of the alien phenomenon.

She glanced at her watch. "We better get going. Any other questions?"

He took a felt tip pen from his pocket and quickly scrawled his signature on the bottom of the contract. He handed it back to her, then looked at the check.

If he were a whistler, he would've whistled softly at the five grand he was being paid. "Not bad for a couple of hours' work."

"David believes you're worth it."

"Very flattering."

They walked out a side door, through a patio, and along a walkway to another building. They entered a large room that looked like a combination of a library and meeting room. Soft music played from hidden speakers. A reclining chair had been placed in the center of the room and several chairs faced it.

"Looks like I'm going to have an audience," Calloway commented.

Before she could answer, the door opened and two men entered. Camila introduced him to the president's chief of staff and his national security advisor. Waters, a pudgy man, wore a sport coat and an open-collar shirt, no doubt his idea of casual dress. Howell wore khakis and a baggy sweatshirt with the words "GUESS WHO" on the front.

Both of them seemed ill at ease in his presence, and uncertain what to say. "We hope you understand the need for confidentiality in this matter," Waters said.

"I signed the agreement," he answered, matter-of-factly.

"I'll tell you, Mr. Calloway, I'm a skeptic." Howell smiled, jammed his hands into pockets. "But I've always had an interest in these matters. Could you tell me something about my future while we're waiting for the president? I'm just curious."

Calloway felt as if Howell was treating him like a carnival side-show. "I don't really do general readings. My work has been specifically directed at seeing distant targets. In other words, I would have a better chance at describing your wife and her surroundings than I could tell you about your future."

"You could call a psychic line later, Harvey," Camila suggested.

"What you do sounds verifiable," Waters said.

Howell ignored Camila. "I'll take you up on that one. What's my wife look like and where is she now?"

"Harvey, we're not here to be entertained," Camila interceded.

Howell raised his hands. "Okay, never mind. I just think it would be interesting to test Mr. Calloway."

"He's been tested by the CIA," Waters said.

The door swung open. Agent Tyler entered and stood by the open door. A moment later, Dustin swept into the room and gripped Calloway's hand firmly. "Trent Calloway, good seeing you again after so many years."

"I'm surprised you remembered. Great to see you, too."

"As I told Camila, that experience wasn't something I would easily forget."

Calloway couldn't help but feel a sense of wonderment at the turn of events. Just a few days ago, he was guiding raft trips and living in a trailer on the riverbank and now here he was conferring with the president of the United States, who was treating him like an old buddy.

"I want to thank you for the work you've already done for us. It's impossible to overestimate the significance of finding that bomb. I told Camila I want to invite you to the White House and maybe even bring your accomplishments to the public's attention. People need to know about what you've done and the amazing way you did it."

"Thank you, sir. But I'll have to think about that public part. I'm not sure I want that sort of attention."

"I understand completely. On the other hand, you have a chance to show how remote viewing can be used in a positive manner." He looked over at Howell. "Considering Trent's recent success, I think we should seriously consider reinstating the program as part of our national defense."

Howell nodded. "We should look into it."

"Whether it's part of the government or not doesn't really matter," Calloway said. "The fact is, remote viewing is being practiced privately for better or worse," Calloway said.

"What do you mean by that—for better or worse?" Waters asked.

"This is a talent that, in the wrong hands, can be abused and the abuse can be very hard to detect. You may actually need some of us to serve as watchdogs over the process."

"That's all for the future," Dustin said. "Right now, we have a pressing matter that could change the way we think about ourselves and our world."

"I'm ready anytime," Calloway said.

He settled into the reclining chair and Camila handed him a pad and pen. "Just give me a few minutes while I sink into my zone. When I lift my hand, that means I'm ready for you to send me to the target."

"But what target?" Camila asked.

"I need a place, date, and time. Nothing more."

Camila moved off with the president and they conferred as Howell and Waters looked on. Calloway closed his eyes, took several long, deep breaths, and imagined his mind as a clean slate ready to absorb impressions. Chairs squeaked as the others sat down. He heard Howell say something and an image appeared on his slate. He pushed it away, drifted deeper. The image appeared again.

He raised his hand. "Okay, Trent, are you ready?" Camila asked.

"Mr. Howell, your wife is a tall, large-boned woman who is very interested in clothing. She may design clothes. She's athletic, maybe a swimmer, but she also beats you regularly at tennis."

"Did Camila tell you this?" he asked, a hint of astonishment in his voice.

"I didn't say anything of the kind," Camila said.

"I see her in a large walk-in closet. She's looking for a dress, a green gown, and wonders what happened to it."

Camila sputtered in a choking laughter.

Something about the missing dress attracted Calloway's attention. He felt an energy around it, a familiar energy that he related to Maxwell's remote viewers. They knew something about the dress and then, for a moment, he glimpsed Howell wearing it. He blinked open his eyes looked from Howell to Camila. They both looked warily back at him. Was he losing his mind? Were they already attacking him?

"Can we move on?" Camila asked in a calm, steady voice.

He nodded, relieved to get away from the confusing matter. "Give me a minute."

He settled down again. He wiped the slate clean with an imaginary cloth, then took a couple more deep breaths. He drifted deeper, raised his hand again, lowered it.

This time, Camila gave him the coordinates. "June third at two A.M., the president's bedroom."

After a few seconds, he saw the interior of a quiet, darkened bedroom. He was vaguely aware of a sleeping couple under the covers. Suddenly, a man sat up, blinked his eyes open. Calloway recognized David Dustin, his hair tousled. He wore silk pajamas. He looked around anxiously. Calloway searched the corners of the bedroom, but didn't sense anyone else in the room.

It appeared that the president had awakened from a nightmare. He looked terrified. Whatever he saw continued to unfold, but Calloway couldn't see any of it.

Calloway searched the room again, this time attempting to feel rather than see. For a moment, he sensed the same energy as he'd felt around the green gown, the energy he associated with the others, the net. Then it vanished. He let the image fade, opened his eyes. He usually began sketching now, but this time he merely tapped the tip of the pen against the paper. He looked up. Dustin stared intently at him, waiting for him to break the silence.

"Are you okay, Trent?" Camila asked.

"I'm fine. Can you give me another time? I didn't get the full picture."

"You mean you didn't see them—the aliens?" Howell asked.

"No, I didn't. But that doesn't mean they weren't there." He didn't want to say anything about the others. He was concerned that he'd sensed them because that was what he'd expected. He'd front-loaded himself. Why else would they appear around the gown owned by Howell's wife?

"That was the date of my first encounter," Dustin said.

"Let's go to the latest one—three days ago at the White House. About the same time."

"How can I help?" Camila asked. "I'm not doing my part."

"You're doing fine," Calloway responded. "Stay focused. You're helping me, even though you might not think so. Give me a couple of minutes, then ask me questions."

Calloway closed his eyes, shifting back easily into his zone. Even though Camila was an inexperienced monitor, her presence provided a sense of stability, an ineffable connection between here and there, this room and the place that he moved to when remote viewing.

He found himself back in the same bedroom. This time Dustin was already sitting up in bed, his body rigid, expressionless. He stared straight ahead as if in a trance. Calloway didn't sense any fear around him this time, just a calm intensity as if he were dreaming with his eyes open. Next to him, the first lady slept peacefully, unaware that her husband was sitting up.

"What do you see, Trent?" Camila asked in a quiet voice.

"I found the target. I'm with the president."

"Can you see anyone else in the room besides the president and the first lady?"

He scanned the room searching for another presence. Again, he saw nothing. He moved closer to the president and willed himself to see what Dustin was seeing. Suddenly, he felt an energy field above his head. It felt as if he were being pulled upward. The sense of here and there vanished. He realized that he was both in the library with the others and in the president's bedroom. He turned his gaze upward and saw a glowing tube penetrating the ceiling. He felt as if he were being pulled up into it, then realized he/Dustin was floating up through the tube, legs and arms spread out.

"I'm being lifted up, up through the ceiling. I'm continuing to rise. I can't tell how far."

"You or the president?"

"I see what he sees."

"Try to observe what's going on from outside of the president," Camila said.

He separated from Dustin and instantly the tube vanished. He found himself in darkness as if a blanket had been dropped over him. But within the darkness, he sensed awareness, that same familiar awareness. For the first time, the net took on a visual dimension—a mix of light and shadow, and eyes, or the sense of eyes, several sets: watching, aware, in contact with one another.

He tried to push past the net, to see Dustin again, but he was trapped in a sticky mesh of awareness. He felt it closing around him and then he heard his name echoing around him as if the room were filled with people rhythmically chanting his name. *Cal-lo-way . . . Cal-lo-way . . . Cal-lo-way*. Endlessly, over and over. He mentally pulled himself sharply back and the chanting ceased as abruptly as it had begun.

"I'm being blocked. I've lost contact. I need to move back into the president's perspective."

"Permission denied," a voice snapped.

Calloway blinked open his eyes. Everyone turned to Howell, who had replied for the president.

"I'm protecting the president and the nation. No telling what might happen," Howell explained. "It's too invasive."

"I thought you said you didn't believe that this really worked," Camila said.

"I didn't say that," Howell said, defensively. "I said I was a skeptic."

Dustin raised a hand. "I understand your concerns. But I believe Mr. Calloway is talking about a very limited access that relates to that particular night and to a particular incident. Am I correct?"

Calloway nodded.

"In that case, I don't see why he shouldn't continue," Dustin said. "I'm finding this fascinating."

"Wait a minute." Waters spoke up. "From what I understand, Trent hasn't seen any aliens in the room on two nights when the encounters took place. Just this floating experience on the second one. Why go any further? Mr. President, I think we should drop this matter right here. It appears to me that you have had a series of very vivid dreams that seemed real to you. I'm not a dream analyst, but these dreams could symbolize your own feelings about the need to unite the world, which we so often talk about."

"Thank you, Todd. Your point is well taken. I'm going to call an end to the session here, but before I leave I want to talk to Mr. Calloway in private."

Calloway expected Waters or Howell to protest, but both stood up and headed toward the door. Camila nodded encouragingly at him, then followed the others out. Tyler remained standing by the door after they left.

Calloway felt awkward in the reclining chair and Dustin suggested they move to the table. "My staff members are concerned about me," he said after they sat down. "Which is understandable and appreciated. However, as you can see, they want only limited information. Something simple and explainable. They want this matter to be over. Considering their sentiments, I thought it best to talk to you alone."

Calloway nodded, but didn't know what to say. So he waited for the president to continue.

"I suspect that you weren't given the chance to tell me everything that you perceived. Am I right?"

He nodded again. "There is something else."

"I'd like to hear about it. And I'd like an assessment of my experience. Please, don't hold anything back."

"I appreciate that, sir. First of all, I did sense an invasive energy essence that is not part of you. However, I don't believe that it's source is alien or extraterrestrial. I also believe the intention is to deceive, confuse, and disrupt."

Dustin looked baffled. "I find this very disturbing. But who or what is it?"

"Earlier, I said that there are remote viewers working for better and for worse. I believe that you've been victimized by a group of very adept remote viewers. They are so clever and manipulative that their leader even managed to address the governors conference."

"What? You mean, Maxwell?"

"Yes sir."

Dustin leaned back into his chair. "But it seemed so real. I was certain that I actually experienced all of it."

"Think of what they're doing as an advanced form of virtual reality that requires only minds, no computers, no accessories. They're linked together and they're strong, strong enough to play very realistic mind games on people who are totally unaware of their presence."

Dustin appeared shell-shocked. "What if they come back?" he asked in a quiet voice.

"Now that you know, it'll be different," Calloway said. "Stay aware of any thoughts or impulses that seem foreign to you. They can push, but there are always tell-tale signs. If you compare your thoughts to a bowl of marbles, watch for the stone among the shiny marbles."

Dustin grinned. "And I'll try not to lose my marbles."

Calloway winced. "Sorry, sir. I guess that wasn't the best analogy."

"No offense taken."

"If you have any more alien experiences, tell yourself it's not real. Say it over and over while it's happening. You should be able to see through it."

"I have to say that I'm still having a hard time accepting this, Trent. I find it incredible that remote viewing has been advanced to such a degree. It's not about viewing, at all. It's about control."

"That's exactly what it's about in Maxwell's hands and it's frightening. It's like a kid carrying around a backpack nuclear bomb. Extremely dangerous."

"Well put." Dustin glanced at his watch. "I need to be on my way."

They both stood up. "Please, keep this to yourself, Trent. For the time being, I'd appreciate it if you didn't tell anyone on my staff about this conversation, not even Camila."

"That's a promise."

They shook hands and Dustin beamed at him with his best presidential smile. "Sorry again that I can't stay for lunch. But I'll let Camila know that you're ready."

Tyler followed the president out the door, paying no heed to Calloway. If he'd overheard any of their conversation, he gave no indication of it.

Calloway walked back over to the reclining chair he'd used and slumped down to await Camila. He felt relieved that it was over. He closed his eyes and within seconds started to drift off. He glimpsed Ed Miller's face. He looked frenzied and was shouting about something. Something was wrong, very wrong.

"Trent?"

His eyes flew open. Camila smiled down at him. "How about some lunch."

"I'd love some. I'm starved."

As they left the room, he thought about Miller and wondered what the image of the old outfitter meant.

Twenty-one

Camila dropped her head back, closed her eyes, and let the warm sun beat down on her. "It's nice out here. Other than talking to the reporters at the gate, I haven't gotten outside since we arrived. Too busy running from one meeting to the next."

He watched her, taking pleasure in the moment, the opportunity to be alone with her again. It had been a long time since they'd sat together comfortable in their own thoughts. But he reminded himself that in a day or two he would be back in his trailer, back to his nomadic life. No longer eating lunch by a pool served by a waiter in a white coat. No longer seeing Camila, either.

He picked up the remainder of his tuna salad sandwich and bit into the croissant roll. His chip and pickles and the crab bisque had already been devoured.

The thought of returning to Bluff reminded him again of the fleeting image he'd seen of Miller shouting in distress. "Camila, do you think I can make a quick call?"

"Of course. Use my phone." She reached down to her case, handed it to him. She started to get up, but he motioned her to stay.

"This'll just take a minute. I want to check with the outfitter in Bluff. Make sure I still have a job."

She smiled. "With your abilities, Trent, you shouldn't have to worry about leading raft trips, anymore."

He dialed the number, thinking he wasn't sure that giving up the river for remote viewing was such a good idea, especially considering what he knew about Maxwell and Wiley.

Again, he heard Miller's recorded voice. "Hi, Ed. It's me again, Trent, just checking in. Guess I'll try later."

"Trent! My God!" Miller gasped for breath. "I'm glad I caught you before you hung up."

"What's going on, Ed?"

"Oh, my God. You won't believe it. The bastards!"

"Hold on, start from the beginning. What happened?"

Camila looked up, gave him a puzzled look. Calloway shrugged.

"There were men here last night looking for you. They were up at the restaurant first, just before it closed, then they came here. They weren't very nice fellows, either. I could tell they meant business, but all I told them was that you were gone and hadn't been around for several days."

"Do you think they were FBI agents?"

"FBI? Hell no, not these guys. They were thugs, the kind of guys the FBI goes after. But let me finish. One of them, a big guy, started twisting my arm behind my back trying to get information out of me. Finally, he must've figured I didn't know anything and they left."

"Are you okay?"

"My arm's sore, but that's not the half of it. Joe, the fellow who runs the restaurant, woke me up early this morning and told me about a fire down at Sand Island. The frigging bastards blew up your trailer, Trent!"

"You're kidding."

"Hey, I wish I were."

Wiley's men were already seeking revenge, he thought. Perez's assessment, *We are in deep shit trouble,* echoed in his head. "Ed, I've got to go. I'll be back as soon as I can get there. It might be a couple of days, though."

"If I were you, I'd stay away from here for a while. What did you do to those guys, anyhow?"

"Listen to the news, Ed. The story coming out of Salt Lake City. That'll give you an idea."

"Hey, I just heard something about a goddamn nuclear bomb found up there. Is that it?"

"You got it. When this thing is over, I'll explain it all to you."

He handed the phone back to Camila and quickly told her what Miller had said.

"Trent, that's terrible. What are you going to do?"

"Don't know."

He thought back to Perez's impression that Maxwell's gang had pushed him when they'd arrived. If Maxwell knew he was staying with Perez, then Wiley could find out. Now he and the others faced a two-pronged attack: psychic and physical. He didn't like either alternative.

Two men in business suits moved across the courtyard. Calloway recognized Agent Clarke accompanied by a black man in his thirties whose intense gaze focused on Calloway. They stopped a few feet away. Camila turned, "Can I help you?"

"This is Special Agent Lewis Fielding of the FBI," Clarke said, "Here to talk to Mr. Calloway."

Camila greeted Fielding, thanked him for coming, then excused herself. She told Calloway to let her know when he was leaving.

He shook Fielding's hand, smiled. "Nice to finally meet you in person."

An eerie feeling rippled through Calloway. Fielding reminded him of his old buddy, Bobby Aimes. Fielding was older, a few pounds heavier, but the way he smiled and a certain look in his eye brought back memories of Aimes. Good memories and bad ones.

Fielding joined him at the table. They talked for more than an hour covering the entire scenario of events from the six-digit number and lightning strike to the point where he and Doc and Perez had discovered the bomb. At first, he focused on Wiley and the bomb and avoided any mention of Maxwell and the other remote viewers. But, as Fielding questioned him, he told him the rest of the story, everything except the connection with the president and the aliens. Finally, he told him about the firebombing of his trailer.

Fielding nodded. "I heard about that on my way over here. I'm glad I didn't have to break the news."

Fielding had done some research on remote viewing since they'd first talked, but he seemed to doubt parts of the story. "Maybe you did find the bomb with your mind. But this psychic hotline stuff, Maxwell and his remote viewers working for Wiley and killing my colleagues, I've got problems with that." He shook his head. "Those deaths were accidents. Same with the two kids."

Calloway nodded patiently. "I can understand your reservations. But believe me, they can kill."

Fielding didn't look convinced. "I need to talk to your friends, Doc and Eduardo, before I leave the area. How about if I follow you back?"

Not a good idea. "Let me talk to Perez first. I don't think he'd like it if I showed up with an FBI agent."

"What's he got to hide?"

"I told you, Lewis, he likes his privacy. That's why he lives underground. Give me a call in the morning. I'll work on him tonight."

Fielding handed him his card. "I'd appreciate it if you'd call me tonight."

They stood up and shook hands. He liked the man and knew the quandary he faced with the psychic-derived material. He probably dreaded the prospect of preparing a report on the meeting for his superiors. "By the way, what do you think it means that the bomb was unarmed?" Fielding asked.

"It worries me," Calloway answered. "My guess is that Wiley's got plutonium and he's going to try to use it. If you get a nuclear weapon from Russia, you probably get the whole package."

Before Fielding could respond, Clarke approached. He asked Calloway to wait for Camila, that she'd be right out. Then he and Fielding left. Camila showed up a couple of minutes later and they walked to the parking lot.

"I'm really sorry about your trailer," she said.

"Yeah, so am I."

They walked in silence until they reached the Range Rover. He could tell that she had something on her mind. "I know that David wants you to keep your conversation with him private," she began. "But I just hope that you were able to tell him something that will make him understand his experience in a new light."

He'd been wondering when she was going to mention the private talk and he admired her reserve. Without saying it directly, she was asking if he'd linked Dustin's experiences to psychic attacks. "I think I did do just that."

"That's good." She smiled. "By the way, you really surprised Harvey Howell with that accurate description of his wife. And you don't know how much that comment about the green gown hit home. Someday I'll tell you about it."

"I don't know what happened, but I'll tell you this: that gown is linked to the same energy as the aliens. There was outside manipulation involved."

She looked stunned. "Oh, God. It fits, Trent."

He nodded. "I better get going. My host will think I'm being held captive."

He extended a hand. She tentatively took it, thanked him for coming. She let go of his hand, but he didn't turn away. She looked up, met his gaze, then reached out and hugged him. She felt great, like old times, like when things were good between them. He held her close, held her a little too long.

Finally, she pulled back, touched her index finger to his chest. "Watch it, Calloway. We're going to get ourselves in trouble if you start that stuff."

That kind of trouble sounded pretty good right now. He brushed his fingertips lightly along her jaw. "I'll see you."

Maxwell had been beside himself all day. Now, five hours after hearing the bad news, he still felt like a condemned man moments before the execution. He expected to see Wiley's thugs show up at the door at any moment.

He froze at the peal of the phone, then relaxed, realizing that it was Marlys's line, not his cell phone. He waited for the recorder to take the call. "Max, are you there?"

He snatched up the phone. "Hi, Maryls. Are you off now?"

"It's after six. I've been off since five-thirty. Are you coming over for dinner or not?"

"Yeah, I'm hungry. Give me ten minutes."

"Okay. I'll wait. How did your business go in Salt Lakes City?"

"Real good," he lied. "I finished my work and decided to drive all night so I could get back to see you tonight."

What else could he tell her, that he'd recovered a nuclear bomb, then had almost gotten blown away in a men's room by one of the most notorious men alive? That he was lucky he wasn't behind bars? Not likely. Nor could he tell her that he was worried that he would be shot the moment he stepped outside her door because he'd lost the nuke to the FBI. No, she wouldn't understand.

"I just wished you'd gotten back earlier while I was still awake."

"I'm here now."

"Good. I may keep you up all night. If you can stay up, Max!"

He laughed. "Just you wait. See you in a bit."

He hung up. His shoulders slumped. He didn't have the heart to tell her that he'd be working tonight, probably working all night. But at least he'd have dinner with her.

Even though Perez now lived far from the sea, he dined on fresh seafood several times a week. Sarah had driven to town earlier and picked up Perez's order and prepared the sumptuous meal, which included grilled salmon, boiled potatoes the size of golf balls, and steamed asparagus spears.

"You've been real quiet, Trent," Doc said, halfway through dinner. "Are you sure you don't want to talk about what happened at the ranch?"

"Actually, I was thinking about my conversation with Ed Miller, the outfitter I work for."

"Oh, no. He didn't fire you, did he?" she asked.

"No, something worse." He told them what happened in Bluff.

"Don't even think about going back there," Perez said. "Stay here until this is over. We're going to nail that bastard, Wiley, even if we have to drag the FBI to his hideout."

"That's right," Doc said. "We'll find him. Let's do it tonight."

He realized the situation presented the perfect opportunity for getting Fielding here. "I think you're right. But we need the authorities involved. I want Lewis Fielding here so he can see us work."

"What?" Perez blurted. "You want to bring that FBI agent here? No way. No federal agents on my property."

"Now you sound like one of Wiley's followers," Calloway said.

"No, I am not like them. I am my own country. I don't need their Freedom Nation. It would be worse than what we've got now. Far worse."

"Eduardo, don't be an idiot. Fielding is not going to destroy your privacy," Doc said. "We've already done that."

He shook his head. "I am not concerned about that. I am worried about what surrounds Agent Fielding, what energies he might bring in here. I don't want this place infected."

"What do you mean?" Calloway asked.

"I understand," Doc said, "you think he may have bad energy around him, because of the work he does."

"I don't think, I know."

Doc beamed. "I've got the answer for that. After he leaves, we'll burn some sage. I brought some with me. We'll cleanse the place."

"Maybe that'll take care of some of the bad energy we've got around us, too," Calloway said, thinking of Maxwell and his network.

"This is nonsense," Perez said. "I do not want your G-man in my house."

Calloway threw up his hands. "Okay. Doc and I will go to Crested Butte and rent a room. We'll go after Wiley there."

"You can join us," Doc said, standing up from the table. "That is, if you dare come to the surface and leave your property."

Perez stared glumly at the two of them. He shook his head in disgust. "I do not want you two to leave. It is far too dangerous out there. Unfortunately, we need to stay together until this thing is resolved and I hope that is not too long.''

Doc placed her hands on her hips. ''Well?''

Perez shrugged. ''Oh, shit. I suppose you can invite the G-man. But only him. No partners.''

Calloway smiled. ''Great. I'll call his pager right now.'' No sense waiting for Perez to change his mind.

He left the table and walked out into the main room under the enormous atrium and over to the phone at a corner table. When Fielding returned his call a couple of minutes later, Calloway told him what they planned to do. Fielding would have a chance not only to talk to Doc and Perez, but also to see them remote view Wiley's hideout.

''Give me the directions,'' Fielding said. ''I'll be out within the hour.''

Perez and Doc sipped coffee when Calloway returned. He sat down and poured himself a cup from a silver decanter. ''All set. He's on his way.''

''I can't wait to nail Wiley,'' Doc said. ''And we'll take down Maxwell with him.''

''They're a dangerous combination,'' Perez said.

More dangerous than either Doc or Perez realized, he thought. In spite of his pledge to Dustin, Calloway felt compelled now to tell them what had happened when he'd remote viewed for the president. They needed to know how far Maxwell had taken remote viewing.

''I've got to tell you about this afternoon.''

''You went after Dustin's aliens,'' Perez said with a smile. ''Did you think you could hide that from us? No way. But what happened?''

He told them about the two short sessions.

Perez shook his head in disbelief. For a change, he seemed to question the extent that one's privacy could be invaded. ''Do you really think they could create aliens and make him believe, make him tell the nation about it?''

''I know it sounds like a stretch, but I think they've developed that far,'' Calloway said.

"Maxwell is flexing his muscles," Doc added. "It makes him feel like a macho man."

Perez crossed his arms. "I still think it might be real aliens."

"Think about it, Eduardo," Doc said. "Trent may be right. Do you remember all those alien sessions we did? Sometimes Maxwell just created alien targets that weren't related to photos or anything, just to see what we would get. And we'd still come up with aliens."

"Right," Calloway interjected. "So let's take it a step further. If he could suggest that we see aliens and we did, a good remote viewer could put a target into anyone's head. Shit, I bet Ritter could put an alien in your head, too."

"Maybe you're right," Perez conceded. "So we have to expose Maxwell and pull the mask off these aliens."

Marlys hadn't bothered changing from her long, purple dress, and that was fine with him. When they were alone, Maxwell liked to run his fingertips lightly over the tops of her breasts exposed by the low-cut dress. He liked to think that he was doing what other men at the bar just imagined doing themselves.

He slid onto a barstool next to her. "Should we get a table?"

She greeted him with a hug and a peck on the lips. He felt the eyes of the other men at the bar judging him, maybe wishing they were in his place.

"How about a drink first?"

He shook his head. "No drinking for me tonight. I've got work to do upstairs."

"Tonight?" She frowned. "I thought we'd have the night together. Rent a movie or something."

"I wish we could do that. But I've got a pressing assignment."

She frowned. "You didn't tell me. What kind of pressing assignment?"

"It's a confidential matter. The party involved doesn't want anyone to know that he's availing the service."

She stared at him as if she were looking through him. Then she smiled. "Mr. Mystery Man."

Maryls was hard to figure sometimes. When he expected that she would be upset, like now, she seemed to take the news in stride. "Will you wait up for me? We could have some late-night fun."

"Depends what time you get in. I don't stay up all night like you."

They got up and moved over to a table. "Say, I noticed I had one of your credit cards with me. I accidentally used it at a motel. I'll pay you back."

She looked suspiciously at the card. "How did you get it?"

"Remember when you insisted on paying for drinks that night? I ended up with your card."

"Oh, yeah." She opened her purse to put it away. He noticed a book sticking out. "What are you reading?"

She held it up. "*Alien Agenda*. It's about UFOs and abductions and all that. I'm fascinated by the president's admission that he's made contact. It's really incredible. Do you believe it? A lot of people think he's nuts, but I say it's true."

Maxwell sat back in his chair and smiled. He'd only known her six months and he found out new things about her all the time. So she was interested in aliens. "I think it's just a hoax of some sort. He probably thinks it'll make him more powerful if people think he's in contact with beings from another world."

"Really? That's what you think? I can't believe he would make it up."

He shrugged. "Maybe I'm just being overly harsh with him. He's not my favorite person in the world."

He'd love to tell her that not only was it a hoax, but that he had perpetrated it, that he could actually manipulate the way the president of the United States sees and acts. Of course, if she knew that, she might get suspicious about her own relationship with him.

He would never tell her that Ritter had "looked in" on her one night and nudged the new waitress to take an interest in Maxwell.

The next evening, Maxwell dined at the hotel and sat at one of Marlys's tables. When he told her that he was a regular here, she'd chatted amiably with him throughout the meal. Later, he'd asked to buy her a drink after she got off work, and she'd readily agreed.

He realized Marlys was talking to him. "Sorry. What did you say?"

"I knew you weren't listening to me. I said why don't you ask Ritter to look into President Dustin's future and see what happens. I really can't think of anything more important."

"That would certainly be interesting, but this isn't a hobby. My guys get paid for what they do and I don't ask them to work for nothing."

"Yeah, but I would think you'd be curious."

He smiled. "Maybe we already know the answer."

"Then tell me. I want to know."

He leaned toward her, slipped a hand under the table, and rested it on her thigh. He whispered, "He's going to get invited for a little ride in a flying saucer. He'll buzz the Capitol Building a couple of times, then he'll fly off into space and never be seen or heard from again."

"What?" She pushed his hand away. "You're spoofing me. You're making that up."

He laughed. "Well, it's still a good idea, if you ask me."

She wasn't laughing though. She stared past him. He heard Ritter's annoying taps scraping the floor. He turned and saw a tall wraith-like figure moving their way. Ritter wore a robe and his street shoes and held his head between his hands. Maxwell stood up, moved over to him. "Steve, what's going on? What are you doing?"

"Lots of static. Too much static. It's strong, getting stronger. It's really bothering me."

"C'mon, let's get you upstairs."

"The others," he moaned. "It's coming from them. They're joining together. They're going to destroy us. All of us."

He placed a hand on Ritter's shoulder. He felt the eyes of everyone in the place on him and Ritter. He turned to Marlys, who looked stricken. "Sorry about this."

"You're not going to eat dinner?" she called out. But he couldn't answer her. Not now. He quickly ushered Ritter away.

Twenty-two

Just as they stepped out of the elevator on the fourth floor, Ritter's legs gave way and he flopped to the carpeting. Maxwell dropped to one knee and awkwardly pulled him to his feet. Ritter wobbled like a marionette and babbled an unintelligible flurry of sounds. Maxwell wrapped an arm around his shoulder and dragged him the last fifty feet.

The door of Ritter's room hung open and Maxwell pushed his way inside with his load. He hauled Ritter across the room and dumped him onto a chair, where he collapsed, his head hanging to one side.

"Steve, are you all right? Talk to me. What's going on?"

No response.

Shit. Maybe he'd blown a fuse. Maxwell had always been concerned about something like that happening. He'd imagined his remote viewers all ending up in mental hospitals staring at the walls. But Ritter and the others had repeatedly exhibited an impressive mental resilience. They excelled in their work, if not their everyday lives.

"Steve, can you hear me?" Maxwell picked up his thin, limp arm and felt for Ritter's pulse. A long thread of spittle seeped from the corner of his mouth.

"We're all here now. We're ready to start," Ritter mumbled.

"What did you say?"

Ritter slowly raised his head. He stared blankly ahead. "I said, we're all here now. They say I can speak for them."

Incredible, Maxwell thought. Ritter had entered a deep trance state, one in which his body was asleep, but his mind was alert, connected with the others. It had never happened this way before. Usually they worked together on conference calls, one or two others at a time, each one sinking into his zone, but keeping in contact by phone. But now Ritter implied that he was aware of all of them—Johnstone, Timmons, and Henderson.

Maxwell wanted proof. "Johnstone, are you there?"

"Yes," Ritter replied in a monotone.

"What's your mother's maiden name?"

"Carter."

"Timmons, can you hear me?"

"I told you we are all here," Ritter replied. "But go ahead and check our IDs."

"Timmons, what your oldest brother's name?"

"Alex."

"Henderson, what kind of work did your maternal grandfather do? You told me once."

"He was a blacksmith."

Fantastic. He doubted that Ritter would know the answers to the questions he'd asked. Ritter took little interest in the personal lives of the other viewers and rarely talked with them outside of their remote viewing sessions.

"Okay. We've got a lot of work tonight. Important stuff. We're going to push beyond our limits. Is that understood?"

He realized he didn't know if the others actually heard him or Ritter relayed his comments. But if it worked, it didn't matter.

"That's no problem," Ritter replied. "No telephones, no problem."

"First, we're going to find Agent Fielding. We need to see if he's getting close to our sponsor. We want to find out what he knows and what his plans are."

"Got him," Ritter said, nearly cutting off Maxwell's last words.

So fast. Maybe they were moving too fast. He needed to keep Ritter and the others reined in. After Ritter's bizarre behavior, anything could happen. He wanted results, not surprises.

Ritter's loss of control reminded him of the old days when they were first developing remote viewing. As part of the training, they would send everyone to the Monroe Institute in West Virginia where they would learn Robert Monroe's method for out-of-body travel. Ultimately, Maxwell had concluded that the out-of-body method didn't work, not for their purposes. He wanted his viewers firmly grounded in their bodies, in contact with him as well as out there with their target. Once he'd made that determination, the remote viewing protocol became linked with bilocation, but not out-of-body experiences.

"We all feel pressure on the net," Ritter said as if responding to his thoughts. "More parts being activated. It links us closer together."

He didn't like the sound of that. "Steve, what about the static you mentioned in the dining room?"

"A temporary block when we tried to look in on the others. Caught us by surprise. Disturbing, disrupting. Static . . . static . . . static."

"Are the outsiders here with us now?"

"Outsiders?" Ritter asked.

"Calloway, Doc, and Perez. You know who I mean." Maxwell had always referred to them as the others or the nonparticipants, but now "outsiders" seemed a more appropriate term.

"We feel them close by. No static now. They're part of the net, not outsiders. But they're not here. Not in the same way."

"Keep in mind that they are working against us," Maxwell said. "They want to destroy everything we've done. Even destroy the net."

"We're ready to swallow them." Ritter spoke slowly, but his voice was firm. When he was working, Ritter usually dropped his annoying habit of incessantly repeating words at the end of sentences.

"That's good, but the FBI agent comes first. Now tell me about Fielding. What is he doing?"

"He's getting ready to leave the hotel where he's staying. He's excited. He senses a break in the case. Ah, how interesting for you, Max. He's going to Perez's place to see our other half—the weaker half. He has his doubts about remote viewing, but if he gets the results he wants, he doesn't care how he gets them.''

So that was it. Calloway and the others had either found Wiley's hideout already or they were about to go after it. Maxwell realized that he'd forgotten to set up the tape recorder. He opened a desk drawer next to Ritter's bed and looked for blank tapes. When he didn't find any, he settled for a notebook and pen. There would be no time for Wiley to listen to any tapes, anyhow. Everything was moving too fast now.

''They haven't looked yet,'' Ritter said as if he'd heard his thoughts. ''Fielding was tempted to tell them to find the location, then they'd talk. But he also wants proof of what they do. He wants to know more about this stuff.''

Maxwell laid the pen down. He recalled Wiley's words when he'd surprised Maxwell in his room in the Brown Palace. If Wiley were caught, he would tell the authorities how he'd used remote viewers to remain hidden. But now Maxwell glimpsed his opportunity to hit hard and crush all of them—Fielding and the three outsiders. Snare them like flies in a web before they found Wiley.

''He thinks he can get there in fifteen minutes if he can find the turnoff to the property,'' Ritter said.

''Okay, just relax now as he drives. If there's anything else any of you pick up, just tell me.''

''Johnstone says this is the way it should always be,'' Ritter said in his monotone voice. ''We're all closely connected. Everything is coming through very clearly. Mind to mind.''

''Good. That's good.''

A red light flashed on the wall. A recorded female voice, rather than an alarm, alerted everyone of Fielding's approach. *Vehicle entering property. Vehicle approaching residence.*

Now Calloway understood how Perez had known of their arrival even though he'd been a hundred feet or more below ground level. ''I have sensors at the perimeters," Perez said. "Video cameras, too. Take a look."

He picked up a remote control device from a drawer in a coffee table and pointed it at a wall. The paneling slid aside, revealing a large-screen television. A dark-colored Ford Taurus rolled into view and stopped in front of the house. Fielding stepped out, looked around, then approached the door. His face now loomed on the screen as he looked up toward the hidden camera.

Perez touched another button on the remote. "Hello, Mr. Fielding. Please wait right there."

"I'll go get him," Calloway volunteered. He walked over to the elevator and rode it up to the surface. He crossed the garage, and opened the door for Fielding.

"Welcome to the mole hole."

Fielding followed him to the elevator. "We're going down three levels."

"I guess I know where to come now in case of an atomic attack," Fielding replied.

"I think you'll find this place interesting."

"I'm not here to be entertained, Mr. Calloway," Fielding answered. "But I hope you have something else for me that's interesting."

"We're going to work on it." The idea of this Bobby Aimes look alike calling him mister bothered him. "And call me Trent."

The elevator door slid open at the third level and they moved out into the central room. Calloway introduced Doc and Perez. Fielding's gaze moved about the large room, then upward into the atrium.

"You ought to see it during the day," Calloway said. "There's a skylight at the top and steel plates that close over it at the touch of a button."

"Impressive," Fielding said in a noncommittal tone. He turned to Perez. "Looks like you can survive anything. But I hope you've got a good collection of videos in case you get stuck in here for a few years."

"Mr. Fielding, I am just protecting myself because I can afford to do it. I came to this country on a raft from Cuba in 1980. Five years later, I went to work for the CIA as a psychic and exposed myself to all sorts of dangers. I don't regret it and I hope that I helped protect this country. Now I am helping myself.''

"Yeah, well, I'd like to see if you could help me tonight. If you can win the lottery, maybe you can find George Wiley.''

Perez smiled. "I am glad you asked. We are ready anytime you are. But do you want something to drink or eat first? My housekeeper will be leaving in a few minutes, so I thought I would ask.''

"No thank you. I'm fine.'' He turned to Doc. "I have some questions for you about your work with Mr. Calloway, but let's put them off until later. I'd like to get started as soon as we can.''

"You're going to see how it happened,'' Doc answered. "You'll be a witness to it all. You should find it very interesting.''

"Everybody wants to make my life interesting. All I want to do is catch that bastard before he blows up something.''

Perez led them down a hallway and into a more intimate room. Dim lighting oozed from hidden recesses in the ceiling. Several candles burned on a low table and Native American flute music played from invisible speakers.

A U-shaped sofa combination dominated the room with a well-padded chair completing the circle. Perez gestured for them to sit down. "Trent, you take the back. Doc and I will be on either side of you. You get the chair, Mr. Fielding. Now we will find the wayward general for you.''

"So give me a clue, how does this work?'' Fielding asked.

"The three of us will go down into what we call our zone, where the remote viewing works. Give us a few minutes. I'll signal you, then ask your question.''

Calloway didn't like working this way. Multiple viewers created distractions. When one saw something, the others tended to look for it and create analytical overlays that short-circuited their efforts. Sometimes, the viewers constructed extravagant fantasies as images built one upon another until they were told that their impressions had nothing to do with the target.

Doc apparently felt the same way. "Why don't I monitor you two? That way Agent Fielding can just observe."

Perez shook his head. "No, we all need to go down tonight. We need to be united. Are we ready?"

Calloway took a deep breath, then another. He sank slowly into his zone. Trouble. They weren't alone. Ritter and the others were here, watching.

Look at the man in front of you.

It sounded like a whisper in his ear. He ignored it.

Look, Trent. It's your old buddy.

He willed himself not to look at Fielding.

"Hi, Trent. We had such a good time as kids."

This time the words sounded as if they were spoken in the room. He blinked his eyes open. Bobby Aimes looked just as he'd last seen him. He hadn't changed a bit. He smiled with that same goofy grin, and spoke aloud.

"You remember when we both joined the air force. It was great. But what happened, Trent?"

It's not Aimes, he told himself, attempting to stay calm. But then he heard himself responding. *"You stole Denise from me, Bobby. You ran off with her. You left the air force and turned into a drug pilot."*

"No, you got it all wrong, Trent. Denise was my girl, not yours. She always liked me, even in high school. You never saw that. You refused to see it. You never forgave me. So you had me killed. You sneaked right into that punk's head and he shot me. Why, why did you do it? It was my last run. I was ready to quit."

"Stop it! I didn't want to kill you, Bobby. Maxwell sent me into the Colombian's head. He pushed me. Made the guy think you were double-crossing him. It happened so fast."

Aimes grinned again. *"Now I can do it to you, too. Watch me!"*

"Steve, what's going on? Where is Fielding now?"

Ritter let out a long sigh. "He's inside. They're all underground."

Maxwell glanced at his watch. A minute passed. Then another. "What's going on now?"

"They're going to look for Wiley." He smiled. "I'm playing with Calloway. Fucking up his mind. He thinks Fielding looks like his old buddy, that guy he knocked off for you, the drug pilot." He laughed again. "You tell him, Bobby. He did you wrong. Now, dead Bobby's going to get him back good."

Maxwell didn't like the distraction. Ritter wasn't following orders again. "Let's focus on Fielding. Let's make him see things. Fielding is our target. Push hard on him. Make him feel threatened. He sees them all pull out knives. They're coming after him. They're crazy. He's got to defend himself. He's got no choice. He's got to shoot them all before they get him."

Ritter's breathing came harder now. He nodded his head and spoke aloud as if talking to Fielding. "Yeah, that's it. They're nuts. Totally nuts. Do it now! Do it now before they get you! Pull the gun! Shoot them! Shoot them!"

Calloway stood up, reached a hand out toward Fielding. "Bobby!"

Doc leaped up. "No, Trent! It's a ruse!"

Perez gasped, bolted to his feet. He slipped a small black object shaped like a fountain pen from his pocket and stabbed at it with his thumb. Fielding reacted to the sudden movement, reached inside his coat pocket and pulled out a gun.

"Drop the knives! Now! All of you!"

Perez let the device fall to the carpeting. He raised his hands. Calloway and Doc lowered their open palms to show that they were unarmed.

Fielding leaned over, picked it up the oblong object. "Jesus. I could've sworn you pulled a knife on me. For a moment, I thought all of you had knives." He turned the device over in his hand. "What's going on, anyhow?"

Perez placed a hand on his chest. "I thought you were going to shoot. We were under attack. They wanted you to kill us.''

''Are you okay, Trent?'' Doc asked. ''It was Ritter and the others, you know. They pushed you hard.''

Calloway felt a sudden flood of relief wash over him. He couldn't take his eyes off Fielding. ''I know. I know.''

''What are you talking about?'' Fielding looked mystified as if he'd found himself in a carnival fun house where nothing seemed real.

''They had me believing you were someone else. I thought you—he—was talking to me.''

Fielding, still looking perplexed, handed the slender object back to Perez. ''What is it?''

''It activates an EMF, an electromagnetic field, around the building,'' Perez explained. ''They can't penetrate it. Now we are safe.''

Calloway remembered seeing Perez holding it in his hands earlier, before Fielding had arrived. He laughed. ''Goddamn, Eduardo, now I know that you've got every imaginable gadget here.''

Doc frowned. ''A lot of people are trying to avoid EMF. They say it causes brain diseases.''

''Short-term exposure, I think, is safe,'' Perez said, seriously. ''We need it to protect us. I hit it just in time. They almost got us.''

Fielding put away his weapon. ''What about Wiley? Can you find him?''

Perez grimaced. ''Unfortunately, when the field is activated, it disrupts us, too. They cannot look in and we cannot look out.''

''It's a stalemate,'' Calloway said.

Twenty-three

Enough. Camila turned off the television. She'd just spent the last hour ferreting out the latest reports about the president, while her roommate, Sally Powers, competed for her attention.

"Don't worry about those polls, Camila. It doesn't matter what Dustin said about aliens. As long as no aliens show up, we're in good shape."

Powers, the old pro, helped stabilize her. In the past couple of weeks, she'd provided Camila with a ton of insight into the inner workings of the press corps. She'd already assured her several times that the attention on the silly alien comments just showed how well the country was being run. The media didn't have any serious problems to tackle.

But neither Powers nor any reporters knew about the real threat, the one that Calloway had told her about. She found herself in an awkward, frustrating position. She couldn't say anything about it, not to Powers, and especially not to the media. At least, not until the president acknowledged the true source of the aliens to her, to his advisors, and to his cabinet. Even then, there would still be a question about how much, if anything, should be revealed to the public about the remote viewing threat.

Meanwhile, the news programs were filled with soft pieces about alien abductees who sympathized with the president and ufologists who made their analysis of what was known about the president's encounter. Very little of substance was leaking out the front gate. In fact, the only leak had been the president's own, and its implications of the contradictory comments were still being discussed.

"I'm going for a little walk. I'll be back in a few minutes. Do you want to join me?"

Please say no. She wanted to be alone for a while.

"No thanks. I'm going to make a couple of telephone calls. Is that all right?"

She smiled. "Fine. See you in a while."

Camila closed the door. She stepped out and let the cool evening air wash over her. She walked to the corner of the building, then across the lawn and past the stables. The sun had just dropped below the trees, but there would be another half hour of light. She kept going and found the trail at the edge of the forest.

Ever since she'd seen Dustin and Kyle Leslie disappearing into the trees on horseback, she'd promised herself she'd take a walk along the trail before she left. Dustin had wanted the media allowed inside for a photo-op, but she'd convinced him it was a bad idea. She'd pictured the evening news opening with the president on horseback and reporters shouting out questions about aliens. It would look ridiculous and unpresidential. Instead, she'd gotten Gerry Davis, the White House photographer, to shoot it and distribute the photos.

She paused near the head of the trail. A rich smell of moist earth and decaying vegetation filled her nostrils. What if there were bears out here? She looked back, then resolutely strode forward. No, she told herself, she wasn't going to be afraid of nature. The chances of encountering anything larger than a squirrel were slim.

She needed this time for herself, away from the other staff members and away from the reporters, who camped day and night outside the gate. The ranch house, all 15,000 square feet of it, disappeared behind her and now she found herself in a majestic forest of tall pines. She continued on, accompanied by a hypnotic chorus of frogs, her feet sinking in the bed of soft brown pine needles with each step. The forest canopy blocked out the fading light, creating an eerie, shadowy world below. Each step seemed to take her deeper into a mythical world of unknown creatures, real and imagined, a world that had vanished from her life long ago.

She walked on and thought back to the summer when she was fourteen. She'd spent a couple of weeks with a cousin who lived on the edge of a state forest in northern Colorado and they'd slept in a tent in the backyard. Late at night, when everyone else had fallen asleep, she and Maya would get up and walk in the forest. At first, she'd been terrified. The forest at night was alive with shadows and unseen creatures. Each night they had gone a little further before running back to their tent, laughing and imagining they were being chased by grizzly bears or other undefined beasts.

Camila recalled what had drawn them into the forest in the first place, something she'd forgotten all about. Maya had told her about the fairy lights that she had seen on summer nights. Then one night they'd seen them, a swirling glow of light that literally lit up the forest. The fairy light, of course, had a logical explanation. On closer inspections, the moving specks of light turned out to be swarms of mating lightning bugs.

Camila suddenly felt as though she were being watched and wished Maya were with her now. A silly thought. She hadn't seen the woman since college days. She'd married and moved to Oklahoma. But the boldness and curiosity of those two teenaged girls steeled her nerves.

Keep going. A little further.

She imagined that at the next turn a fallen tree would block the trail and that would mark the end of her hike. But nothing impeded her, and she continued farther and farther into the forest.

She stopped. Something had changed. At first, she couldn't pinpoint it. Then she realized she no longer heard the frogs. Time to go back. God, she must've walked nearly a mile along the winding trail. Then she noticed an opening just ahead where the forest gave way to a field. Her legs carried her forward and she felt the density and darkness of the tall, huddled trees lift away as she entered a grassy clearing.

The sun had disappeared behind the mountains. Dusk settled across the landscape. She inhaled the fragrant air. She'd like to come here at midday, maybe for a picnic, she thought. Maybe with Calloway. Jesus, what a thought. What was wrong with her? Calloway was merely an echo from the past, her old life. Still, there was something appealing to that life, at least the early part of it before it had turned sour like a carton of milk ignored in back of the refrigerator. She had to admit that in spite of the frenzy and swirl of activities around her day after day, she was lonely. A long-term relationship sounded appealing right now. But with Calloway again? Face it, she told herself. She had traveled a million miles since the breakup. Miles that she would never retrace.

She stopped, looked around. Again, she felt as if she weren't alone. Silly thought, she told herself. She walked on. But the oppressive sense of being watched intensified. She looked slowly around her again, turning in a circle. She felt the hair on her arms standing on end as gooseflesh erupted. Then she raised her gaze, inch by inch, until she saw it. A bright, oval light moved quietly above the forest on the far side of the clearing.

It moved closer and became distinct in shape, a metallic disk-like object that glimmered with a burnt reddish hue in the last rays of sunlight. It hovered above the field, three or four hundred feet overhead. She noticed its grid-like underside. No sound emanated from the vessel. Wasn't that what the alien abductees said about their captor's crafts? She remembered hearing something to that effect during the last couple of days. It must be a joke, an experimental vessel, someone capitalizing on the president's problems. Certainly it wasn't remote viewers. She was wide-awake, not like the president in his bed. No way could they create anything this real.

Of course, there was one other alternative, that Calloway had been wrong about the remote viewers, that it was the real thing, that the craft contained aliens, the very same creatures that had contacted the president. Maybe they were aware of her and had followed her here. Calm down, she told herself. Don't let your imagination run wild. Stay with the rational, the logical, the most likely. It was just a silly hoax, she told herself. What was she afraid of—the boogie man from outer space? Whoever was up there most likely didn't know she was down here.

Yet, in spite of her efforts to calm herself, she felt her body shaking. She wanted to turn and run, but she was too frightened. She couldn't move. Finally, she forced herself to back away toward the forest. One step back, then another and another. She kept her gaze on the craft. She couldn't rid herself of the idea that there were aliens inside and they were watching her.

As soon as she reached the trees, she would dash for it. She would set a new world record for the mile. Ten more yards. Almost there. She started to turn toward the trail when a thin beam of blue light penetrated the dusk and struck her in the forehead. Instantaneously, she saw herself from a distance connected to the ship by the thread of light. She felt pressure against her forehead, throbbing, but not painful, just uncomfortable. Her heart pounded. She couldn't run, couldn't move. Then it all faded.

She felt the damp grass and pushed herself up. She looked around confused for a moment, then recalled the walk and the incident. She gazed up and spotted a moving dot of light like a distant airplane. It shrank and disappeared.

She touched her forehead, recalling the beam of light. She stood up, brushed herself off. The time. Still dusk . . . or was it dawn? She glanced at her watch. Seven-twenty-two P.M., she told herself. Evening. She tried to recall when she'd left the room. Just after the six o'clock news. That seemed about right.

She moved toward the trees. Dim, shadowy. She didn't want to go in there. She wasn't even sure of the direction back to the compound. Then she saw the trail and hurried ahead. She started to trot, anxious to get back to the room, but soon slowed to a fast walk.

Had others seen the object in the sky? Should she report it right away? Better to remain quiet, she thought, at least for a while, and see what happened. Besides, what would she report, that she'd seen a UFO and it had beamed a light at her? No, definitely not. She wasn't going to exasperate the situation.

Yet, she should talk to someone about it. Maybe Waters. He would want to control it. Keep it under wraps. He might even send her away on an assignment or an unwanted vacation. She saw lights from the stable. Closer now. Maybe she could confide in Powers. But Sally didn't want any real aliens around. She wished Powers had gone with her on the walk. Then she would understand.

She reached the room, tried the door. It opened. A single light burned between the two beds. No sign of Powers. Maybe she'd gone to alert the Secret Service about her disappearance. If that was the case, then she should report what happened. Maybe others had reported it already. She moved into the room and saw the note on her bed.

Camila—Celebrity sighting at the cocktail party. Bruce Willis is here! You coming?

She recalled that Kyle Leslie was hosting a cocktail party on the president's last night. No thanks. She didn't feel like mingling or drinking or eating. She felt empty, confused, tired. She sat down on the bed and started laughing. No one missed her. She could've gone to the moon and back and no one would've known.

She felt a faint tingling. Something passed through her like a warm breeze.

In the near future, people will travel to the moon, to other planets, and elsewhere. But not in spaceships. They will project a nonphysical part of themselves to their destination.

Where did that come from? She felt a wave of panic. Someone was inside her head.

In the future, we will connect with the president through you. You are our conduit.

What? No, this wasn't happening to her.

The choice is yours. We can recede. You will be left alone. We will approach again at another time.

Who are you?

Watchers.

A chill ran through her and panic bubbled up into her throat. She rubbed her arms and blurted aloud. "Go away. Go away. Go away. Go away. I don't want this. I don't want this."

Call Calloway.

Yes. The one person she knew who could understand, and maybe even make sense of what was happening to her. She reached for the phone and flipped through her address book.

She punched the number. Waited. A man answered. She identified herself and asked for Calloway.

Please be there.

A couple of agonizing moments passed. "A minute please," the voice said in a faint Spanish accent.

Thank God.

"Camila?"

"I'm so glad you're there. I went for a walk," she blurted and told him what happened, exactly as she recalled it.

"Okay, calm down," Calloway said when she finished. "You've got to understand what's going on. These are not aliens. These are remote viewers working with Gordon Maxwell. They are getting in your head now just like they did to the president. Don't trust any thoughts that seem like they're coming from outside of you. That's the important thing."

"But Trent. I saw the disk. It was there."

"You thought you saw it. Did anyone else see it?" he asked.

"I don't know. I haven't seen anyone. They're all at a party looking at a star—not a UFO."

"What?"

"Never mind."

"Okay. Here's what I want you to do. Relax yourself, take several deep breaths, and imagine an invisible wall around you that will keep out any invasive thoughts."

"Will that work?"

She heard another voice in the background and Calloway excused himself. He came back a few seconds later. "Camila, what I suggested can help. I don't want to scare you, but it might not be enough."

"What do you mean? Do you think they might come back?"

She listened as he told her about how Agent Fielding had seen knives and nearly shot Perez. "I know this sounds crazy, but we're protected here now by an electromagnetic field. They can't penetrate it. It might be a good idea if you come over here. I don't think you should be anywhere near the president tonight."

"You're scaring me, Trent."

"I'm sorry, but I'm concerned about you."

"Okay. I'll see if I can get a car."

"Good. Head to Crested Butte and give me a call on the way. I'll give you directions."

She hung up. Definitely a crazy idea. But what else was she going to do? She certainly didn't feel like going to a party.

Twenty-four

Maxwell looked around the dining room and bar for Marlys. But she'd left and he could hardly blame her. She'd been waiting on tables all day expecting to go out with him. Then he'd just abandoned her before dinner in favor of Ritter. Not a good move for the relationship, a repeat of the old pattern, his passion for his work threatening to destroy his hopes for a stable relationship. He'd have to make it up to her. But he'd had no choice, not with Ritter collapsing as if he'd left his body in mid-stride.

He started back to Ritter's room, but instead sidled up to the bar and ordered a beer. He took out his cell phone and rang up Marlys. "Are you there? It's me. Pick up. Sorry about dinner. Can I make it up to you?" She didn't answer. "Okay, I'll try later."

He sipped his beer and puzzled over the static barrier that had interrupted Ritter and the others. Just a few seconds longer and Fielding would've blown them all away—Calloway, Doc, Perez. Bang, bang, bang. But Perez took his paranoia seriously. He'd raised a wall of static that had blocked Ritter and the others. Now Maxwell knew what had happened earlier when Ritter had complained about static. At least this time, Ritter had quickly dissociated with the target.

Years ago, he and Perez and a couple of others had experimented with electromagnetic fields. Activating such fields at a target site could cause minor confusion on the part of distant viewers. But when the task involved entering the mind of a target and affecting his actions,

EMF disrupted the connection, destroyed any chance of entering and manipulating the target's conscious thoughts. Unless . . .

He snapped his fingers. He'd overlooked the obvious solution. He quickly finished his beer and headed back upstairs. He found Ritter seated in the same chair busily scrawling on a notepad.

"Steve, can you contact the others? I think I know what we need to do."

He put down the pen, then dropped the pad on the floor. He gazed blankly ahead. After half a minute, he spoke in a monotone. "We're waiting."

"Okay. Find Lewis Fielding again. Can you tell if he is still underground with Perez?"

"He's driving away from Perez's place. He's upset by what happened." Ritter responded so quickly that Maxwell wondered if he knew what he'd been about to ask.

"Good. Very good. I need all of you to press hard. You've got to get into Fielding and make him go back. He needs to get inside the house again."

A couple of minutes passed and Maxwell started to wonder if Fielding had pushed them away this time.

"He turned around," Ritter said in a weary voice. "It was harder than before. He's aware of us, but he forgot about something. So he had a reason to go back. We hooked into that and it worked."

"This time we've got to go a step further. Once they let him back in the house, Fielding will be out of reach, out of our immediate influence. So you've got to program him to do our work. He's got to go into that house committed to killing all of them. Can you do that? Can you push that far?"

Ritter laughed, his fatigue vanished. The challenge apparently energized him. "We can. Of course we can. But he might shoot himself when he's done. His mind will be about as useful as a bowl of clumpy oatmeal."

"I think the general will appreciate that," Maxwell said.

Ritter turned quiet.

Maxwell leaned forward in his chair, reached down, and picked up the notebook that Ritter had been scrawling on. He saw a crude drawing of a disk with a beam of light shooting down from it and at the head of a woman. He wondered what it meant.

Vehicle entering property. Vehicle approaching residence.

Calloway looked up at the now familiar sound of the recorded voice. A red light flashed on the wall and Perez turned on the monitor. A dark-colored Yukon eased up to the building. The driver's door opened and Calloway recognized Nick Tyler. Then Camila stepped out of the passenger side.

"I'll go let them in," Calloway said. "It's Camila and a Secret Service agent."

Perez turned off the monitor. "Great. *Mi casa es su casa,*" he said, glumly. "Yes, go get them."

"Cheer up," Doc said. "Before you know it, you'll have your house back to yourself and you'll probably miss all the activity."

"Maybe so. But maybe no. I like my privacy."

Calloway couldn't help laughing to himself at the irony as he stepped into the elevator. So much for Perez's seclusion. First, he and Doc had arrived, then they brought in an FBI agent, and now comes a Secret Service agent and the president's press secretary. But he sympathized with Perez. He completed understood his desire for privacy and looked forward to returning to his old life. But at the moment, he wondered if that would ever be possible.

It was supposed to be an underground house, but it looked like a garage to Camila. "Well, we're not in Washington, anymore, Nick."

Tyler looked toward Crested Butte Mountain, its peak bathed in moonlight. "It would be a nice view if he had some windows."

Camila had told Tyler what little she knew about Perez and warned him to expect an eccentric multimillionaire. He'd seemed particularly interested in the fact that Perez supposedly had remote viewed his winning lottery numbers.

"Let's go knock. I hope they can hear us down there." Just then she heard the sound of an engine and turned.

"Looks like we've got company," Tyler said as a dark blue Taurus approached. "Let me check it out."

The window rolled down and she saw a black man behind the wheel. He held up an ID just as she recognized Agent Fielding. "He's okay, Nick. He was at the ranch this afternoon."

"Hello, Ms. Hidalgo," Fielding said as he stepped out of the car. She extended her hand and he shook it. "I guess I'm as surprised to see you two as you are to see me."

Camila let go of his grip as quickly as she could. She'd felt a chill as if icy fingers had squeezed her stomach and at the same time a feeling of dread had closed around her heart. She took a step back, quelling an urge to run, to get away as quickly as she could. What was wrong with her, anyhow? She'd never reacted that way before, even when encountering someone she didn't like.

To her relief, a door opened and Calloway stepped out. He flashed a smile at her, but the smile vanished as he saw Fielding. "You're back. What happened?"

Fielding turned up his hands. "I got halfway to town when I realized that I'd forgotten to interview Ms. Boyle and Mr. Perez. I thought I better get it done tonight."

"Okay. Fine with me. I don't think they will mind, but I guess you better ask." Calloway waved a hand toward Tyler. "Good to see you again, Nick. C'mon join the party."

"Yeah, my second one tonight."

Camila had asked Tyler to find her a car. He'd done so, and when he'd volunteered to drive, she'd readily agreed.

"You okay?" Calloway asked in a voice just above a whisper as they headed toward the door.

"I think so." She wanted to tell him not to say anything about her experience in front of either Tyler or Fielding, but there was no opportunity.

She felt a combination of exhilaration and wonder as well as fear and confusion in the aftermath of the incident. She also sensed a nearly imperceptible change that had something to do with that beam of light that had struck her forehead. As soon as they returned to Washington, she would get a full checkup.

En route, she had jokingly asked Tyler if anyone had reported any unusual flying objects over the ranch. "No UFOs to speak of," he'd replied in a tone that neither suggested humor nor sarcasm. If no one had mentioned it, she wouldn't either.

Calloway opened the door and led the way through the garage to a sturdy oversized steel door. "This place is like a fortress, Trent," Camila said.

"You haven't seen anything yet."

The evening was turning into a party, but a peculiar one that lacked a festive mood. Beneath the smiles, Calloway sensed wariness and tension as if everyone expected something unpleasant to unfold. He felt vaguely confused about exactly what everyone was doing here and wondered if it was related to the EMF. He could only imagine how Perez felt.

After Calloway introduced everyone, Perez took him aside. "Why did you let Fielding back in here?" he asked through gritted teeth. "He could've been exposed to them again."

"But he's in *here* now. We're protected," Calloway protested.

"Before, yes. Now, I do not know."

Doc moved over to him. "Too many people," she said, nervously. "I'm going to go disappear in the media room."

"Okay. But Fielding wants to talk to you."

"Fine. Send him in. I'll be waiting."

Calloway moved over to Fielding, who was talking with Tyler. "So, do you want to interview Doc? Now's a good time."

Fielding frowned at Calloway as if he'd just been interrupted from something important. "Oh yeah, the interview."

"Jeez, the guy forgot what he'd remembered he'd forgotten," Calloway said as Fielding walked off toward the media room.

Tyler stared after the FBI agent. "You remember when you asked me about how I locate someone in a crowd who might be a threat to the president?"

"Yeah?"

He shook his head. "I don't know why, but that guy just gave me the same feeling I get when I'm suspicious about someone like that."

Fifteen minutes had passed since Ritter said Fielding had gotten back inside. Maxwell impatiently moved about the cramped room. "Steve, can you tell what's going on?"

"It's difficult, but we know that he hasn't killed anyone yet."

"Why not? Isn't it working?"

"Too many people. More than he thought," Ritter said. "Two others showed up. He knows one of them. Somebody related to the president."

"Why didn't you say so before?"

"You didn't ask."

Great. What else didn't he know? "Can you push him? Can you force his hand?"

"We can try, but there's so much goddamn static."

"No excuses. Push hard. Push him over the edge."

Camila felt light-headed as if she'd drunk several glasses of wine, even though Perez hadn't even offered her water. Maybe it was the after-effects of her encounter with the unknown. She wanted to talk to Calloway about it, but there were too many people around. Or, maybe it was just the effect of this incredibly wonderful and strange underground mansion.

"What do you think of my place?" Perez asked.

"Very impressive. When you see that little garage up there, you don't have any idea that there's something like this below the ground. I don't feel a bit claustrophobic, either.''

"It's the atrium of course. Let me show you something.'' He took out a remote control device from his pocket, pointed it upward, and clicked. A faint humming sound emanated from above. ''I just opened the steel plates that cover the skylight.''

Camila caught her breath. "What's that?'' A bright, oval-shaped object floated high above them.

Perez looked up. "That, Ms. Hidalgo, is the moon.''

"Oh.'' She laughed nervously.

"I can close it, if you like.''

"No. I like it open. As long as you think it's safe.''

Perez considered her question. "You know, people think I am paranoid and Doc thinks I might be a coward living down here. But I am just being cautious. To answer your question, I think we are safe from any physical attack.'' He smiled confidently. "I have sensors and detectors to alert me of any intruders or even changes in weather conditions. I can close it again within seconds.''

"You're well prepared, Mr. Perez. Trent told me about the electromagnetic field, too.''

In spite of what Perez said, Camila couldn't help feeling that the danger might already be inside. She looked around. "Do you know where Agent Fielding went?''

"He's interviewing Doc in my home theater.'' His eyes narrowed as if something disturbed him. Then, he turned to her, smiled, and played host again. "It's a comfortable place. When they're done, I'll show it to you.''

She nodded. Comfortable or not, she felt an overwhelming sensation that something horrible was about to descend upon them.

Calloway approached Camila as Perez moved off. He knew she was confused by her experience and had come here to talk about it as much as to seek sanctuary. "I want to hear more about what happened.''

"I still find it hard to believe that what I experienced was implanted in my mind. I mean I wasn't in bed. Like I told you, I was out walking when I saw it. I was wide-awake."

"Maxwell and his remote viewers are way out of control. He has taken this practice to a new level, a very dangerous one."

A red light began blinking on the wall. She didn't know what it meant, but it went along with how she felt. "Trent, I've been getting the worst feeling that something horrible . . ."

Vehicle entering property. Vehicle approaching residence.

"Who the hell is coming now?" Perez said, raising his voice. "This is unbelievable."

His words were punctuated by the report of a gunshot from within the house. Calloway tensed at the sound. Doc, where was Doc? Tyler, the first to react, rushed forward, gun in hand. But Fielding stepped into a doorway and aimed his gun at the Secret Service agent.

Belatedly, Calloway realized he'd made a big mistake letting Fielding back inside, and he'd ignored Tyler's subtle warning. The FBI agent had been infected. Somehow, he had to make up for his blunder.

"Put it down right now or you're dead!" Fielding shouted.

Tyler hesitated, then laid his gun on the floor. Calloway stared at it. He could dive for the weapon, but he might never have a chance to fire.

"Everyone get in the middle of the room where I can see you," Fielding ordered.

"Do what he says," Tyler said in a low voice, stepping back. "Don't challenge him."

Calloway hesitated, then moved back with the others. He didn't agree with Tyler. Maxwell's gang had turned him into a killing machine and unless they could stop him, they would all die.

Fielding aimed his weapon at Perez. "Turn the static off. I don't know what the fuck that means, but you better do it now, or you're dead."

Perez held up his hands. "Okay. Okay." Slowly, he reached into his pocket and pulled out the oblong, electromagnetic field regulator. "There, I turned it off."

Not much time now, Calloway thought. "Snap out of it, Fielding. You're an FBI agent. You're not a killer. They're controlling you."

Fielding smiled, aimed the gun at Calloway. He knew he was about to die. At that moment, Tyler stepped in front of him.

Fielding's smile faded. "What? You want it first? Okay."

A single shot struck Tyler in the forehead. He dropped to the floor in front of Calloway. Blood pooled around his head.

"Next!"

"What the hell's wrong with you?" Camila shouted. "You're out of your mind."

He aimed at Camila.

"No!" Calloway shouted. He took a step toward Fielding. "No! Don't shoot!"

"Okay. You want to be next!"

At that moment, Doc stumbled out of the room holding a hand to her chest. Blood spilled over her white blouse. She reached out toward Fielding, but crumpled to the floor.

Camila rushed toward Doc and Fielding swung the gun in her direction, aimed at her head. Calloway lunged forward, tackled Fielding, knocking his arm in the air just as the gun fired. They rolled over, struggled for the weapon. Calloway pinned his arms to the floor, his face just inches from Fielding's.

He felt the others, all of them inside the FBI agent, pressing around him. He saw their faces—Ritter, Henderson, Johnstone, Timmons— one after another superimposed on Fielding's features as he stared up at him.

Ritter: *We're in, Trent!*

Henderson: *Gotcha now!*

Johnstone: *I see, I feel, I touch!*

Timmons: *Checking in!*

Ritter: *And you're checking out!*

Startled, angered, frightened, Calloway shoved a hand under Fielding's jaw and squeezed his cheeks as if he were trying to rip off his face. With the other hand, he continued to struggle for control of the gun. Fielding groaned, shifted his weight, and suddenly with an unexpected burst of strength threw Calloway off him. But as Calloway rolled away, he reached for the gun. He twisted Fielding's hand and pried the weapon loose. He grabbed it, rolled over, and aimed it at Fielding, who had just gotten to his knees. Calloway moved closer, grabbed Fielding by the collar, and pressed the muzzle to his forehead.

"Shoot him if he moves!" Perez shouted from behind him. "I'll get some rope."

"Don't kill me, Trent. Please, Trent." Bobby Aimes stared up at Calloway.

Not Aimes, he told himself. Couldn't be Aimes. Yet, a part of him wanted to believe a fantasy that Aimes never died, that he'd become an FBI agent.

Aimes flashed his goofy grin. *"Your turn to die, Trent."*

Calloway slowly pulled the gun away from Fielding, turned it toward his own head, pressed it to his temple. He couldn't stop himself and he knew he was about to fire. He tightened his finger around the trigger.

"No, Trent!" Camila shouted. "No! Don't do it!"

"Like scratching an itch, Trent. Squeeze."

At that moment, an explosion rocked the building. Glass shards showered down. Calloway dropped the gun. Slivers of glass struck his arms and back. A hand pulled on his arm. Movement swirled around him. He crawled away from Aimes. No, not Aimes. He glanced back and saw Fielding reaching for the gun.

Shots fired from above, the bullets just missing Fielding, who rolled over, aimed up into the atrium, and returned the fire. To Calloway's amazement, a half dozen men wearing camouflage uniforms and carrying automatic weapons rappelled the wall on long lines. Others, draped over the opening, fired down.

"Run!" Camila shouted. She pulled on his arm. Calloway lurched to his feet and they scampered toward the elevator.

Twenty-five

T he field is down," Ritter said.
"What happened? What do you see?" Maxwell demanded.

Ritter didn't respond for nearly a minute. "It's confusing. I see long lines hanging down. Men with guns. Dressed in camouflage. Like military. Militia."

Wiley's men, Maxwell thought. They'd found the place and gotten inside. "Is George Wiley there? Can you find him among the soldiers?"

Ritter cocked his head to the side as if listening to a voice in his head. "He's nearby. But he's not at the target."

Maxwell was about to ask him to clarify the comment when Ritter bolted upright in his seat and twitched his shoulders from side to side as if someone had just jabbed a cattle prod into his back. "The target is dead," he blurted.

"What do you mean?"

"Fielding is dead."

"What about Calloway?"

"On the run, but not Doc."

"What happened?"

"Doc is out of the picture." He laughed. "She can't run. She's too busy bleeding."

"What else happened?"

"Lots of shooting."

"Where is Calloway and Perez?"

A sharp rap at the door interrupted Ritter's reply. Maxwell jerked around. Who the hell could that be? "Stay with the target. I'll take care of it."

Probably someone from the management complaining about Ritter's behavior. A payoff might be in order. He took out his wallet and found five one-hundred-dollar bills that he kept tucked away. He slipped them into his pants pocket. He straightened his back and opened the door ready to stare imperiously down at any hotel employee who might dare to disturb them.

His jaw dropped an inch. For a change, he didn't know what to say. He finally uttered a simple question. "What's going on?"

"Can we come inside?" Marlys asked. She didn't look a bit disturbed and that bothered Maxwell.

He stepped aside and she moved into the room, followed closely by George Wiley.

Calloway and Camila hurried out of the room as the flurry of gunshots rattled from above. With each step, he recovered more of his sense of self as the contact with the others—through Fielding—faded. The elevator door hissed open. They stepped inside, but just as the door slid closed, a hand reached in and opened it.

"Oh, no!" Camila cried out.

Calloway expected to see Fielding aiming and firing.

"Get out of there!" Perez barked. "Follow me. The elevator is not safe anymore."

They dashed through the kitchen and out a door that led up a stairway. "You see, they got to him," Perez exclaimed between gasps of air. "He was completely in their control and so were you for a while. But who are these other invaders? What is going on here?"

Calloway didn't know any more than Perez, but he guessed that Wiley's militia had just attacked the underground fortress, and the attackers had inadvertently saved his life.

They climbed one level and Perez opened the door. "This way."

Bending low, they rushed along the open walkway past the dangling lines. Shouts echoed from below. Perez turned into a room that was lined with shelves stocked with enough dry goods to last several years. He opened a door and stepped into a long, walk-in closet stacked with more boxes of canned goods. At the back of the closet, he reached up, touched something, and the wall turned on a central axis.

They moved into a tunnel with rough-cut stone walls. Perez found a flashlight and turned it on. "This comes out on the other side of the butte. I have a Jeep parked there."

"You thought of everything, Eduardo," Camila said.

"Did you think I would build a house with only one way out? No way."

Maxwell suddenly understood what Ritter meant when he'd said that Wiley was nearby, but not at the target. He held up a hand. "Let me bring Ritter back."

He walked over to his chair and sat down. "Okay, Steve. I want you to come fully back into the room."

"They're getting away," Ritter responded. His eyes were open and staring straight ahead. If he was aware of Wiley or Marlys, he didn't show it.

"Come back now."

"Let him finish," Wiley said, moving closer. "Who's getting away?"

Maxwell figured that Ritter would instantly snap out of his zone at the sound of another voice. But to his surprise, Ritter responded.

"Calloway, Perez, and a woman."

"Who's the woman?" Wiley asked.

Ritter bent over and picked up his notebook. He pointed to the woman in the drawing. "That one."

Wiley took the notebook. "I don't understand."

Maxwell shrugged. "Who is she, Steve?"

"She works for the president."

"It must be Camila Hidalgo, Calloway's ex-wife." Maxwell looked at Wiley, then at Marlys, wondering again what they were doing together.

"What does this drawing mean?" Wiley asked.

"It's something she saw," Ritter answered, cryptically.

What the hell was he doing? Ritter wasn't supposed to work on his own, especially not on presidential targeting. But he didn't want to get into it now, especially in front of Wiley.

"Where are they now?" Maxwell asked, changing the subject.

"Coming out of a tunnel, an escape route. It leads to the back side of the butte."

Wiley took out a cell phone and walked into the bathroom. As soon as the door closed, Maxwell turned to Marlys. "Where did he come from?"

"He came to the house looking for you." She sounded a bit too smug. "You never said you worked for him."

He tried to assess the damage. "Do you know who he is?"

She laughed. "Don't be an idiot, Max. Of course I do. *People* magazine called George Wiley the most dangerous man in America. He looks a little different than his pictures, but that's him."

"Well, I'm not one of his followers, if that's what you're wondering. I'm just someone he hired."

"I know all about it. You're a mercenary. You and your psychics are his extrasensory security team."

Maxwell tensed. She knew too much. Wiley must've been doing a lot of talking. The bastard.

"Right on the money," Wiley said, returning to the room. "They did get away."

He folded up his phone and put it in his pocket. He didn't seem particularly concerned. "But they're not going far. All the roads are blocked. The dogs will get them."

Maxwell barely heard what he'd said. He didn't like the way Wiley stood next to Marlys, how fit and good looking he appeared, how Marlys regarded him. Then Wiley slipped an arm around her shoulder and grinned at Maxwell. "Don't look so dumbfounded, Max. Did you think I wouldn't have someone checking on you?"

Maxwell couldn't believe it. He'd been set up.

"Sorry, Max," Marlys said, "but I'm with George and Freedom Nation all the way. Unlike you."

Maxwell leaped to his feet "You sonofabitch, Wiley. I stuck my neck out for you."

"You did it for money and power, nothing more," Wiley responded. "You're not committed, Max. You're unprincipled. You don't have any ideals. You're a user. You tried to use me just like you use your psychics."

"That's not true," he stammered. "I never used you. It's the other way around. That's the way it looks to me."

"I know what you've been doing," Wiley said. "So don't try to hide anything from me."

"I've never hid anything from you," he sputtered. "Except for the bomb, of course, and I contacted you right away."

"Max, cut it out," Marlys said. "George knows all about your secret alien work with the president and how you got the vice president's wife to threaten divorce, and how Dustin's national security advisor nearly went to a formal dinner in a dress," Marlys said.

"What are you talking about? You don't know anything about that. I've never mentioned any of that to you."

"I did." Ritter smiled inanely up at him.

Oh, shit. He'd kill the bastard. His ears burned, his nostrils flared.

"Steve was very cooperative," Marlys said. "If you remember correctly, Steve gave you the idea to put aliens in the president's head."

"You think of it as your project," Wiley said. "But guess what? The aliens were part of my plan. I saw that Dustin was vulnerable and Steve liked the idea."

"Liked it a lot," Ritter put in.

"And he said you would like it, too," Wiley added.

He didn't want to hear any more. They'd all turned on him. His anger surged and he lunged for Wiley, grabbed his throat, squeezed, jamming his thumb deep into his neck. He'd kill the fucker. They fell over backward, toppling over a chair, and Maxwell pinned Wiley's arms to the floor with his knees.

He squeezed harder. Wiley gagged, his eyes bulged. Marlys pounded on his back, tried to pull him off, but he was too strong. His rage had doubled, tripled his seething, adrenaline-fueled strength. He could lift a car from a body right now, or snap a neck like a twig.

"You're dead, George," he hissed between his clenched jaw.

No, you are!

Then he felt them. All of them inside his head—Ritter, Johnstone, Timmons, and Henderson. He could see their faces, feel them pushing on him. The pressure increased as if invisible thumbs were pressing hard against his temples.

No, no, stop! You work for me.

He struggled against them, but the pain intensified even further. He released Wiley, grabbed his head, and rolled onto his back, curling into a fetal position.

Now you die, Max. Ritter's voice. *We can't let you kill him.*

He vaguely heard the words through another wave of intense pain. His brain felt as if it were about to explode. Then they backed off. The pain started to recede like the tide rolling out.

Ritter hovered over him. "Guess what, Max? They have another backpack nuke, and this time it's loaded, loaded and ready to rock 'n' roll. They're going to deliver it themselves—George and Marlys—and we will protect them the entire way. Your team, Max."

"I don't care. Just leave me alone."

"Sorry, Max."

The pain suddenly surged forward, an enormous tsunami of agony. Battering him. Crushing him. Choking him. He gagged. Swallowed his tongue.

He felt his brain shattering, exploding. He couldn't breathe, couldn't move, couldn't think, couldn't feel anything. His life ebbed away.

"I think he's dead," Marlys said. "Are you all right, George?"

Twenty-six

They reached the end of the tunnel and pushed aside the underbrush that blocked the entrance. Calloway climbed out into the night and took a deep breath of the cool evening air, relieved to be out of the cramped tunnel. Hounds barked in the distance. He scanned the craggy moonlit landscape and spotted a strip of pale brown dirt a couple of hundred yards away, the road out of here.

Perez pointed to the right. A four-wheel-drive Jeep was parked between the butte and a huge boulder. They hurried over to it.

"I hope you've got the key," Calloway said.

"Of course I do," Perez answered with an indignant snort. "Right on my key chain. There's also one hidden under a rock near the right front tire."

"You amaze me," Camila said as she climbed into the backseat.

"The Jeep is no good if you can't drive it," he replied.

"You better keep the lights off," Calloway said.

"I know. I wish a cloud would cover the moon, too. It seems very bright out here after walking in that tunnel."

They bounced over the rocks as Perez drove down a steep incline. For a moment, Calloway thought the vehicle would flip over, but Perez maneuvered it expertly through the rocky field. He reached a gentle incline and the Jeep scrambled up onto a dirt road.

"Glad that part's over," Camila said from behind him.

"It's the next part that worries me." Calloway had no sooner spoken when several headlights appeared in the distance moving their way. "What do you think, Eduardo?"

"I don't like it. There shouldn't be anybody driving back here at this time."

"Unless they're looking for us," Calloway said.

"You got it."

Perez crossed the road and drove down a rugged slope. He continued on until a wall of rock blocked him from going further. He turned off the engine. "I hope that's far enough away."

Three pickups crawled along the road, moving at no more than fifteen miles an hour. "They're definitely looking for us," Perez said.

The vehicles passed within a hundred yards of them and continued on. As they disappeared around a bend in the road, Perez turned on the engine. "Now we make a break for it."

They bounced back to the road and turned left, opposite the direction the pickups were moving. They'd driven about half a mile when Perez stopped on a rise. He pointed to the right. Moonlight illuminated at least a dozen vehicles parked at the base of the butte near his garage. The baying of the hounds sounded louder and Calloway could see several dogs scrambling over the rocks in the moonlight.

"Look at that. How could this happen to me?" Perez sounded indignant, unconcerned about the dangers. "That is my place and those bastards are overrunning it."

"Christ, Eduardo. Let's get out of here," Camila said in a panic-riddled voice. "I'll call for help."

Calloway pointed ahead. "More company."

A predatory-looking Humvee rolled over the next rise and headed toward them. No time to run. No place to hide. "Oh, oh!" Perez snapped out of his funk. "What are we going to do?"

"No choice," Calloway said in a firm voice. "We go to work. We use our abilities."

"What do you have in mind?" Perez asked.

Calloway watched the approaching vehicle. "We make them believe we are with them."

"Oh, wonderful," Camila groaned. "I don't know about you two, but I can't do that!"

"Don't worry about it. Eduardo and I will take care of them." But Calloway had his own concerns. If these guys were Wiley's white supremacists, as he suspected, they were going to have trouble accepting him as one of their own.

Perez seemed to pick up his thoughts. "We make them see white, Trent. That is how we do it."

"Smart thinking. Get ready. You take the driver, I'll take the passenger."

"But what should I do, duck down?" Camila leaned forward, gripping the back of Calloway's seat.

"No, just relax," Calloway said. "Help us out. When the door opens, you say, 'Now!' That's when we go for them."

In spite of his confident tone, Calloway couldn't help wondering what was going to happen. He had never done anything like this, especially under these conditions. No time to prepare and armed targets approaching them. Nothing remote about this at all. No need to locate the target. Just get inside immediately and twitch the man's conception of reality.

Impossible, he thought. But then his abilities were much improved, he reminded himself. Far superior than his days on active duty. The link among them—the net—had enhanced their skills.

He took several long, deep breaths, letting his eyelids droop until he could barely see. Flaring headlights suddenly blocked what little vision remained. He heard the rumble of the other engine. Surprisingly, the lights and sound helped. He felt himself slipping down.

"Now!" Camila hissed.

Calloway saw the silhouette of a man with a rifle emerge from the passenger side. He easily read the man's thoughts. *It must be them. Yes. That's the fuckin' nigger. We got 'em now. Shoot if they make any sudden moves.*

Calloway struggled to contain his panic. He threw everything at him. He pushed hard, harder than he'd ever done. He told the man to see white, to see one of their own. The man moved closer.

Maybe not them. For a moment there . . . must be the shadows, the moonlight or something. Just one of ours. Let's see what they're doing.

Calloway raised a hand, greeting the man, a towhead in his mid-thirties. He felt oddly dissociated with himself as he spoke. "We're watching from here. In case anyone tries to walk away."

The man nodded, grinned. "You mean run away."

"Yeah."

He looked toward the rear seat. Calloway pushed again. *Just two of them here.*

"I believe my eyes are playing tricks with me tonight," the man said. "I could've sworn there was someone in the backseat." He laughed. "And you looked a little dark there at first."

"What, you don't like my moon tan?"

He pointed at Calloway. "Funny guy."

Perez ended a brief conversation with the driver. He tapped Calloway on the shoulder. "Come. We are going to trade vehicles with these guys. It is our turn to drive the Humvee."

Calloway nodded. A part of him wanted to laugh, but he forced himself to stay focused, making certain that his target didn't start reassessing. Camila walked in front of them, not saying a word.

Perez flipped him the keys. "You want to drive?"

"Why not."

He got behind the wheel, started the engine. Camila sat up front, Perez climbed into the back. Calloway made a U-turn and drove away.

"If I hadn't seen it with my own eyes, I never would've believed it," Camila said, turning in her seat, looking from one to the other.

"I know what you mean," Calloway said. "But they're going to figure it out pretty damn quick. They're not robots."

"True. They may be starting to wonder what happened already," Perez said. "Especially since I took the key with me."

"That's great!" she chortled. "So they're stuck."

"Hey, look at this." Calloway held up a walkie-talkie. "Too bad they left their two-way radios."

"Stay to the left where the road splits up ahead," Perez said.

Camila took out her cell phone. "I'm calling the cops right now."

"You better tell them what they're up against," Calloway said. "I don't know if the Crested Butte police department is prepared to face an army."

"I am not so sure about calling the police, Camila," Perez worried. "I hear that Freedom Nation has sympathizers in lots of these police departments."

"Don't worry, Eduardo," Camila responded. "I won't give away our position. But they'll respond when they hear an FBI agent and a Secret Service agent are down. They have no choice. That place will be blanketed with federal agents within an hour."

"Yeah," Perez said, glumly.

Camila made the call, identified herself, quickly explained the situation, and told the dispatcher to alert state police, federal authorities, and the military. She disconnected the call before the dispatcher could ask any further questions. "That should do it. This could be the beginning of the end of Freedom Nation."

Calloway heard a beep and saw a red light blinking on the two-way radio. He picked it up and turned it on. "Attention, Freedom Nation fighters. I have word that our commander in chief is airborne and carrying the payload! It won't be long now!" The man let out a gleeful yelp, then added: "Over and out."

"I wonder what exactly that means," Camila said.

"I don't like the sounds of it," Calloway said, glancing into the rearview mirror to make certain they weren't being followed.

Perez slid down into his seat in the rear. "Let me work on it. I'm going to find their commander in chief—George Wiley."

Five minutes passed before Calloway asked him if he was okay. "I'm fine. But I'm not getting anything. It's like there's a shield around him," Perez explained.

"He's being protected by the others," Calloway said. "I'm certain of it."

"I think you are right," Perez said. "They are blocking me."

"But what's the payload and where is he going?" Camila asked.

"I bet the walkie-talkie man knows," Calloway said. "Can you try him, Eduardo?"

"Give me a minute, then lead me to him."

Calloway drove on. He looked over at Camila and smiled. She reached out and took his hand. She'd been through a lot tonight, but she was strong, stronger than he remembered. He thought about Doc. There'd been no time to help her. But maybe she didn't need help anymore. Maybe it was too late. The same for Tyler. He didn't know the Secret Service agent well, but he'd liked him, and the guy had saved his life.

Perez cleared his throat, indicating he was ready. "Okay, Eduardo," Calloway said. "Go to the walkie-talkie man. Find him now. Describe him to me."

"He is in his mid-fifties, gray hair, overweight. Vietnam vet. His name is Sumner, no Sudner. Thinks the world has gone to hell. Wants to see things change in his lifetime. Change in a big way. But he feels all torn up. He lost his daughter in this thing somehow, and he thinks that Wiley might kill him."

Calloway didn't want to pursue the man's personal problems. He wanted to stay with the present and push further for details. "Okay, good. What's he doing now?"

"Oh, he is angry about something. Us. They found the guys who lost the Humvee."

"What are they going to do?"

"They are ending the operation and pulling out. They figure we are headed to the Crested Butte PD. They have a couple of guys back in town monitoring the police scanner. They told them to watch for us."

"What will they do if they see us?"

"They are supposed to hit us with everything they've got, take us out."

Perez provided the information in a matter-of-fact manner, as if he were talking about someone else's life. That didn't surprise Calloway, since part of Perez remained with his target. He needed to move on, then get Perez back so they could figure out what to do.

"Okay, what does Sudner know about the general and the payload?"

"That is easy. He feels very emotional about this. He has something personal at stake. The daughter. I am not sure what happened. He is blocking it out. But he wants this to work. He wants Wiley to take out Washington, D.C., with the bomb. The real one. A backpack nuke. The other one . . . his daughter had something to do with it. Okay, she was in the car and died. That's it. A big sacrifice and now he wants Dustin and the rest of the federal government to pay. Really pay."

Camila pointed to a sign that said five miles to Crested Butte. Calloway nodded, but pushed on. "What else does he know about it? What other details?"

"Wiley is in a rented private jet. He left from the airport in Durango. The whole thing is going to happen fast. He has a remote trigger on the bomb and he will detonate it from the air tomorrow morning just after Air Force One lands."

"Okay, one more question. Where will the bomb be placed?"

"He doesn't know. Probably somewhere in the airport. That's what Sudner thinks."

"All right. Come back now, Eduardo. Release the target and bring yourself completely back here."

Perez blinked, exhaled loudly, and leaned forward focusing on the road. "Where are we?"

"About two miles from Crested Butte," Calloway said.

"Just keep going toward Gunnison," Perez said. "Don't stop. They are nearby, watching. Close to the police department."

"Go directly to Leslie's ranch," Camila said. "We've got to warn the president. He can't leave in the morning. We've got to alert Washington National. That's where the president is scheduled to land."

"Wait a minute. There's something wrong here," Calloway said.

"What is it?" Camila asked.

Calloway hesitated, putting together disparate thoughts. "Okay, let's look at what we know about General Wiley. He's a clever strategist. He throws feints to mislead anyone after him. That's what he did with the fake bomb. He wanted to see what would happen, and when it failed he had a backup—the real bomb. So my guess is that he's not telling his lieutenants the full story."

"You mean you don't think that he really plans to bomb Washington?" Camila asked.

"Yes, I do. But not tomorrow morning and not from the ground. Think about it. Why would he take the chance of getting caught on the ground or losing the bomb when he has a remote trigger?"

"I understand," Perez said. "Shit, you are right. I did not see it."

Camila shook her head. "Oh, no. What are you saying?"

"He's not going to land at all. He's going to drop it from the jet tonight and set it off before it hits," Calloway explained. "It's twelve-thirty now. My guess is that he could be over Washington in a few hours."

"But the president won't be in Washington then. And do you really think he'd lie like that to his own men?" Camila asked.

"Yes, definitely," Calloway answered. "There's a good reason, too. He doesn't want to tell them how he's going to kill the president."

"You got it, Trent!" Perez shouted from the backseat.

"Wait. You guys are going too fast," Camila said. "What do you mean? How is he going to kill him?"

"He will kill him with his secret weapon, the remote viewers," Perez answered.

"That's what I think," Calloway said. "He doesn't need Dustin in Washington when he destroys it. He'll take care of him soon enough. It'll look like a brain hemorrhage or a heart attack."

Camila shook her head. "I still find it hard to believe they can do that. Did they do that when you were in the military, Trent?"

"Towards the end, yes. But only through indirect means. They'd push an intermediary into the act. He tricked me into doing it once. That's when I left."

She looked over at him. "We've got to stop them, but I don't know if anyone will believe us. The air force certainly won't shoot a private plane out of the sky based on a psychic impression. We don't know if they can even identify the plane."

Calloway peered into the rearview mirror, studying a vehicle that suddenly loomed in his vision. "We've got a pickup coming up fast on us."

He'd no sooner spoken when he heard an automatic weapon coughing bullets. Several struck the back of the Humvee.

"Get down!" Calloway yelled out and stepped on the accelerator.

The back window shattered. Calloway glanced into the mirror, saw the pickup ten feet behind them, a rifle from the passenger side aimed down at a back tire. He slammed on the brakes and his seatbelt tore into his shoulder, chest, and hips. An instant later, the pickup slammed into the rear of the Humvee.

He held tight to the steering wheel and stepped on the accelerator. The pickup remained several feet behind the Humvee and another round of bullets struck the frame and ricocheted off the passenger side of the vehicle.

Calloway focused on the road, picking up more speed. He hit fifty, sixty, seventy. The road suddenly curved sharply and he turned hard on the wheel to keep from flying off the road bed. An ordinary Jeep would have risen on two wheels and rolled over. But the Humvee, with its extraordinarily wide wheelbase, hugged the pavement. Behind him, he heard tires screech and a moment later the pickup catapulted off the road, flipping over and over down an embankment.

Calloway eased off the accelerator and looked over at Camila, who was crumpled on the floor. "Camila?"

She raised her head. "I'm okay."

"Eduardo?"

No answer.

Camila looked back and climbed into the rear seat. "Oh, God, Trent. He's hit. We've got to get him to a hospital."

"I guess they did not order the bulletproof windows," Perez groaned.

"Don't talk, Eduardo," Calloway shouted. "Camila, call 911. Get an emergency helicopter to the ranch fast. We'll be there in ten minutes."

She snapped up the cell phone. "Hang on, Eduardo. Hang on!"

Twenty-seven

Calloway drove up to the gate of the ranch and signaled frantically. A state trooper approached just as a helicopter circled overhead.

Camila held Perez's hand. "We've got help coming, Eduardo. Stay with us."

"Don't move him," the trooper said. "Just stay right here. The emergency medical team is landing."

Several sleepy reporters and cameramen peered into the Humvee. "Hey, Camila," one of them said. "What happened? What's going on?"

Calloway pushed through the reporters and opened the back door. He told Camila that he'd like to be with Perez before the medics arrived. Camila patted Perez's bloodied arm. Tears streamed down her cheeks. She crawled out the vehicle and moved away, trailed by several reporters.

Calloway held on to Perez's hand and tried to reach him. He knew Perez had been badly wounded. To his surprise, he heard Perez's voice in his head.

Now you can crack the net. With me gone, the web has a hole. Go through it. You can still stop Wiley. You can do it.

"But how, Eduardo?" He didn't know whether he spoke the words or communicated them telepathically.

Hands fell on Calloway's shoulders and the connection broke. Men and women in green jumpsuits moved in and eased Calloway out of the Humvee. "We'll take it from here," one of them said. "We'll do everything we can for him."

Calloway stumbled away, Perez's words still in his mind. A state trooper escorted him through the gate and into the entryway of the house. He leaned against the wall amid a flurry of activity.

Camila appeared out of nowhere, her T-shirt stained with blood, her face streaked with tears. "Trent, you remember Agent Clarke?"

He nodded, forcing himself to snap out of the disjointed space he'd drifted into after his contact with Perez.

Clarke moved forward. "We can track any private jets coming into Washington, but there's very little we can do unless the plane lands."

"You're looking at the end of Washington, at the end of the United States the way we know it, and you're telling me you can't do anything?"

Clarke raised a hand, then touched his ear, listening through a tiny transmitter. After several seconds, he looked up. "We just contacted La Plata County Airport in Durango. No private jet filed a flight plan for Washington, D.C., during the last eight hours. However, a Gulfstream jet took off at nine-twenty-five this evening. It filed a flight plan for Great Falls, Montana, and it's an hour overdue."

"That must be it."

Clarke nodded. "We're working on that possibility." He listened again, then spoke softly into a wrist transmitter, acknowledging that he'd received the information.

"Okay, here's what we know. A Gulfstream jet's cruising speed is 459 knots. A direct flight from Durango to Dulles would take approximately five hours. So, it's possible that he could arrive over the capital by two-twenty."

"That's less than an hour," Camila gasped.

Calloway heard the helicopter carrying Perez lift off. Too late, he thought. Perez would be dead on arrival. He pushed away the thought, not wanting to believe it.

He remembered Perez's final message to him. He turned to Camila. "Is there some place quiet we could go so I can work?"

She looked to Clarke, who nodded. They followed him outside, past the swimming pool, and into the library where Calloway had worked hours earlier.

"What's your plan, Trent?" Camila asked.

"I don't have one. But I'll see if I can find Wiley. What else can I do?"

"I'll monitor you," Camila said. This time there was no hesitation on her part.

He found a comfortable chair and began to relax himself. In spite of everything that he'd been through tonight, he quickly sank down into his zone. He signaled with his hand when he was ready.

"Go to George Wiley and describe his surroundings," Camila said.

He felt swift movement, the sensation of flight. For a moment, he glimpsed the interior of a private jet. Three men and a woman were aboard, including the pilot. Then the image vanished as if invisible blinders had cut off his vision.

"I got a brief look. Wiley's in flight."

"Is Maxwell with him?" she asked.

"I don't think so. I didn't sense him there."

Maxwell has disappeared from the radar.

An odd thought. Not his own. Then he felt the presence of the others.

"Hey there, Trent. Long time no see. Hey, what happened to Perez? I don't feel him around."

"Is that you again, Ritter?"

"We're all here—watching you. By the way, too bad about Doc."

"I know you did it. You pulled that trigger, Steve. The blood's on your hands."

"Don't see any." Ritter cackled. *"So what are you up to? Looking for someone? Hope it's not Maxwell. He'd dead, too. We killed him. He taught us well."*

"Then you can stop Wiley, too, before it's too late."

"Stop him? We're helping him, Trent. Protecting him. That's why you can't see anything."

In spite of his variety of experiences in the psychic world, communicating in a telepathic mode, as if he were on a conference call, was new and strange. The powers of Maxwell's creation—the PSI/ NET—as Perez had described it, astonished him. In Wiley's hands, the possibilities were utterly frightening.

"Your block isn't working very well, Steve. Wiley's flying in a Gulfstream jet. He left the Durango airport at about nine-twenty-five. He'll pass over Washington, D.C., within the hour."

"Not bad, Trent. Not bad. You're good. You're one of us. But you can't stop us."

He and Ritter had never been close, even when they saw each other every day. Ritter had always been more competitive than personable. He'd always considered himself the best of the team and Calloway his main competition.

"Trent, can you tell us what you're seeing now?" Camila asked.

"Tell her to stick it up her twat and go look for a UFO. That was clever back at the ranch, Trent. Very clever. But what was your point? That was you playing with her, wasn't it?"

He ignored Ritter. "I'm communing with the bad guys, Camila. They're trying to block me from zeroing in on Wiley. You could say that they are right here with us."

"Do you want to come back?"

"No, not yet."

"Fly with us, Trent-o. It's a free trip. Your last journey to D.C."

Calloway pushed harder. For a moment, he glimpsed the interior of the eight-passenger plane again. He saw Ritter sitting across the aisle from Wiley, who sat next to a woman he didn't recognize.

"You're up there with him."

"Guessing or seeing?"

He ignored Ritter. The mind chatter formed part of the block.

"We can kill you, Trent. We will kill you."

He felt pressure on his temples. He willed them away, but the pressure increased. Invisible hammers pounded on either side of his head from the inside out.

"You won't kill me. It would weaken the net."

"We can do without you. The net molds exactly to our needs."

He pushed back, but they were too strong. He pushed again. Desperate this time. He sank beneath their weight, his resistance weakening. He saw their eyes now, glowering, searing into his brain. He gasped for air, but they had stolen his breath. He heard Camila calling to him, calling from far, far away. He couldn't come back. They wouldn't let him. He'd misjudged their strength, their ability, their willingness to destroy a part of their net. He'd escaped Wiley's militia only to fall to his own kind.

All at once, the pressure vanished. He sucked in a deep, reviving breath of air. He opened his eyes, expecting to see Camila in front of him. Instead, he found himself aboard the jet, no longer peering in from afar, but fully fixed in his surrounding. They'd let go of him. Something had distracted them and he'd done just as Perez had said to. He'd fallen through a hole in the net.

Wiley and the woman peered intently out the window. Ritter looked around, confused. Calloway, baffled by the sudden shift and still apprehensive from the attack, just wanted out. He drifted up, up through the top of the plane and that was when he saw what had caught Wiley's attention. A disk-shaped object, no, two of them, accompanied the plane, one off each wing.

At the same time, Calloway remained aware of himself sitting in the chair in the library, where Ritter's voice had whispered in his head. He was vaguely cognizant of Camila kneeling in front of him, a hand on his knee, attempting gently to bring him back. She was talking in a firm voice, but her words didn't register. Instead, he heard Ritter again.

"Now I see why you created the UFO for your ex-wife. You were practicing for this trip. Very clever. I've totally underestimated you, Trent. But if we kill you, the UFOs vanish, right?"

Calloway realized that Ritter actually believed that the crafts were his creation. He didn't disagree. He shifted his focus back to the plane and moved into the cabin again, hoping to make the best of the distraction.

"They're locked on us," the pilot said. "I can't move. They're controlling our movements."

"No!" Ritter shouted. "They're not real. It's implanted in your head."

"Bullshit!" Wiley snapped. "Cut the double-talk. I see what I see. Those things are out there. I bet they're secret military crafts. Put out your antennae. How do we break away from them? What do we do?"

"I'm already in contact with their creator. It's just Calloway. They're not real."

"I don't know what the fuck you're talking about." Wiley dismissed Ritter and yelled to the pilot. "Where are we now? How close?"

"Three minutes out of Washington."

"Perfect."

The woman pointed at something outside the window. "What, Marlys? What is it now?" Wiley asked.

"We've got more company," she responded.

"Two air force fighters are coming up fast," the pilot reported. "They're trying to make radio contact."

"For chrissake." Wiley moved aft and dragged a backpack from behind the last seat. He ripped away the floor covering, revealing the emergency exit, a hatch in the floor. He took hold of the lever, pulled on it.

Calloway pushed harder, moving up to Wiley, working his way inside him. Ritter, preoccupied, no longer blocked him, and he easily read Wiley's thoughts as he zipped open the backpack.

An SS-22 primary with a plutonium core and a trigger detonator. Hit the switch on the right side for activation and the core's ready to go into nuclear yield. Enough power to demolish twelve square blocks and kill half a million people in the capital and surrounding area. That'll wake them up.

Calloway needed to nudge Wiley now, change his mind, delay his response. Something. But then he struck a wall. The others—Johnstone, Timmons, Henderson—were there waiting, protecting, blocking. And they came directly at him, dark psychic knights charging with poison lances, aiming for his mind.

Calloway dodged them as best he could, sending them terrifying images of the plane on fire, spinning out of control, and of Wiley's head in flames. The effort seemed to distract them momentarily. He remained hovering just outside of Wiley, aware of his thoughts.

He directed Wiley to close the hatch. But the others blocked him again, pushed him away. He threw out an image of Wiley tumbling out the hatch, but they didn't buy it. A distorted chorus of voices echoed in his head.

No, Trent. No, Trent. We know your tricks. We know them now. You can't get to him. Not now. Not ever. It's all over.

Wiley zipped up the backpack, slid open the hatch a few inches. He clung to a handle on the wall as he felt the suction. He pulled the hatch open several more inches, then kicked the backpack. The bomb tottered a moment.

"Crossing the Potomac now," the pilot announced.

Wiley touched the backpack with the toe of his shoe and the bomb vanished through the hatch. Calloway looked on, helpless, still in the grip of the others. Wiley deftly pushed the hatch closed, locked it, then hurried back to his seat.

He opened a briefcase and took out the triggering device. "Bon voyage, Washington, D.C," he shouted. "Dustin, your next."

He tapped in the activation code. One click and Calloway knew that his vision of a destroyed capital would be real. He pushed on Wiley again, pushed harder. Again, he felt of wave of energy blocking him. He couldn't get to him, couldn't change his mind, couldn't stop him.

"They're real," Ritter yelled. "It's not Calloway; it's not the military, either. Those things out there are real."

"Shut up!" Wiley yelled. "One thing at a time."

Ritter's shout momentarily distracted the others. Calloway pushed at the triggering device, pushed with everything he had left. He glimpsed the tiny circuit board, poured heat into it. Melted it. Fried the circuit.

Wiley pressed the red button. Waited. He pressed again. He looked out the window waiting for a bright flash, an eruption far below. Nothing. "What the hell's wrong? Why doesn't it blow?"

"Oh, no!" Ritter said. "He got in. Somehow, the fucker got in. He got the trigger."

"What!"

Wiley hurled the box at Ritter. It bounced off his shoulder, fell harmlessly to the floor.

"The disks are gone," the pilot reported. "I don't see them anywhere."

Calloway moved back, away from the jet, and saw the fighters moving closer, closing in on their prey. This time, Wiley wouldn't get away.

"Trent, can you hear me?"

The image faded. He blinked, rubbed his face with his hands, then opened his eyes to see Camila crouched in front of him, staring intently at him. He took her hands. "I'm back. It's okay. We beat 'em. Barely, but we did it."

Twenty-eight

FIVE WEEKS LATER

Calloway guided the raft out of the white water and along a curving sandstone wall. The choppy water settled as they eased into a quiet pool. The familiar sandy beach, the place where he'd briefly reached across time and glimpsed a scene from the ancient past, marked the end point for the trip.

They would picnic here and browse along the pale brown cliffs that had once served as a canvas for Anasazi artists. Then the president, his press secretary, and the rest of the entourage would depart in a helicopter that waited above the cliffs.

Camila leaped out as the raft touched shore. "This has been great, Trent. I really needed this break."

In the weeks since a nuclear bomb had fallen harmlessly into a tree in Arlington and George Wiley, the bomber, had been captured, the resulting media frenzy had overwhelmed all other events. Each day, it seemed, new revelations came out: the deaths of Fielding and Tyler were connected to Wiley and Freedom Nation. Wiley was linked to remote viewing and questions were being raised about the deaths of two former CIA remote viewers—Maxwell and Perez. Even the buzz surrounding the president's comments about aliens faded until Steve Ritter boasted from his jail cell that he and other remote viewers had engineered Dustin's alien encounters.

"I'm just glad that you've been kept out of it," Camila said after a pause.

"I've noticed that nothing has been said about the UFOs that attracted the fighter jets to Wiley's plane," Calloway said.

"I'm sure that it'll spill out at some point. There's just been so much being exposed about the psychic-induced encounters that no one is ready to look at the possibility of a real UFO. Whatever that is."

"I don't know what it was, either," Calloway conceded. "But I think it was related to your own encounter."

Camila frowned. "I thought that was Ritter's work."

"He thought it was my work." Calloway shrugged. "So I don't know. Except, I keep thinking about something Maxwell told me a long time ago. He thought that aliens would make themselves known when people believed they were here. Maybe the president's false experience created the real thing—at least for a few minutes."

She laughed. "I'll have to think about that one."

Calloway looked up as Dustin approached him. "Trent, this has been fantastic. Just fantastic. I'd like to do it again sometime."

"It's been an honor, sir. Anytime you're ready, let us know."

"I'd like to have you out to my house for dinner one of these nights, too." He smiled. "You know, that big white place on Pennsylvania Avenue."

Calloway smiled. "I've seen pictures of it. I'd like to get out there when I've got some time. My new RV arrives next week."

"A remote viewer living in an RV. I like that. Why don't you drive it and park it in my backyard. Just don't drive on the roses." They laughed, then Dustin added: "I know Camila would like you to spend some time with us."

"I want to spend some time with her, too, and I'd like to visit Doc. I heard she's recovering nicely."

Dustin took a step closer and lowered his voice. "In spite of what happened regarding my alien encounters, I still believe there's something to the phenomenon. Those UFOs that showed up before the bomb was dropped were tracked on radar. I think your talents could be used to find out a lot more about the source of those vessels."

"That could be," Calloway said.

Camila held up a hand. "Hold on. David, if you want me as your permanent spokesperson, then I would really prefer if you waited until you were out of office before you take that path again.''

Dustin laughed. ''Maybe so.''

''Hey, you guys!'' Ed Miller called out from a picnic table that he'd set up. ''Lunch is all ready.''

They walked back to the table and he took Camila's hand. ''How's it been, living with Ed?'' she asked.

''He's okay. But I'll be glad to get my own place again.''

''It was real nice of him to make you his partner.''

''Yeah, now I've got more work to do. But I enjoy it.''

''What about remote viewing?'' she asked.

''It's dangerous stuff. But under the right circumstances, and for the right reasons, I'm ready . . . as long as either you or Doc, when she's ready, monitor me.''

She smiled, hugged him. ''That's a deal. It's a new tool. We need to explore it more thoroughly.''

At that moment, Calloway glimpsed an Indian man walking along the base of the cliff near the walls of petroglyphs where ancient shamans had entered trances and traveled to other worlds. The man looked up at Calloway and he recognized him as the one he'd seen before. A shaman. A warrior. A remote viewer. The man walked on and faded away.

''Agreed. Except, one thing. It's not exactly a new tool, Camila. It's been around a long time.''